DEATH
IN THE
RIVER

A gripping British crime mystery full of twists

P.F. FORD

A Slater & Norman Mystery Book 7

Originally published as *A Skeleton in the Closet*

Revised edition 2024
Joffe Books, London
www.joffebooks.com

First published as *A Skeleton in the Closet*
in Great Britain in 2016

This paperback edition was first published
in Great Britain in 2024

Cover art by Dee Dee Book Covers

ISBN: 978-1-83526-551-2

*With thanks to my amazing wife, Mary — sometimes
we need someone else to believe in us before we really
believe in ourselves. None of this would have happened
without her unfailing belief and support.*

PROLOGUE

Tuesday, 7 September 1993

It was the end of the first day back at school after the summer
holidays, and the three bullies were back in action already.
The small twelve-year-old boy who was their intended victim
was running as fast as he could, tearing across the grass and
up the steps that led onto the bridge across the river. He was
still a fair way ahead, but they were gaining, and it was only
a matter of time before they caught up with him. There was
just one last chance. He looked back over his shoulder to
make sure he was far enough ahead.

The three bullies raced up the steps onto the bridge.
'The little bugger's got away,' said the first of the three as he
reached the top.

'He can't be far ahead. Come on, we can still catch him,'
said the second.

'No, leave it,' said the third, who was obviously the
leader of the gang. 'I'm knackered. Teacher's pet may have
escaped today but we'll catch him next time, and then he'll
just have to pay double.'

He leaned on the side of the bridge and looked over
at the river flowing lazily past beneath them. A path ran

alongside the river, and at weekends it would be busy with people out enjoying the fresh air, but at 4 p.m. on a grey Tuesday afternoon it was completely deserted. But then, coming around a bend not too far away, the leader saw a schoolboy on a bicycle, heading their way.

'Oh look,' he said. 'It's target practice time.'

The other two boys joined him and watched the approaching schoolboy.

'He looks like a first year,' said one of the boys.

'Perfect,' said the leader. 'Let's see how good my aim is.'

They stood back from the edge of the bridge so the approaching boy couldn't see them, but they needn't have worried. He was enjoying riding along by the river and was blissfully unaware of their presence up above him.

As Adam Radford rode under the bridge, he savoured the sudden change in light, just as he always did. This was one of his favourite rides, and now he would be able to come home this way every day, something he was looking forward to. Looking ahead through the tunnel, he could see the next bend in the river where he could turn onto the path that took him off towards home. Just five more minutes and he would be there.

Up above, the lead bully watched as the boy disappeared under the bridge. Then he raced across to the other side, counting to himself as he went. He leaned over the wall at the far side, reaching out to suspend the brick he was carrying above the path. He was still counting. He had watched people cycling under this bridge loads of times and he knew exactly how long it took for them to emerge from the far side.

'Twenty-five,' he said, quietly.

He let go of the brick and watched, fascinated, as the front wheel of the bicycle appeared from under the bridge. His timing was perfect, and the brick turned end over end before smashing into the top of the small boy's skull. For just the briefest moment, the boy continued onwards as if nothing had happened, but then he slumped forward and the bike wobbled slightly before turning towards the river.

With a quiet splash, boy and bike plunged into the river and disappeared.

'Wow! How's that for a good shot?' cried the ringleader.

'Bloody hell,' said one of the others. 'D'you think he's alright?'

'He'll have a headache and his mum won't be too happy that he's dumped his bike in the river,' said the ringleader. 'Just remember, we weren't here, okay? We were all over at my house. No one has seen us, so it's nothing to do with us. Now we'd better get out of here.'

They began walking away from the scene, quickly breaking into a breathless, giggling run, both exhilarated and scared by what they had done.

As soon as they had gone, their original victim crawled out from behind the bushes where he had been hiding. From his vantage point, he had been able to see them leaning over the bridge, but he had no idea what they were doing. Cautiously, he leaned over the bridge. He couldn't see anything on the path below, just an old brick off to one side. He wondered why they found dropping a brick off a bridge so exciting.

Out in the centre of the river, carried by the gentle current, what could have been a bundle of clothing floated slowly downstream.

CHAPTER ONE

DS Dave Slater had been hoping for a quiet first night back on duty. The victim of an unfortunate accident which had seen him concussed and subsequently hospitalised for two days, and then signed off for a further week, he had been looking forward to easing himself back into work and finding out what he had missed. The normal night roster at Tinton Police Station allowed for one detective to be on-site, with another on call if necessary. As Tinton was normally a pretty quiet, law-abiding town, this was usually sufficient to cover the workload, and Slater was happy enough to return to what should have been an easy enough shift.

His pleasure had been short-lived. On his arrival he had been told he was required to be interviewed about the night of his accident. The interview would take place around 8 p.m. that evening.

Bloody health and safety, thought Slater. They were police officers, after all, and they sometimes had to deal with violent people, so there were bound to be times when they were at risk. Sometimes people got hurt. It was part of the job. It went with the territory.

He rubbed his head. The whole sorry affair had come on the heels of the Wild Boar Woods case. He could have done with something a bit less dramatic after that. Even another flasher would have been preferable. But, of course, it *would* have ended with him getting cracked across the head and spending two nights in hospital. That was just typical.

* * *

As Slater looked across the table at the man opposite him, he thought DI Grimm had a most appropriate name. He was a hard-faced man who seemed to be totally devoid of any sort of good humour. He hadn't even managed to say hello when Slater had entered the room. The blonde DS sitting to Grimm's left seemed equally unhappy. Her hair was tied back in a rather severe bun. He wondered if that was why her face looked so pointed and pinched, or if she had simply spent too much time working with Grimm. She said her name was DS Fury, and he felt that was a good match for her appearance.

He could feel animosity building up within him. He had been in quite a good mood earlier, but he knew his face was now as grim as theirs. He had been waiting around for almost two hours before he had been called in, and now he had been sitting here, waiting for them to start, for what seemed like an age. As yet, no one had said anything apart from the curt introductions.

He'd been injured before and had to attend these interviews, but they were usually conducted by people he knew in a rather friendlier atmosphere. Come to think of it, they didn't usually involve a DI. An uncomfortable awareness began to creep up on him at the dawning realisation this interview probably had nothing to do with health and safety.

As if reading his thoughts, DI Grimm looked up from the notes he had been reading. 'How's the head now?' he asked.

'It seems to be working alright since they put the stuffing back in and sewed me up.'

For a moment, Grimm looked at Slater as if he'd spoken a foreign language, but then his face broke into what might have been a half smile — or it could have been a grimace. Slater couldn't be sure, one way or the other, but he was pretty sure Grimm had no sense of humour.

'Oh, I see,' said Grimm. 'You think it's a laughing matter.'

'I didn't at the time, nor when I woke up in hospital with a pneumatic drill hammering away inside my skull, but these things happen, don't they? No one died.'

There was a stony silence following Slater's comment. Grimm narrowed his eyes and gave Slater a piercing look, and DS Fury's head snapped up from her note-taking.

'What?' Slater looked between the two interrogators. 'Well, no one did get seriously hurt. I'm here, aren't I?'

'Do you understand why you're here, Detective Sergeant Slater?' asked Grimm.

Slater thought about a smart answer but resisted the temptation. He shifted uncomfortably in his chair. He didn't know what was going on, but he had been around long enough to understand that Grimm and Fury weren't here to make friends.

'I assumed this was going to be an interview about my accident,' he said. 'But those interviews are usually a bit more on the warm and fuzzy side. I've been around long enough to know an icy atmosphere like this means disciplinary hearing. What I don't know is why I wasn't warned and what I'm supposed to have done.'

Fury went back to scribbling her notes, while Grimm placed his elbows on the table and steepled his hands in front of his face.

'Hmmm. Yes, I'm sorry about that,' he said from behind his fingers. He placed his hands flat on the desk. 'You've been kept in the dark at my request. I thought it in everyone's best interests.'

'You mean you thought I might have time to prepare some lies for you if I knew this was coming,' said Slater. 'Whereas this way I don't even know what I'm supposed to have done.'

Grimm looked puzzled. 'What you're supposed to have done?'

Now Slater was confused. 'Well, if I'm not in the shit, why am I here?'

Fury looked up and studied his face. 'You really don't know, do you?' It was a statement not a question.

'What?' asked Slater, exasperated. 'What the hell's going on?'

'I'm sorry,' said Grimm, who obviously wasn't. 'You seem to have the wrong idea. You're not the perpetrator here. We're hoping you're going to be a witness.'

Slater sat back in his chair and folded his arms. 'A witness to what? I've been off sick for ten days.'

'A man has been seriously injured and is now recovering in hospital,' said Grimm. 'He nearly died while in custody. Your body language tells me you don't care and you don't want to help. I have to say, DS Slater, I find that to be a very disappointing attitude.'

Slater bit his tongue while he thought about how to respond without insulting a superior officer. After a few seconds, he unfolded his arms and leaned forward.

'You find my attitude disappointing, do you, sir?' he said, leaving a long pause before the 'sir'. 'Well, let me explain why my attitude is so unhelpful. Ten days ago my colleague and I tried to arrest two suspects. One of them, a great big bugger, excuse my language, who was about twice the size of me, resisted arrest and attacked me. As a result, I ended up in hospital and I've just spent ten days off work, recovering.

'On my first evening back at work I'm informed I have to attend an interview. I then spend the best part of three hours waiting to be called to that interview. When I finally get in to the interview room, I'm met by two stony-faced officers who don't even have the good manners to say hello. I then spend the next five minutes staring at the top of your heads while you ignore me, and then by some miracle I'm supposed to know what I'm here for when you've knowingly kept me in the dark. Do you *really* think that's the best way to nurture a good attitude in me? Sir?'

Slater had been stabbing at the table with his finger to emphasise his points. Now he sat back in his chair.

Grimm's face was a picture. It looked as though he was considering reaching across the table and placing his hands around Slater's throat to emphasise his own point. Fury's eyes had grown wider and wider as Slater had made his speech, and he was sure he caught the flicker of a smile as she put her head back down and started writing.

'You don't like me, Slater, do you?' asked Grimm.

'I don't know you so I have no opinion one way or the other,' said Slater. 'But I'll tell you this: I don't like being kept in the dark, I don't like being treated like an idiot, and I don't like people wasting my time.'

'We're only doing our job, you know. Have you ever thought of that?'

'Maybe it's not what you do, but the way you do it,' said Slater, leaning towards Grimm. 'Have you ever thought of that?'

Grimm and Slater glared at each other across the table. Slater knew he would have to back down, but he was determined he wasn't going to be bullied by the likes of Grimm, even if he *was* a DI.

* * *

In the observation suite, DCI Goodnews was regretting agreeing to keep Slater in the dark. She should have known Grimm was going to play it this way and put Slater's back up. This whole situation was a mess and she had probably allowed it to get even worse. She had always prided herself on her loyalty to her own officers, so why hadn't she warned Slater what was going on?

Back in the interview room, it was DS Fury who gave Slater a reason to break eye contact with Grimm.

'The point is, you *are* here,' she said. 'So why don't you tell us what you remember about the night you were injured? The sooner we get this over with, the sooner you can get back to work.'

'I wrote a statement while I was in hospital,' Slater said, turning to Fury. 'You must have read it.'

'Yes, but that was almost two weeks ago and you were concussed. I'd like to hear it again, in your own words.'

Slater sighed. 'What's this really about?'

Fury and Grimm exchanged a look.

'One of the suspects you and DC Darling were trying to arrest that night has accused DC Darling of assault causing grievous bodily harm,' said Grimm.

'But they got away,' said Slater. 'And anyway, he was trying to strangle me! Darling took a swipe at him with a cast-iron frying pan and took me out. That's when they got away.'

'Are you sure you don't want to press your own charges against her?' asked Grimm.

Slater couldn't quite believe his ears. 'No, I bloody don't. It was an accident. The guy saw her coming and swung me round so my head was where his should have been.'

'But she knocked you out cold! She could have killed you.'

'If she hadn't intervened, *he* would have killed me. Perhaps you would have preferred that. At least then you'd have something worth investigating, but it still wouldn't have been her fault.'

'You know very well,' snapped Grimm, 'that we have to investigate when a member of the public has made a complaint.'

'Even when that same member of the public was trying to strangle her colleague at the time?' asked Slater. 'What was the girl supposed to do, stand there and let him kill me? Surely we're allowed to defend ourselves.'

'Yes, but she went a long way beyond just defending herself. She put the man in hospital!'

'No. She put *me* in hospital. They got away because she stopped to make sure she hadn't killed me. I thought she was in the ambulance when they were taking me to the hospital.'

Grimm sighed. 'Yes, she did accompany you to the hospital. It's what she did two nights later that's the problem.'

'What did she do?' asked Slater, puzzled.

'She tracked down your attacker and his accomplice and arrested them.'

'What? Alone? But that big guy must be six feet four and weigh about sixteen stone. Darling's a midget and doesn't weigh half that soaking wet!'

'It appears DC Darling practises martial arts.' Grimm pulled a face as he said the last two words.

'Well, good for her,' said Slater, appreciatively.

'Are you saying you condone her behaviour?' Grimm glared at him.

'I condone her right to defend herself.'

'She wasn't defending herself. We have a witness who backs up the victim's story that DC Darling went berserk and attacked him.'

'Don't tell me,' said Slater. 'This witness is his accomplice, right?'

'The identity of the witness is immaterial. We cannot allow police officers to act as vigilantes and lose control like that. We all have a duty of care to the public—'

'Yeah,' said Slater. 'But what about the public? Don't they have a duty of care to us, as human beings?'

'I'm not here to debate the rights and wrongs of the public attitude to the police,' said Grimm. 'I'm here to ensure public safety at the hands of the police and to ensure the police carry out their duties in the correct manner. Unfortunately, it appears they won't be safe if we allow DC Darling to continue in her role as a police officer.'

Slater sat back in his seat, momentarily gobsmacked. 'Why exactly am I here? I'm not a witness to the incident, and it sounds as if you've already made up your mind what happened, based on the evidence of two thugs, one of whom had been fighting with me just a couple of nights before.'

'Yes, he mentioned that,' said Grimm. 'Apparently Darling told him it was "payback time". Was she referring to you? Was she paying him back for beating you up?'

'I don't know,' said Slater. 'I wasn't there.'

Grimm gave Slater a hard stare and Fury looked up from her notes again.

'Now what?' It began to dawn on Slater what he had said. 'Hold on a minute. You're not suggesting I had anything to do with this, are you?'

Grimm looked down at the notes before him. 'I see from your record you've been in trouble before.' He looked back up at Slater.

'Am I in trouble now?'

'That's what we have to decide,' said Grimm. 'The thing is, we have a man recovering in hospital with ruptured testicles, a ruptured spleen, several cracked ribs, and multiple bruises. She only used martial arts to bring him down. After that, she resorted to giving him a good old-fashioned kicking.'

Slater swallowed hard. This was all news to him. No wonder he hadn't seen or heard from Darling. But why had no one else told him? Did his colleagues really think he would be a party to something like this? And what about Goodnews? Surely *she* didn't think he would have asked Darling to do this for him?

His thoughts were interrupted by a dull booming sound from somewhere below them in the building. The building seemed to shiver and a split second later, a fire alarm began to ring. Without thinking, Slater jumped to his feet and started for the door.

'Detective Sergeant Slater,' spluttered Grimm, furiously. 'Get back here, we're not finished yet.'

'That sounded like an explosion to me,' said Slater, as he dragged the door open. 'This is my station and these are my mates. You sit there like some puffed-up ponce if you want. I'm going to see if I can help.'

'You'll pay for this insubordination,' roared Grimm, but Slater was already flying down the stairs.

* * *

The purple-faced Grimm was apoplectic with rage, so angry he could barely speak. Next to him, Fury was neither

11

surprised Slater had so little respect for her boss (after all, he was *such* an arrogant prick), nor was she surprised at the display of barely suppressed rage going on next to her. She had seen it so many times before. She was quite looking forward to the day when he really lost control and attacked someone. She would be volunteering to lead that investigation herself.

'Sir,' she said. 'The alarm. I think we should evacuate, don't you?'

CHAPTER TWO

Goodnews had reacted as quickly as Slater and they raced down the stairs together, bursting through the doors into the downstairs reception area. The noise from the alarm was even louder down there. A shocked-looking Sandy Mollinson, the night shift duty sergeant, was manning the desk, a phone pressed to his ear. He put the phone down as they entered.

'It's down in the basement,' he told them. 'The forensics lab.'

'Is there anyone down there?' asked Slater.

Mollinson shook his head. 'I've checked the log. The last one signed out hours ago.'

'What about a fire?' asked Goodnews.

'I haven't been down there yet,' he said, 'but there's CO_2 extinguishers so it should be okay.'

'I'll go and check,' said Slater, heading off towards the basement doors.

'Can you turn that alarm off?' asked Goodnews. 'I can't hear myself think.'

Mollinson reached down and hit a button. 'Fire service will be here any minute. There's no one down there, all my lads are out on the road and the two killjoys are upstairs. That means no one's unaccounted for, so there's no need for any heroics.'

In the near distance, sirens could be heard, getting louder.

'Thanks, Sandy,' said Goodnews. 'Any idea what happened?'

'My best guess is some sort of system failure,' said Mollinson. 'Gas, maybe, or something chemical.'

'Gas would have been a bigger explosion, don't you think?'

'The experts are here now,' said Mollinson, over the sound of heavy vehicles pulling up outside. 'Best let them tell us what happened.'

'Aye,' agreed Goodnews, 'you're probably right there. At least we've got no casualties. If it had happened during the day, there might have been four or five people down there and this place could have been heaving.'

Slater came back up from the basement just as the front door clattered open and the first of the firefighters burst through.

'Down there.' He pointed to the basement doors. 'It looks like there's a small fire, but the CO2 seems to be killing it.'

He joined Goodnews and Mollinson as more fire crew poured through the doors and down into the basement.

'Shouldn't we be assembling outside?' asked Mollinson, looking to Goodnews.

'I know that's the correct protocol, but as the senior officer, I think I can safely say I can account for all the staff who should be here. I think we'd be better served starting our investigation rather than standing outside like a bunch of lemons.'

Slater reached for the log book they kept at the front desk. It might be the old-fashioned way of doing things, but as long as everyone signed in and out it was still a great way of keeping track of who was in the building at any given time, and it had the advantage of still working, even if there was a power cut.

Just then, the door from the basement opened and a worried-looking fire officer appeared. 'I'm going to have to ask you to evacuate the building,' he said.

'But the fire was almost out,' said Slater.

'The fire *is* out. But this was no accident. It was started by an explosive device and until we've made sure there aren't any more I need to clear the building.'

'Yeah,' began Goodnews, 'but I'm the senior officer here, and—'

'It might be your station under normal circumstances, Miss, but right now it's my fire and I'm the senior fire officer. I need you all outside, please.'

They had been joined by Grimm and Fury.

'What's going on?' demanded Grimm. 'I'm trying to conduct an investigation here.'

Goodnews gave him a withering look. 'We have to leave the building. It appears we may have had a bomb go off in the basement, and they want to make sure there aren't any more devices down there. Follow me.' She turned to lead the way out of the building.

'This is outrageous,' said Grimm. 'Your man walked out of an interview. I demand you suspend him immediately.'

Goodnews swung round to face Grimm, who almost walked into her. 'May I remind you, Detective Inspector, that I am the senior officer here, and I don't take orders from you. My officer responded with selfless devotion to duty when that bomb went off, which is more than can be said for one or two other officers who were in the building. Right now I need all my officers to help with my own investigation. You can finish conducting your interview when it's more convenient.'

'But I've come all the way from—'

'I don't care if you've come all the way from bloody Mars,' said Goodnews. 'I think you'll find a bomb going off in a police station ranks as a fairly important investigation, don't you agree? Would you really like me to broadcast the fact that you obstructed such an inquiry?'

Grimm spluttered impotently, his face a picture, as Goodnews turned and led them from the building. As they walked down the short flight of steps outside, Slater found himself alongside Fury.

'He's gonna burst a blood vessel if he's not careful,' he muttered to her, nodding at Grimm.

She cast a quick look around and then lowered her voice. 'Let's hope so.'

Slater was so surprised he almost missed the next step and had to stop momentarily.

Well, there you go, he thought, watching Fury in surprise as she stepped out ahead of him. *I got you all wrong*. He felt a brief moment of sympathy for her having to work for an arse like Grimm.

As they reached the bottom of the steps, Goodnews turned to Grimm and they exchanged a few brief words. Slater didn't hear the exchange but he could work out what she had said, as Grimm marched furiously away, Fury almost having to run to keep up.

'Poor cow, having to work with an arsehole like that,' Slater muttered to Mollinson as they walked across the car park.

'Aye,' said Goodnews, who had caught them up and wasn't supposed to have heard the remark. 'You might bear that in mind next time you're having a moan about me.'

Mollinson couldn't hide his grin and Slater felt his face burning.

The car park would normally be empty at this time of night but for a handful of cars, but tonight it was heaving with fire engines and fire officers. There was a small group of outbuildings across the car park beyond the fire crews. Mollinson led them inside the nearest one and switched on the lights.

'I'd better go and get on the radio,' he said. 'I need to make sure no one comes back until we're given the all-clear.'

'Of course,' said Goodnews. 'You carry on, Sandy.' She turned to Slater. 'Okay, what do we know so far?'

'Looks like we've had a bomb go off in the basement. And looking at this log, the last person from the forensics lab to sign out was Ian Becks. That was just after 6 p.m.'

'Have you got his phone number? We could do with his help.'

'I'll try him.' Slater reached into his pocket for his mobile phone.

'I'd better call the chief constable and tell him the good news,' said Goodnews. 'This is just what I need after one of my officers beat someone up last week.'

'About that,' said Slater, listening to the Becks' phone ringing endlessly in his ear. 'It would have been nice if you'd told me instead of letting me go into one of those interviews blind. Do you really think I'd tell her to go and beat someone up?'

'Of course not,' she said. 'It's been a difficult week and I got it wrong. I'm sorry.'

'Sorry?' said Slater, angrily. 'Sorry? Bloody Grimm seems to think I'm head of some sort of vigilante group.'

'Look, I've said I'm sorry. I understand you're angry, but can we talk about this another time? I need to call my boss before he hears about this from someone else. Damage limitation and all that.'

'Yeah,' said Slater, cutting off his call to Becks. 'You go ahead and protect your reputation.'

Goodnews bristled at that. 'That's not what I meant,' she snapped.

'No. Of course not.'

She looked as though she was about to unleash a torrent of anger on him, but then seemed to think better of it. 'I'll go outside and call him. Perhaps in the meantime you'd like to grow up,' she said, and walked off into the night.

Slater decided against answering back and turned his attention to the log book. Once again, he mentally ticked off all the forensics team to make sure they were all accounted for. Sure enough, they were all there, the last signature being Ian Becks' untidy scrawl. And that was about all he could do until the fire chief told him they were allowed back into the building.

He thumbed his way to Becks' number, pressed redial, and held the phone to his ear, then he closed the log book, tucked it under his arm, and began to amble back in the direction of the building. All they could do was wait, and he hated waiting around. And why wasn't Becks answering his phone? It wasn't even going to voicemail, just ringing and ringing.

CHAPTER THREE

It was twenty minutes before Slater saw signs of activity from the back doors of the police station. The fire crews seemed to be making their way outside at last. Maybe now they could get inside and start working.

'What's going on?' asked Goodnews, walking up behind him.

'Dunno,' he said. 'Hopefully they're going to tell us it's all clear.'

'Let's hope so. Hold on, what's that?'

'They're carrying a stretcher. One of them must have got hurt.'

'Or killed,' said Goodnews, grimly. 'That body's covered.'

The stretcher-bearers lowered their cargo carefully to the ground as Eddie Brent, the lead officer, headed in their direction.

'Has one of your guys got hurt?' asked Goodnews.

'He's not one of ours. My lads are all accounted for. This guy must have been right in front of the bomb when it went off. He got blown backwards and was buried under the debris.'

'Christ,' said Slater. 'He might be the guy who planted the bomb.'

'So who is he, then?' asked Goodnews.

'I've no idea,' said Brent. 'We probably wouldn't have found him yet, but his phone kept on ringing and ringing. That's what made us look under all the rubbish.'

Slater was starting to feel an uncomfortable coldness in the pit of his stomach. 'Can I take look?' he asked.

'Sure, go ahead, but I warn you, he's a bit of a mess.'

They walked over to the stretcher and Slater knelt down alongside it. He took the corner of the sheet that was covering the body and pulled it back. The top of the head was badly scorched, but enough of the face was preserved to identify the victim. Goodnews peered over his shoulder.

'Bloody hell,' said Slater.

'Jesus,' she said. 'Is that who I think it is?'

'It's Ian Becks. What the hell was he doing in there? According to the log, he signed out hours ago.'

'Are you sure it's him? Only he's a bit of a mess.'

Slater pulled the sheet back a bit further. 'I'm pretty sure. And look, he's still wearing his motorcycle leathers. How many guys do you know who wear bright red leathers and have reason to be in our forensics lab?'

He re-covered the body and stood up, turning to Goodnews. He thought she looked a bit dazed and seemed to have gone a funny colour, but then it could have been the lighting outside. He felt a bit weak at the knees himself, struggling to comprehend that his colleague and friend Ian Becks was lying dead in front of him. Surely this wasn't really happening.

'Are you okay?' he asked Goodnews.

'What? Oh, yeah, I just wasn't expecting to find one of our own guys murdered while I was in the building.'

'You can't blame yourself for this,' said Slater. 'We don't even know what happened yet.'

Goodnews didn't look convinced but turned her attention to the fire chief. 'We could have done with the body being left *in situ*. You've probably destroyed evidence moving it.'

Slater watched the other man's face. If he was offended by her attitude, his expression didn't show it. His response said it all, though.

'We thought there was a chance he might still be alive when we found him. I suppose we could have stood around and waited to make sure he was dead. At least that would have preserved your precious evidence, but that's not what our job's about. We're here to try to save lives and that's what we tried to do. If you have a problem with that, I suggest you take it up with my superiors.'

Goodnews looked chastened, but before she could speak, he carried on making his point.

'You told me there was no one inside the basement. We might have found him early enough to save him if we'd known he was in there.'

Slater's head was reeling at what was unfolding, but he took the initiative and stepped in between them before things got out of hand.

'I think you need to go and call the chief constable, don't you, guv?'

Goodnews hesitated for a moment and then stomped off.

'I'm sorry, mate,' he said, turning to the fire chief. 'This has come as a shock to all of us. Ian was a key part of our team and he logged off three hours before the explosion. We're just trying to get our heads around why he was in there.'

'I understand that, but she needs to understand we're lifesavers, not crime-solvers. We don't have time to worry about preserving evidence.'

'I know, I know,' said Slater, soothingly. 'The problem is, she's a fast-rising star and I don't think she's ever had anything go wrong on her watch before. Right now, everything's going wrong and she's struggling to cope.'

'That's not my problem,' said the fire chief. 'I admire your loyalty, but at the end of the day it's a piss-poor excuse, isn't it?'

Slater couldn't argue with that. He angled his head in acknowledgement of the fact. 'Can we get inside that building now?' he asked.

'You can go inside but keep out of the basement for now. We don't think there are any more bombs but we can't be sure. We've got an explosives team on the way down from London. They're going to want to check it out before they'll let you in there. Perhaps you can make sure your hot-headed boss understands that.'

'Okay,' said Slater, with a wry smile. 'You've made your point. Let's not overdo it, eh? She is still my boss, and I am still on her side.'

At last, Slater saw a smile creep across the other man's face.

'I'm sorry about your mate,' he said, nodding across at the stretcher. 'If it's any consolation, I doubt he would have known much about it. It wasn't a big explosion, but if I'm right and he was right in front of it . . .'

'Yeah,' said Slater. 'I just can't figure out why he would have been in there. He was one of those blokes who was a stickler, you know? Even if he had come back for some reason, he would have signed back in. It doesn't make any sense.'

CHAPTER FOUR

'Are you alright?' asked Slater as Goodnews joined him in the incident room.

'I don't think I've ever had such a bollocking,' she said, glumly. 'The chief constable is going nuts. He's suggesting our security must be worse than hopeless.'

'Ah,' said Slater, not knowing what else to say. He knew Goodnews had been instrumental in reviewing the security at Tinton. The implication was obvious.

'What with the Darling fiasco last week and now this,' she said, 'I feel as if I've taken two enormous strides backwards.'

'Really?' Slater heard the disappointment in his own voice. 'We've got a colleague lying dead on a stretcher downstairs and all you're worried about is how this could affect your career?'

Goodnews looked as if she had been slapped. 'That's not what I mean at all. Of course what's happened is more important.'

'Good. I'm pleased to hear it,' he said, not convinced.

Goodnews sighed. 'I don't care what you think. There's nothing wrong in having a bit of ambition and wanting to get on in life. You should try it some time, then you might not have such a big problem with it.'

'I don't have a problem with it,' replied Slater, 'as long as it doesn't involve using other people to get there.'

'Is that what you think I do?'

He shrugged his shoulders, wishing he hadn't started this conversation. 'I'm sorry, I'm probably speaking out of turn.'

'No, actually, I'd like to hear what you think.'

'You would?' he said, surprised.

'Aye,' she said. 'I know you think I'm some thick-skinned bitch who doesn't care what anyone else thinks, but it's not quite like that.'

Now Slater felt uncomfortable. Was he pushing her into revealing some sort of vulnerability? This was something he had never expected and he didn't think it was a good idea. Then again, he *had* started it.

'I don't think this is really the time, do you?' he asked her.

'I suppose not,' she admitted, 'but you seem to be challenging me. Do you think I'm going to back down?'

He smiled. 'That's the last thing I would expect you to do. I don't think it's in your nature, is it?'

'You'd better believe it,' she said. 'And you'd better believe we will come back to this conversation at a later date, but right now we should put it on hold.'

'Fair enough,' he agreed.

'Okay, then,' she said, at once all business-like. 'Have you called everyone in?'

'I was going to,' he said. 'But then I thought that was a bit of a knee-jerk reaction. I might be wrong, but in my opinion there's not much point in flooding the place with bodies who are just going to be hanging around until we can get into that basement. We're limited to what we can do right now and they'll think better on a few hours' sleep. So I've only called Steve Biddeford. He's probably the best of the bunch.'

'You're probably right,' said Goodnews. 'But what about you?'

'I was on nights anyway, remember? I'll be good for the rest of the night and maybe a full day tomorrow. How about you?'

'I'm good for now. I don't think I dare take much time out while I'm under the microscope.'

'You can't function on no sleep,' said Slater.

'I know that,' she said. 'But sometimes you just have to make do. Anyway, what have we got so far?'

'I'm struggling to understand why Ian Becks, one of the most anal rule followers I've ever met, would sign out and then come back in again without signing in. It's just completely out of character. We need to go through the CCTV footage from the reception area and see if we can find out what happened.'

'Does he have any family?' asked Goodnews. 'There must be someone we should notify.'

'He's never mentioned anyone,' said Slater, 'but his personnel record should tell us that. Oh, and it might be an idea to take a look at whatever he's been working on. Maybe someone had a grudge because he caught them out.'

Goodnews looked doubtful. 'I'm sure it won't be that,' she said, hastily. 'We've not had anything major in months.'

'Yeah, but we can't ignore it, though, can we?' he said. 'What about anyone who's just been convicted because of Becks? That might be worth checking out.'

She pulled another face. 'Alright. Get Biddeford to take a look at that CCTV footage when he gets here. I'll check his file and see who we have to notify. I'll be upstairs in my office. Let me know when those bomb guys get here. We need to know what they find.'

CHAPTER FIVE

Goodnews had soon discovered Ian Becks' personnel file wasn't going to be much help with finding next of kin. His mother was the only person listed, but she had died two years ago. For whatever reason, Becks' next of kin had never been updated, so Slater had volunteered to go and see what he could find.

It was close to 4.30 a.m. when Slater pulled up outside Ian Becks' flat. He'd had a pint with Becks enough times to have considered him a mate, but he'd never been here before, and now he thought about it, he realised he actually knew very little about him. They had always tended to talk shop, or football, or bicker about who brought more to an investigation, but they had never spoken about their families or anything even vaguely personal.

He had felt rather uncomfortable rifling through the dead man's pockets earlier, but having a key to unlock the door was preferable to breaking in. He slipped on a pair of latex gloves, slid the key quietly into the lock, and turned it. The door swung open and he walked inside, flicking the lights on as he passed the switch.

There was a small hall with four doors leading off. The first one was half open and was obviously the kitchen. He pushed the door fully open and looked inside. As he expected, everything was very neat and tidy. There wasn't so much as a single thing out of place that he could see. He opened one of the cupboards and peered inside. A smile crept across his face as he noticed every can was carefully lined up with its neighbours, all the labels facing the same way.

'It wasn't just at work then, Becksy,' he said, quietly.

He quickly opened the other cupboards and drawers, but he wasn't surprised to find nothing of interest. Becks wouldn't have considered the kitchen the right place to keep paperwork.

He went back into the hallway and pushed open the next door. It was a tiny bathroom. A quick glance told him he wasn't going to find anything of interest in there so he moved on. The next doorway was opposite the front door and opened to reveal the lounge. At first glance, Slater thought it must be furnished in a style that would be labelled minimalist. But as he scanned the room, he was surprised at the sparseness of the furniture. There was a large, slightly threadbare armchair in one corner, a quite small TV in the opposite corner, and an ancient desk standing against one wall. He thought this wasn't so much minimalist as almost non-existent. This was a surprise. He knew Becks must have been on a pretty good salary, so how come he didn't have any decent furniture?

His eye was drawn to a photograph in a silver frame on the sideboard. It looked like someone's wedding. He picked up the photo and stared at it. He had been correct; it was a wedding photo. It was a classic wedding pose, clearly showing a beautiful, smiling bride and her equally happy groom. This was a bit of a shock. Slater had known Becks for three years and he had never once mentioned that he was married.

For a moment, he had the horrible thought that this mystery wife might well be asleep in the bedroom while he was poking around in her home, but that thought quickly receded as he realised this flat bore none of the hallmarks that would suggest a woman lived here. Even so, he held his breath as he quietly crept over to the bedroom and gently pushed the door open. He peered inside. To his great relief, the bed was empty and he noisily released his breath.

So where was this mysterious beauty? Perhaps they were divorced. It seemed most people were these days. Then he had another thought. What if she had died of some illness? Cancer didn't care how old you were, did it?

He suddenly realised he was just speculating and rather wildly at that. He was supposed to be a professional, investigating a murder. Instead of making wild guesses, he should be looking for a clue that might identify her or tell him what had happened to her. He went back to the desk in the lounge. If Becks kept paperwork anywhere, this would surely be the place.

It was an old kneehole desk with three narrow drawers down each side and two wider drawers across the top. He started with the bottom drawers and worked his way up. Most of the paperwork seemed to be old household bills, bank statements and junk mail. Slater flipped quickly through the paperwork. He absently thought it rather odd that Becks should keep junk mail, but he would worry about that later when they came back to carry out a more thorough search. For now, he was just looking for a letter, a birthday card, or anything that might give him a clue as to the mystery wife or any other next of kin. He found it in the very last drawer he looked at.

There was a small bundle of letters from someone called Beth. As Slater read the first one, he could see she was now an ex-wife. It was obvious they were either divorced or living apart, but it was equally obvious they were still very fond of each other. There was an address at the top of each of her letters, so Slater took the bundle and slipped it into his pocket.

He turned off all the lights and made sure the door was locked behind him. He glanced at his watch as he climbed into his car. It was just coming up to five a.m. There wasn't much point in calling the former Mrs Becks just yet. It wasn't as if she could do anything to bring him back, so he might as well give her a couple more hours.

CHAPTER SIX

The explosives team had refused to give Goodnews permission to access the basement, but even so, she had decided to call the entire day shift in early. As Slater arrived back at the station, the first few bleary-eyed officers were arriving. One of the new arrivals was the day shift duty sergeant, Tom Sanders. He had just climbed from his car as Slater pulled up, and by the time they reached the back doors Slater had caught him up.

'And you're sure he signed out and didn't come back, Tom?' Slater asked him as they signed the log.

'Let me think,' said Sanders, as he flipped the page back and studied the previous day's log. 'Here it is. Ian Becks, 18.09, signed out. Something else happened about then. Yeah, here we are, look. Those two miserable gits from out of town turned up.' He pointed to the two signatures of DI Grimm and DS Fury, signed in at 18.10. 'I seem to recall a courier coming in at the same time, but the parcel was for Becksy and I was busy with DI Misery Guts, so he said he'd deal with it and not to worry.'

'So what happened with the courier?' asked Slater.

'I don't know. Like I say, it was for Becks. He dealt with it.'

'And did the courier sign in?'

Sanders looked at the log. 'Obviously not,' he said.

'Did you see Becks come back out?' asked Slater.

'Yes,' said Sanders. 'I was still busy but he waved as he came through.'

'How long was he down in the basement?'

'Five or ten minutes. I can't be sure. That moron Grimm was giving me a hard time. He was such an annoying bastard. It'll be on the CCTV though.'

'Okay, thanks, Tom,' said Slater. 'You know we'll have to take a proper statement from you later, right?'

'Of course. Anything I can do to help. Old Becksy was a bit weird, but he was a bloody genius and he was *our* bloody genius. We'll all want to help if we can.'

Slater didn't want to spoil Sanders' day before it got started, but he could see there was going to be a shit storm over the security at the front desk, and blaming Grimm wasn't going to help, especially if *he* ended up leading the inevitable investigation.

* * *

When Slater reached the incident room, he was pleased to see it was becoming a hive of activity. There was only a small team at Tinton so their resources were limited, but Goodnews had been busy while Slater had been out and she was delegating tasks as people arrived.

'Any luck?' she asked him.

'I think so,' he said. 'It appears there's a Mrs Becks, but I think they're probably divorced.'

'Christ!' said Goodnews. 'He kept that bloody quiet. But you were his mate. You must have known.'

'You'd think so, wouldn't you? But the more I think about it, the more I realise he never, ever mentioned anything about his personal life.'

'But you used to go to the pub together, didn't you?'

'Well, yeah, now and then, but it was never a regular thing. And we were never really close, you know? We just exchanged banter about work, and football and stuff like that.'

'Oh, sophisticated stuff then.' Goodnews smiled. 'I suppose page three would have been a hot topic.'

'Actually, now I think about it, I don't think we ever talked about anything like that,' said Slater.

'Oh, come on. I thought beer, football and sex was all you blokes ever talked about,' she scoffed.

'I admit they would normally be hot topics with most blokes, but I swear Becks never spoke about sex, or women, or his past.'

'Do you think that's significant?'

'I haven't a clue if it's significant,' said Slater, 'but you have to admit it's a bit strange.'

Goodnews sighed. 'Aye, but then he was one strange guy, wasn't he?'

Slater smiled sadly. 'I can't argue with that.' He emptied the letters from his pocket and sat down. 'So where have we got to?'

'I'm waiting for Tom Sanders to come in,' she said. 'He was on the desk when Becks signed out. We need to get a statement from him.'

'He's just come in,' said Slater. 'I signed in with him.'

'I take it you had a little chat with him.'

'He remembers Becks signing out but he was also dealing with the happy twins, Grimm and Fury. And then, just to add to the general chaos, a courier arrived.'

Goodnews suddenly perked up. 'Oh aye,' she said. 'Go on.'

'According to Tom, the parcel was for Becks. He could see Tom was busy so he dealt with the courier himself. He says he's pretty sure Becks must have taken the parcel back down to the basement, and he thinks he left five or ten minutes later.'

'What do you mean he "thinks" he saw Becks leave?'

'DI Arsey was still giving him a hard time so he was distracted and not sure about the time, but he says Becks made a point of waving to him as he left.'

'So Becks signs out, receives a parcel while he's in reception, takes it back downstairs, and then leaves a few minutes later,' summarised Goodnews. 'Is that right?'

'That's how it looks,' said Slater. 'CCTV will prove it. Has anyone looked at it yet?'

'Steve Biddeford's working on it. He's working backwards to see if we can find out when Becks came back into the building. If he timed it right, and the front desk was unmanned for a minute or two, he could have got in without signing.'

'But why would he want to?' asked Slater. 'And anyway, he knows there's CCTV watching reception. He's not stupid enough to think he can get in unnoticed.'

Goodnews was looking through the letters Slater had brought back from Becks' flat. There was a photograph in amongst them and it slipped out on to the table.

'Is this her?' she asked, looking up at Slater.

He nodded. 'Yeah, that's her.'

'Wow! Talk about batting above your average. Who would have thought a nerd like him could pull a lovely looking girl like this?'

'Not just pull, but tie the knot as well,' said Slater. 'And from what I've read in those letters, they're still pretty close.'

'Have you called her yet?' asked Goodnews.

'I thought I'd leave it until seven,' he said. 'She's not down as next of kin and she can't bring him back . . .'

'Go and get yourself a cup of coffee. I'll have look through these letters and see if I can learn anything useful.'

CHAPTER SEVEN

'Coffee?' asked Slater, pushing open the door to the tech room.

Steve Biddeford looked up from his position in front of the bank of screens as Slater walked across with a steaming cup.

'Thanks,' he said. 'Look, I'm sorry about Becks. I know we all knew him and appreciated his work, but you and him were mates—'

'It's okay,' said Slater. 'We shared a few pints now and then but I'm just learning we weren't really mates. It turns out I hardly knew anything about him. Three years, and I've only just found out he had been married and was divorced.'

'Really? He kept that bloody quiet.'

Slater smiled. 'That's just what Goodnews said.'

'So where are we?' asked Biddeford.

'All we know so far is that he signed out at 18.09. As he was signing out, a courier arrived with a parcel for him. He took the parcel back downstairs to his office, then five or ten minutes later he walks back through reception and out of the building. So he was gone by about 18.20, but then about three hours later, he's sat at his desk down in the basement when something explodes, blowing him over backwards and causing bad enough injuries that when the fire service guys find him, about half an hour or so later, he had just taken his last breath.'

'I've gone backwards from the time of the explosion,' said Biddeford. 'I've got back to 7 p.m., and so far the only sign of life in that reception area is the hands on the clock moving.'

'Are we missing something?' said Slater. 'There isn't any other way in, is there?'

'There's always the fire exit. He could have left it open before he went home and then sneaked back later.'

'The fire service guys assure us the fire exit was still locked and the trip switch was still working. You can only open it from the inside, and if you did open it for more than fifteen seconds it would trigger an alarm out here as a potential security breach,' said Slater. 'And if he had come back, where's his motorbike? He went everywhere on that.'

'He could have left it somewhere and got a taxi,' suggested Biddeford.

'I suppose that's something we need to check out. I wonder if Goodnews has got onto it yet.'

'What are you on now?' asked Biddeford.

'I'm just going to see his ex-wife. It seems they were still close, so maybe she can shed some light on his state of mind. Maybe he had an enemy we don't know about.'

'Ah, the crappiest job of all.' Biddeford aimed a grim look at his colleague. 'Good luck with that.'

Slater returned the look. No one ever wanted to notify family members about a death. 'Someone's got to do it,' he said.

'What about what he was working on?' asked Biddeford.

'The boss seems to think he wasn't working on anything that would warrant a bomb,' said Slater.

'Yeah, but we've got to check it out, haven't we? It sounds like a no-brainer to me.'

'We're agreed about that. Maybe if we both keep suggesting it we can wear her down.'

'She probably won't like me suggesting it,' said Biddeford. 'But then it won't be the first time I've got on her wrong side.'

'Just mention it in passing,' said Slater. 'If enough of us talk about it, she can't ignore it.'

'But why would she want to?' asked Biddeford. 'Start with the obvious. It's basic police work, isn't it?'

'Maybe she just sees it different to us,' said Slater. 'Right now she needs a quick result and that's clouding her judgement. Perhaps we just need to do a little bit of managing upwards.'

'Okay, I'll drop a hint when I see her.'

'I'd better go. Perhaps by the time I get back, the CCTV footage will have revealed the answer and we can all relax.'

'I think you'll find that's called wishful thinking.'

'Optimism,' said Slater. 'That's what it is.'

'Yeah, right.' Biddeford returned to his TV screen. 'Good luck with that.'

* * *

'I've circulated a description of his motorbike,' said Goodnews, 'and I've asked for his private mobile phone records and emails. We should be able to access his work emails and phone records from our own servers.'

'What about what he was working on?' asked Slater.

'That won't tell us if he's received any sort of threat, will it?' she said.

'No,' agreed Slater, 'but it might point to someone who uses this sort of extreme violence to make a point.'

'I think we should go through the phone and email records first.' Goodnews's voice was firm. 'Then, if we find a threat we can see if there's a job we can link it to.'

The situation was making Slater feel slightly uneasy but he couldn't put his finger on why. Anyway, her tone made it quite clear she wasn't prepared to negotiate so he decided to let it go for now.

'We could do with someone like Norm in this situation,' said Slater. 'He probably dealt with this sort of crime all the time when he was based up in London.'

Slater's thoughts drifted to his former colleague, DS Norman Norman. He missed Norm's portly frame pushing its way through the double doors, a tray of coffees and bacon rolls announcing his arrival. He'd only been in Tinton for a couple of years but Slater had immediately taken to Norman and vice versa.

Slater looked at DCI Goodnews, standing in front of him, looking frosty. It was her fault in a way that Norman wasn't around any longer. She had made it clear she had no room for a Mister Roly-Poly figure in her team, and when Norman refused to lose weight and get fit, he had been pensioned off at the first opportunity. Slater felt irritated all over again — Norm had been a bloody good officer. So what if he couldn't run a marathon?

He wondered briefly if Norm would come back as a civilian researcher again, like he had on the last big case. Unlikely, he thought sadly, as Norm had left proclaiming he wouldn't work with DCI Goodnews again.

'I think you'll find it was Mr Norman's choice to leave.' Goodnews's icy voice broke through Slater's ponderings. 'I even found a way for him to use his experience to assist the team, but he has some sort of grudge against me that he couldn't get past.'

Slater felt a smartarse retort on the way but he managed to stop it right on the tip of his tongue. He chose instead to say nothing, wondering how his relationship with his boss had got to this point. It was as if they were tiptoeing around some sort of flashpoint that could only end in an almighty explosion. He knew he was just as much to blame as her, but he couldn't for the life of him say why.

CHAPTER EIGHT

Bethan Becks had been horrified when Slater had broken the news to her, and it had taken the family liaison officer a good twenty minutes and a cup of strong, sweet tea before she had become composed enough to answer his questions.

'It's such a shock,' she said. 'Can you tell me what happened?'

'All we know so far is that he signed out of work just after six p.m. and left the building, but then, somehow, three hours later he was at his desk when there was an explosion,' said Slater. As he said the words, he realised how little they really *did* know.

'But how did he get back in without anyone noticing?' asked Beth.

'That's just one of the things we're trying to figure out,' he admitted.

'And you say there was an explosion. Was it a bomb?'

'It's too soon to say for sure, but at the moment it looks the most likely explanation.'

'But who would do such a thing?'

'That's what we're trying to work out,' said Slater. 'I was hoping you might be able to help us out there. I know you and Ian were divorced, but I believe you still kept in touch.'

Beth looked at Slater and bit her lip. He felt as if he were being assessed. 'How well did you know Ian?' she asked.

'Not as well as I thought,' he replied, carefully. 'For a start, I didn't know he'd been married.'

'He only ever told people what he wanted them to know,' she said, mysteriously. 'It's been very hard for him to face up to reality and deal with everything.'

'I'm not with you,' said Slater. 'I've only worked with him for three years, and as far as I'm aware he's not had any problems. If there's something you know that might help us, you should tell me.'

She looked long and hard at his face, then she sighed. 'He had a secret,' she said. 'I promised I would never tell anyone, but I suppose it can't hurt now, can it?'

Slater held his breath.

'Ian was always quite prim and proper,' she began. 'We went out together for four years before we married, but in all that time we never once had sex.'

Slater found that hard to believe. Beth Becks was a very attractive woman.

'He used to say he wanted to wait. I didn't mind. He was quite religious, so I just assumed he was doing the right thing, you know?'

Slater nodded encouragingly. He had a feeling where this was going, but surely he would have known, wouldn't he?

'But then, when we were married, he found it difficult. I was sure he loved me, but he just didn't seem to be able to show it in the way a man should, if you see what I mean.'

Slater nodded again.

'You know what I'm saying, don't you, Mr Slater? Poor Ian was gay, but he'd never been able to admit it. He thought if he married me . . .'

She stopped speaking and turned to stare out of the window. Slater gave her a few moments before he spoke. 'Is that why you divorced?' he asked.

She nodded her head and turned back to face him. 'We still loved each other. But I needed what he couldn't give me,

38

and he needed what I couldn't give him. I suppose we could have carried on, but who really wants to live a lie? You have to be who you really are, don't you? He was trying to come to terms with it, but he'd been hiding it for years. It was very difficult for him.'

Even though Slater had guessed where the conversation was leading, he was still finding it hard to take in. It wasn't that he cared about Becks being gay, he was just finding it hard to believe he knew so very little about someone he had worked with for over three years.

'I know you still kept in touch,' he said. 'I had to go to his flat, and I found your letters.'

'Did he keep them?' she asked.

'I think they meant a great deal to him. As far as I can tell, he had never confided in anyone at work, so it's possible you were the only person he trusted where this was concerned.'

'Poor Ian,' she said. 'He must have been so alone.'

A small sob escaped from her and she reached for a tissue. Slater had an uncomfortable, guilty feeling. If only he'd known. He would have been happy to talk to Becks, but he'd had no idea what the poor guy was going through.

'Did he ever mention being worried about anything?' he asked. 'Did he ever suggest he was in any sort of danger or being threatened by anyone?'

Beth thought for a moment. 'I'm not aware that he felt in danger. There was the incident a few weeks ago, but he thought that was a one-off and he was just in the wrong place at the wrong time.'

'What incident was that?' Slater asked.

'A few weeks ago,' she said. 'Someone attacked him with a baseball bat or a cricket bat. I think he was the victim of a "gay-basher". He said it wasn't that, but he'd been talking about going to a gay bar and it happened at night. I think it's too much of a coincidence, don't you?'

'I remember that,' said Slater. 'It was about eight weeks ago. He told me he'd been trying out for his village cricket team. He said he'd been too slow getting out of the way of the fast bowler and the ball had smacked against his arm.'

'He's never played cricket in his life,' said Beth.

'Do you know where this gay bar is?'

'It's called Dickie's Bar,' she said. 'He was hoping he might meet someone.'

'I know where Dickie's Bar is,' he said. 'We can pay them a visit. Maybe someone will remember something. Is there anything else you can tell us?'

'There was one thing but I'm not sure how it would be relevant. Apparently there was a lot of bullying when he was at school.'

Slater frowned.

'Like I said, it's probably completely irrelevant, and I wouldn't have taken much notice except in all the time I'd known him, he had never mentioned it. Then, suddenly, someone attacked him and out it came.'

Slater found it easy to imagine the geeky Becks being the victim of a school bully. 'Did he think it was the same person who had bullied him at school?'

'I have no idea, he didn't say. But it's not likely, is it? We all had bullies at school, but even the bullies grow up eventually.'

'Like you say, it's probably unlikely, but right now, I'm open to all suggestions,' said Slater. 'Do you know any names?'

'Good grief, no,' she said. 'That was before I met him, but I can tell you the name of the school if that helps.'

Slater didn't really think it would add anything to their enquiries, but he made a note of the school anyway. He felt it was time to go.

'Look, Beth, I'm sorry we got to meet in these circumstances, but I'm going to have to get back. The family liaison officer will stay with you, but is there anyone we can call?'

'That's alright,' she said. 'My boyfriend will be home later.'

'What does he think about Ian?'

'Oh, they get on just fine,' said Beth, then corrected herself. 'Or should I say, they *got* on fine. It was Jimmy's idea that

40

Ian should submit his manuscript. Jimmy works for a pub-lisher, you see, and Ian had written this novel about a forensic scientist who solved all the crimes the police couldn't.'

Slater couldn't hide his smile. 'He was writing about him-self,' he said. 'He always used to tell me I'd be lost without him.'

This brought a smile to her face too. 'Yes,' she said. 'When he came to work he knew exactly who he was and what he was supposed to do.'

'He was very highly thought of,' said Slater. 'Someone said to me earlier today that everyone at Tinton saw Ian as "our genius".'

'That's nice to know,' she said. 'He would have liked that.'

'If you think of anything else that might help, just give me a call.'

'Thank you,' she said. 'I'll do that.'

CHAPTER NINE

'Right,' said Biddeford, addressing his audience, notebook in his hand. 'I've reviewed all the CCTV footage from the reception area from the time of the explosion right back until the time Becks signed out. I'm not going to run the footage now, but I've picked out the relevant events.'

Goodnews had called a full briefing so everyone would know exactly where the investigation had got to and where it was going next. She had given them a brief update, and now Biddeford was adding his findings from the CCTV footage. She listened intently — she *had* to solve this fast, or all her hard work over the past few months would have been in vain. Her ears were still smarting from the chief constable's comments.

'At 18.08, DI Grimm and DS Fury enter the building. They engage Tom Sanders at the counter and, being an arse, Grimm gives him a hard time, just because he can.'

There were one or two murmurs of agreement.

'Let's save the editorial comments for another time, can we?' interrupted Goodnews. 'A colleague has been murdered. I think that's more important than what anyone thinks of DI Grimm, don't you?'

Biddeford's face turned a deep shade of red. 'Sorry, boss,' he mumbled, awkwardly.

'Move on,' said Goodnews, a small smile playing about her lips. She actually agreed with Biddeford's assessment of Grimm's behaviour, but now wasn't the time.

Biddeford fidgeted awkwardly, coughed, and began again. 'Okay. 18.09. DI Grimm is still hogging the desk sergeant's attention when Ian Becks comes through the doors at the back of reception and makes his way over to sign the log. He's wearing his distinctive red motorcycle leathers and he's carrying his crash helmet. He signs the log and then it looks like his phone rings. He answers and is on the phone for a second, then hangs up and stands in reception. Sadly, it's a blocked number so we've no idea who he was speaking to. Could just have been a wrong number.

'18.11. The front door swings open and a motorcycle courier comes in carrying a package. From Becks' body language, it looks as if he's been waiting for the delivery. He walks up to the courier and speaks to him, then leads him back through the doors at the back of reception. My guess is the courier has agreed to carry the package down to the lab where Becks is going to sign for it.

'18.20. Becks comes back through the doors. This time he's wearing his crash helmet and he heads straight for the front doors. Tom Sanders is still tied up with Grimm and Fury, but he glances up as Becks walks through. Becks raises a hand to acknowledge him and makes his way out of the doors. And that's the last time he appears on the front desk CCTV.'

'You're sure it was Becks?' asked Slater.

'For sure,' said Biddeford. 'His crash helmet's as distinctive as those red leathers.'

'So, what happened to the courier?' asked Goodnews.

'I suspect Becks would have let him out the back way through the fire exit,' said Biddeford. 'Couriers have to park around there. It would have been the quickest way out for him. Saves him having to walk all the way back through and around the building.'

Goodnews sighed in frustration. Their security was so lax as to be almost non-existent. 'So he didn't sign in and he left by the back door,' she said. 'What's the point in us having a bloody security system if no bugger sticks to it?'

'It gets a bit worse, actually,' said Biddeford. 'Anyone wearing a crash helmet is supposed to take it off when they enter the building.'

'But the courier didn't?' she asked.

Biddeford gave her a helpless little shrug.

'Oh bloody hell,' she said, exasperated. 'So you're telling me some faceless guy walked in and was taken downstairs, and we have no idea who he is?'

'We should be able to get the registration number of his bike from the cameras outside,' said Slater.

'Let's bloody hope so,' said Goodnews. 'Steve, I want you to get onto that as soon as we finish up here. I want to know who this guy is, and then I want him interviewed.'

'Yes, boss.'

'Right,' she said, trying to maintain a good humour. 'Next. DS Slater has been to see Ian Becks' former wife.'

There was a lot of surprised murmuring at this piece of news.

'Aye. It came as a bit of a shock when we found out earlier this morning, but it gets even more interesting.'

She nodded at Slater and he made his way to the front of the room.

'I had a long chat with Bethan Becks earlier this morning,' he began. 'It was quite an eye-opener for me. I don't know about the rest of you, but I always thought I knew Ian quite well. Now I've been nosing into his life for a few hours, I realise I actually know almost nothing about him. He was a very private person who would talk all night about football, and how we'd never solve any crimes if it wasn't for his team, but he never actually revealed anything about himself.

'I only found out this morning that he had been married. I was trying to find some evidence of any next of kin and I found some letters she had written to him. The letters show, quite clearly, they were still very close. When I met

Beth, I couldn't understand why Ian would have divorced her. And then she told me.

'Ian had a secret. He was gay. The poor bloke had thought that if he married Beth everything would be alright, but it doesn't work that way, does it? Although they still loved each other they decided it wasn't fair on either of them to carry on as they were, and so they divorced.

'Ian was going to try become the real him and was trying to pluck up the courage to come out. He had recently started going to gay bars, hoping to meet someone. Unfortunately, he met someone who took exception to him being gay and went after him with a baseball bat. Some of you may recall that a couple of months ago he had his arm in a sling for a few days. He said it was an accident playing cricket.'

'A bomb's a bit extreme for a gay-basher, isn't it?' asked Biddeford. 'Battering someone with a baseball bat is the sort of thing we've come to expect from those people, but a bomb?'

'Yeah,' agreed Slater. 'It does sound a bit extreme, doesn't it? I agree with the boss that the courier should be our priority, but at the moment we have to consider all our options.'

'Okay everyone,' said Goodnews. 'Now you know as much about this case as we do. We should be getting a full report on the actual explosive device soon, but until we know more I think we should assume it was a small bomb. What we need to know is how did it get there? We also need to know how the hell Ian Becks got there and *why* he was there. Who was the faceless courier? Why would Becks take him downstairs, and where did he go? How did he get out of the building? Where is Becks' motorbike? And, of course, the million-dollar question: why was Ian Becks a target?'

She left a brief silence and looked around the faces before her. 'He was one of us,' she said, finally. 'As someone said earlier, he might have been a bit weird, but he was a genius, and he was *our* genius. He can't help us with this one so we owe it to him to make sure we don't need his help. I know we can do it, so let's get busy.'

* * *

'What would you like me to do next?' Slater asked Goodnews, when everyone had left the room.

'Have a cup of coffee and take a look at these emails and phone records.' She pointed to a pile of paperwork on her desk. 'Then I've got something I'd like you to do quietly.'

'What's that then? You make it sound like a mission for James Bond.'

'You're not going to like it,' she said.

'Why not?'

She looked around to make sure everyone had gone and no one was within earshot. 'I want you to take look at that CCTV footage from reception.'

'But Steve's already done it,' said Slater. 'Don't you trust him?'

'Aye, I know he's already done it, but I've got a nagging doubt. I seem to recall another case where he reviewed some CCTV footage and missed not one, but two clues.'

'So why did you ask him in the first place? We're just wasting time this way. And he's gonna be well pissed off when he finds out I'm checking up on him.'

'I'm going to ask him to take a couple of uniforms and go search Ian Becks' flat. That should keep him occupied for three or four hours,' said Goodnews. 'And if he does start to whinge I'll make sure he knows it was my idea and not yours. Okay?'

'You're the boss,' said Slater. 'Of course I'll do it if you think it's really necessary.'

'I'd be a lot happier. At least then I'd know for sure we haven't missed anything.'

'See,' said Slater, 'that's where Norm was worth his weight in gold.'

Goodnews stiffened at Slater's reference to Norman. She felt bad enough without having the spectre of Norman rising up. She'd given him a chance, she really had. She'd offered to help him lose the weight and then she'd given him another opportunity to keep on working as part of the team. She couldn't have done anything else, could she? She stood up, feeling exhausted.

'Aye,' she said, pushing her chair back under her desk. 'And what a lot of good that was.' She started to walk towards the door. 'I'll go and tell Biddeford he's relieved from CCTV-watching once he's found that registration number,' she said. 'Then I'll be in my office if you want me.'

Slater felt guilty as he watched her walk from the room and wondered why he'd made that remark. He knew exactly why Norman had quit working with them, and he knew it had been his own choice. Goodnews had created the opportunity for him after he had retired. It wasn't her fault he had felt trapped behind a desk. Come to think of it, she had given him plenty of chance to get himself fit before he had retired. It had been his own choice not to bother, even though he knew it would mean he had to retire.

He turned his attention to Becks' emails. Maybe there would be something useful in there.

CHAPTER TEN

Goodnews looked up, startled, as her office door burst open to reveal Slater, a murderous look in his eyes.

'Did you forget to knock, or what?' she said. 'I could have been on the phone or interviewing someone.'

'What have you done?' he asked, as he approached her desk.

'I'm sorry? I'm not with you.'

He was right in front of her desk now, and he placed his hands along the front edge and leaned towards her. 'What have you done?' he repeated, angrily.

She pushed her chair back and stood up. 'How dare you barge in here and raise your voice at me?' she snapped. 'Who the bloody hell do you think you are?'

'You said at that briefing you wanted to know why Becks was a target, didn't you?' snarled Slater.

'Yes, of course I want to know. We all want to know.'

'I'll tell you why he was a target. And I'll tell you whose fault it is.'

'What the hell are you talking about?' She felt her face redden. 'You're not making any sense.'

'Oh, you know what I'm talking about,' said Slater. 'I'm talking to the person who made Becks into a target.'

He snapped upright, his fists clenching, and began pacing up and down.

Goodnews was genuinely alarmed now. 'I think you need to remember who you're talking to,' she said. 'Now, you either calm down or I'll have you removed from this office.'

'How could you have been so stupid?' he asked.

'A little respect for my rank wouldn't go amiss right now, Detective Sergeant Slater,' she said menacingly. She placed her hand on her desk telephone. 'Now, you either explain yourself or I make a call. What's it going to be?'

'Why did you ask him to contact Interpol?' asked Slater.

'I'm sorry?'

'Oh, don't pretend you don't know. You're copied in on all the emails.'

'Since when do I have to explain my actions to you?' she asked.

He looked at her in dismay. 'Since you're putting my life, Norman's life and Ian Becks' life on the line, I would have thought it would have been reasonable to consult us first!'

Goodnews was fair-skinned anyway, but now she felt the blood draining from her face and knew she probably looked like a ghost. 'But it was confidential,' she said. 'It was just possible we had a fingerprint. We had to try.'

'This is the man who had Norman's flat turned into an inferno and had my car cremated,' said Slater. 'You should remember. It was you who came and rescued me after that Russian bloke had pointed a bloody gun at my head and left me handcuffed.'

'Yes,' she said. 'Of course I remember, and that's exactly why I thought we should find out. When Becks asked me what he wanted me to do with that fingerprint, I thought why not?'

'That case was shelved because there was no money for that sort of investigation and because we were no longer thought to be in any danger,' said Slater. 'It was like all the hornets had left the nest for one much further away and we wouldn't get stung as long as we left them alone. Now you've gone and whacked the nest with a bloody great stick. My guess is the hornets are back!'

'You think it's my fault?' she asked, horrified.

'The reason me and Norm were happy to let it lie was because we knew they had to have a mole over there, even though Interpol would never admit it. We knew if we made any sort of move they would know straight away and the shit would hit the fan. You were here at the time, so how come you seem to be unaware of that?'

The full extent of what Slater was suggesting was beginning to sink in, but Goodnews wasn't having it. 'This is rubbish,' she said. 'We've already got a motorcycle courier as a likely suspect. Are you trying to tell me he came all the way from Serbia?'

'You were just glory-hunting, weren't you?' asked Slater. 'Trying to make a name for yourself by going after the big one the old Serious Crime Unit had let get away. You thought you could make a name for yourself and now Ian Becks is dead, and quite possibly Norman, me, and you are next in line.'

'I've heard enough of this drama queen nonsense,' Goodnews roared, banging her fist on her desk. 'You will not talk to me like this.'

There was a loud cough from the doorway. She looked across to see a very uncomfortable-looking Steve Biddeford standing in the doorway.

'Yes?' she snapped.

'I've got the registration number of that motorbike,' he said, waving a sheet of paper in the air. 'It's registered to a courier company in Winchester.'

'I'll have it here, please,' she said.

'Oh,' said Biddeford. 'I thought—'

'No, I told you earlier I want you to take a couple of uniforms and search Ian Becks' flat.'

Biddeford walked across to her desk and she took the sheet of paper from him. She glanced at it then slid it across in front of Slater.

'DS Slater will be following up on the courier.'

'I'll be off then,' said Biddeford, clearly keen to get out of the firing line.

As he headed back for the door, he glanced back, and then quickened his pace when both Goodnews and Slater glared at him.

Goodnews waited until he had left the room, then she got up, walked across to the door and closed it.

'I think you need to catch up on some sleep,' she said to Slater as she walked back to her desk. 'Becks was your mate. I understand. It gets to you. If you want to get away, I can find someone else to chase up the courier.'

'I'll sort out the courier,' he said, getting to his feet. 'Maybe he didn't come from Serbia, but that doesn't mean the package wasn't sent from Serbia. When I've done that I'll be going off duty for a while — I need to warn Norman he's going to have to watch his back. You should watch yours too. These people aren't amateurs.'

'I don't want to hear any more talk about Serbian gangsters. At this stage there's no reason to think they've got anything to do with it.'

'Oh, I think there's plenty of reason to consider the possibility they're responsible.' Slater's voice was still angry but his body language was now much calmer. 'And if I can find even the slightest link, I'll make sure to remind you that I told you so.'

Goodnews took some deep, slow breaths as she watched Slater grab the sheet of paper and march out through the door. She had sounded a lot more confident than she actually felt when she told Slater he was talking rubbish. She knew there had always been a risk involved in asking Becks to send the fingerprint to Interpol but she had been assured the mole had been removed.

She had been so keen to impress, but as she sat at her desk, a horrible thought occurred to her. Had she ignored the possibility that there might have been more than one mole?

CHAPTER ELEVEN

Slater decided it wouldn't be fair to inflict his current mood on anyone else, so he walked straight down to the car park and jumped into his car. He shoved the sheet of paper onto the passenger seat, fumbled for his mobile phone, found Norman's number, and pressed call. He listened to Norman's phone ringing for what seemed like an age, and then sighed impatiently as it went to voicemail.

'Norm, it's Dave. I need you to call me as soon as you get this message, mate. And don't ignore me, it's important.'

He cut the call and tossed his phone down on the passenger seat. Norman could be a pain when it came to returning calls; he just hoped this wasn't going to be one of those occasions. He started the car and pulled out of the car park.

He couldn't quite get his head around the idea that Goodnews had done this without even bothering to mention it to him. Fair enough, she was the boss and it was her call, but he and Norman were under a death threat. Surely she ought to have told them? It's not as if she didn't know all about it. The last time they had clashed with these people had been during her first case at Tinton, which had led directly to Norman having to retire. It wasn't that long ago; she couldn't have forgotten.

Slater could still vividly recall his terror when he'd found Norman's flat a raging inferno and his friend nowhere to be seen. Then, a few days later, his own car was torched before he had spent a very uncomfortable few minutes staring down the barrel of a pistol being wielded by a Russian who, Slater had no doubt, knew exactly how to blow his brains out and would have enjoyed doing it. They had been very clearly warned that there would be severe consequences should they not back off. And now Interpol had been contacted and Becksy was dead. It couldn't be a coincidence.

* * *

The thirty-minute drive was just about far enough to allow Slater to restore some of his good humour. ASprint Courier Company was located in one corner of a small industrial estate on the outskirts of Winchester. There was a small warehouse with office space above. A handful of small and medium-sized vans were parked outside, and as Slater waited, a forklift truck whined its way out of the warehouse doorway and across to a flatbed truck. The pallet it was carrying rose smoothly into the air and was deposited on the back of the truck, before the forklift eased back and the forks wheezed their way back down to ground level. The driver stopped and looked at Slater.

'Yes, mate?' he said. 'Can I help you?'

'Where's the office?' asked Slater.

'Through the warehouse door, turn left and up the stairs,' said the driver. 'You can ignore the "beware of fork trucks" notice. We've only got the one and I'm out here.'

Slater made his way into the warehouse. Off to one side, three motorcycles were parked. He stopped to ease his notebook out of his pocket, flipped it open, and looked across at the bikes. The middle one had the registration number he was looking for. He made his way up the rickety staircase. There was a small landing area at the top, and a door with a large window allowed him to see into the office. A dark-haired woman with huge round spectacles was talking on the phone, but her face lit up when she saw him and she waved him in.

'I'll talk to you later,' she was saying into the phone as Slater walked in. 'Bye for now.'

She put the receiver down, looked up at Slater, and gave him another beaming smile. 'Good afternoon,' she said. 'How can I help you?'

Slater produced his warrant card and showed it to her as he announced himself. 'I'm DS Slater from Tinton CID.'

Momentarily caught off guard, the woman's smile faded briefly, but she quickly recovered. 'There's nothing wrong, I hope,' she said. 'Is there?'

'I'm investigating an incident which happened at Tinton Police Station yesterday evening,' said Slater. 'It may concern a package delivered by one of your motorcycle couriers.'

'Oh, right,' she said, doubtfully. 'So how can I help?'

'The motorbikes downstairs. Do they belong to you?'

'Not me personally—' she was beginning to sound worried — 'but they do belong to the company. I just look after the office and dole out the work. Mr Armstrong owns the business but he's out at the moment.'

'What's your name?' asked Slater.

'Angie. Angie Banks.'

'Right, Angie, don't look so worried. A package was delivered to our station late yesterday afternoon. Whoever delivered it was riding one of your bikes from downstairs. I'm trying to find out where the package came from and who delivered it.'

'Is the driver in trouble?'

'I don't think so, but he might have seen something or heard something that could help us.'

'Let me have a look,' Angie said, turning back a page in the diary on her desk. 'What time did you say it was delivered?'

'It would have been just after six p.m.'

'Oh yes, here we are. Justin delivered it. Bit of a rush job.'

'Can you tell me who sent the package?'

'P&P Publishing,' she said. 'We do quite a lot of work for them. I remember now, they didn't book us until just after five so it was always going to be a late delivery. They said the guy at the other end was going to be waiting, but he would be in a hurry to get away.'

'Is it possible to speak to the driver?' asked Slater.

'I think he's downstairs. Hang on a minute.' She rose from her chair, crossed beyond Slater, and opened the office door. She leaned over the top of the stairs and called out Justin's name.

'Yeah?' called a voice.

'Can you come up a minute?'

'Sure.'

She came back to her desk and sat down. 'He's just coming. His name is Justin Wells. He's one of our more reliable drivers,' she said, conspiratorially. 'I wouldn't give house room to some of them, but Justin's a good one.'

The door squeaked open and a fresh-faced young man appeared, dressed in black leather motorcycle trousers and a denim shirt. Slater guessed he was in his mid-twenties. He certainly didn't look like a bomb-maker.

'Ah, Justin,' said Angie. 'This is Sergeant Slater. He'd like to ask you some questions about that late delivery you made yesterday afternoon.'

Slater nodded. 'Hello, Justin.'

'What's this about?' asked Justin. 'I just deliver the packages. I don't know what's inside them.'

'It's alright,' said Slater. 'No one is accusing you of anything. I just need you to tell me what happened when you delivered a package to Tinton Police Station yesterday afternoon.'

'I'm not sure what you mean. What's supposed to have happened?' Justin looked uncertain.

'Why not start from when you got the job?' suggested Slater. 'Everything you can recall.'

'Angie gave me the job just after five,' he began.

'5.05,' she said, reading from her diary.

'I whizzed down to P&P,' continued Justin. 'I got there about twenty-past. The package was waiting at the reception desk so I was in and out really quick.'

'D'you know what was in the package?' asked Slater.

'Not for sure, but then, like I said, I don't have to know, I just deliver it. It felt like a big wodge of paperwork, like a manuscript. I think that's what we usually carry for them. They are a publishing company, after all. There was a note on it to say the guy at Tinton would be in a hurry to get away and he might meet me outside.'

'Is that unusual?' asked Slater.

'It is a bit,' said Justin, 'but then it seemed as though it was all a bit last minute so I saw no reason to question it. Instructions are instructions, you know?'

'Okay. So what happened when you got to Tinton.'

'I gave the guy the package, he signed for it, and I came straight back here.'

'You're quite sure you came straight back here?' asked Slater.

'Of course I am,' said Justin. 'I got back just after six thirty.'

'Blimey, you must have been going some,' Angie piped up. 'I hope you didn't trip any speed cameras.'

Justin looked suitably embarrassed.

'You're quite sure about this, are you, Justin?' asked Slater. 'Only we've got you on CCTV coming into our reception area at 18.11. You met the guy the parcel was for and followed him into the back of the building. You were still carrying the package at that point.'

'No way, mate!' said Justin, indignantly. 'I never even went in the building. The bloke met me outside on the front steps, as per the instructions. He signed for it there and then.'

'What did this guy look like?' asked Slater.

'I didn't see his face. He was in his leathers with a crash helmet on. I assumed he was in a hurry to get home.'

'What colour were the leathers?'

'Red,' said Justin. 'You don't see them that colour very often. Most people wear black. Look, he was waiting for me and he signed the right name. That's good enough for me, especially at that time of day.'

Slater was confused. This didn't make sense but Justin seemed genuine enough. He would bet good money he wasn't lying, so what was going on here?

'And you're sure you were back here at six thirty?'

'Thereabouts,' said Justin. 'Andy'll tell you. He was here when I got back.'

Slater looked at Angie. 'Who's Andy?'

'Andy Armstrong,' she said. 'He owns the business.'

'You say the guy at Tinton signed for the package,' said Slater. 'Can I see the signature?'

'It'll be on his job sheet.' Angie got up from her desk and walked over to a filing cabinet. She opened a drawer, pulled out one of the files, and carried it back to her desk. She opened it and turned a couple of pages over.

'Here you are,' she said, laying it down for Slater to see and pointing to the bottom of the sheet.

Slater stared at the form. The time was noted down as *18.10* and the signature read *I. Becks.*

Slater scratched his head. Something was definitely not right, but he couldn't argue with the evidence before his eyes. 'D'you think I could have this job sheet?' he asked.

'Let me take a copy,' said Angie, 'just to keep my records up straight. Then you can take it.'

'Right, thanks,' he said, absently, his mind struggling to understand what he had just heard.

'D'you need me anymore?' asked Justin. 'Only I've got a job in a few minutes.'

'Err, no. I think that'll do for now,' said Slater, not sure if he should let the courier go or not. 'You've been very helpful. If I need to speak to you again, I'll be in touch.'

'Yeah, no problem,' said Justin.

Slater turned back to Angie. 'Can you give me the address of P&P Publishing?'

'I'll write it down for you,' she said. 'It's across the other side of town.'

* * *

Slater climbed back into his car, closed the door, gripped the steering wheel, and stared through the windscreen at nothing in particular. It was gone four p.m. and he had been on duty for more than twenty hours. That would have been enough to make his head ache, but on top of that he'd had a bust-up with Goodnews, and now he had another problem. How had Ian Becks managed to sign for a package on the doorstep of the police station at 18.10 when they had footage clearly showing a courier entering the reception area and meeting him at 18.11?

He closed his eyes and rubbed his face with his hands, but it made no difference — when he opened his eyes again, the problem was still there.

CHAPTER TWELVE

Half an hour later, Slater was climbing back into his car, no less confused. His visit to P&P Publishing had only proved Ian Becks *had* actually written a novel and submitted it to P&P for review. So the package really *was* a manuscript, and it really *had* been a last-minute job because there had been a cock-up in the dispatch department. And, as far as he could see, there didn't seem to be any way he could connect it to Serbia, no matter how he tried. The only thing he was sure about, right now, was that he needed to get away from this job for a while before his head exploded.

He reached for his mobile phone and tried Norman again. This time he answered after just three rings.

'Norman Norman, style guru and freelance detective at your service,' said the familiar voice in his ear.

'Norm! Jeez, I am so pleased to hear your voice,' said Slater.

He heard Norman laugh down the phone. 'Don't tell me, you miss me so much you don't know how you can ever live without me.'

'Yeah, something like that,' said Slater. He let out a big sigh.

'Wow. You sound like shit. Do you want to tell Uncle Normy all about it?'

'You haven't heard, have you?' asked Slater.

'Heard what?'

'Ian Becks got killed last night. Blown up in his own lab.'

'No way,' said Norman. 'If this is your idea of a joke—'

'It's no joke, Norm. He's dead, seriously.' For the first time, there was a lump in Slater's throat as he spoke about Becks.

'It sounds to me like maybe you *do* need to come and have a chat with someone,' said Norman. 'How long have you been on duty?'

'Since seven last night,' said Slater. 'I was supposed to be having a nice, easy first night back at work.'

'You wanna come over?'

'Are you okay with that? I could certainly do with a friendly face right now. I just need to go and report back, and then I'll get away.'

'No problem,' said Norman. 'I'll be here when you arrive.'

No sooner had Slater ended his call and tossed his phone down onto the passenger seat than it started to ring. He picked it up and looked at the incoming number. He sighed heavily. It was Goodnews. *What the hell did she want now?* For a few moments he considered ignoring her, but his professionalism soon won out over his inner child. She might not be his favourite person right now, but they still had a case to solve. He owed it to Ian Becks.

'Boss?' he said into the phone.

'Are you coming back here?' she asked.

'Yeah, I want to write these notes up while it's all still fresh in my mind.'

'Anything interesting?'

'Interesting and confusing.'

'I know you want to get off home,' she said, 'and I know you're hacked off with me, but there's something you need to know. Can you make sure you come up and see me before you go home?'

'Can't it wait?' he asked. 'Only this case—'

'It's about this case, and if I thought it could wait I wouldn't ask.'

Slater closed his eyes and cursed quietly. 'Okay,' he said. 'I'm on my way back now.'

* * *

It was well after six p.m. by the time Slater was standing before Goodnews's desk. She was sitting before a huge pile of paperwork.

'The gist of it,' he told her, 'is that Becks had written a book and sent the manuscript to P&P Publishing in Winchester. It seems the package that was sent yesterday contained the manuscript which was being returned to him with their report. The reason it was late was because of a cock-up in their dispatch department.'

'You said you were confused,' Goodnews reminded him.

'The confusing bit comes when the package is delivered. We've got Ian on CCTV meeting the courier in reception and taking him through to the basement. The courier I spoke to swears he met Ian Becks on the front steps and he signed for the package there and then. The courier says he never even came through the front doors and certainly didn't go down to the basement. I've even got the job sheet with Ian's signature on it.'

'He must be lying,' she said.

'I don't think so,' said Slater. 'His sheet is signed at 18.10. He was on his way back to Winchester when our CCTV says he came through the doors. I would swear he's telling the truth. He certainly convinced me.'

'A minute or two either way can be very significant and some people can be very convincing,' she said, thoughtfully.

Slater frowned. He felt he'd been doing this long enough to know when someone was lying to him. Goodnews obviously caught his expression.

'Sorry,' she said. 'I didn't mean to imply you're stupid or anything. Look, I know you're not happy with me, but we still have to work together to solve this case.'

'That's not going to be a problem,' he said. 'What's happened has happened and it can't be undone. I still think I need to warn Norman, and I still think you and I need to watch our backs, but the most important thing is we owe it to Becksy to find out if they really are behind this.'

'Good,' she said. 'That's what I wanted to hear.'

'Is that what was so important to tell me before I went home?'

'I wish it was that simple,' she said, getting to her feet. 'Come and sit down for a minute.'

She led him across her office to a pair of comfy chairs either side of a small coffee table.

'This is starting to look serious,' he said. 'Are you going to suspend me too?'

Goodnews flared her nostrils angrily. This was obviously a sore point.

'DC Darling has been suspended pending an investigation into allegations she beat up a suspect causing grievous bodily harm,' she said sternly. 'I don't like it any more than you do, but I have no choice when it comes to the procedure I have to follow. You know that.'

He held up his hands in surrender. 'Whoa! Sorry,' he said. 'Now who's taking offence at nothing?'

She looked a little sheepish but she obviously wasn't going to apologise. 'This afternoon,' she began, 'DC Biddeford took two uniforms and a couple of forensics guys over to Ian Becks' flat.'

'I bet they've never seen anywhere in such good order,' said Slater. 'Even the tins in the cupboards all face the same way.'

'I'm afraid it wasn't *all* perfect,' she said. 'They found a large amount of cash and some evidence that had obviously been removed from the lab.'

Slater's mouth dropped open, and he sat in stunned silence for few moments. 'No, that can't be right.'

'I'm sorry,' she said. 'I know he was your mate—'

'There's no way he was bent,' said Slater. 'I don't care what was found, you couldn't meet a more honest bloke. He wasn't capable of stepping outside proper procedure.'

'I'm sorry, but ten thousand pounds in cash and a bundle of evidence says otherwise,' she said. 'Believe me, I don't want to believe it, but you can't argue with the evidence.'

'Where did they find it?' he asked.

'In his desk.'

'Then there's been some sort of mistake. I checked his desk when I went over there early in the morning. I couldn't have missed that amount of cash.'

Goodnews looked at him for a moment and then shrugged. 'I'm sorry,' she said. 'I know it's hard to believe . . .'

'I'm telling you, that stuff wasn't there earlier.'

'So how come they found it?' she asked, gently.

'I don't know. Maybe someone's fitting him up,' Slater said, aware he sounded just a little desperate. He raised his hands and rubbed his face. None of this made sense. It made no sense someone had seen fit to end Becks' life, and it was inconceivable he could have been a crook. He suddenly became aware of just how highly he had regarded Ian Becks, and felt a pang of sadness alongside his desperation.

'I know none of this makes sense right now,' said Goodnews, 'but you've been here for nearly twenty-four hours. I think maybe you need to get off home and get some sleep. Perhaps in the morning we can take look at all the evidence afresh.'

Slater dropped his hands and looked across at her. 'You started almost twelve hours before me,' he said. 'When are *you* going to sleep?'

'Aye,' she said, with a sad little smile. 'That's a good question. With the CC breathing down my neck I have to be seen to be doing, but that's all the more reason to make sure my second-in-command gets some sleep. I've got a camp bed in here, maybe I can steal a few hours later.'

Slater winced at the idea of anyone trying to sleep on an uncomfortable camp bed, knowing they could be interrupted at any minute. But then it was her choice to chase after the top job.

'Okay,' he said. 'I'll take you up on the offer to go home for a few hours. Maybe I need to sleep on it to start making some sense of it.'

CHAPTER THIRTEEN

When Norman's flat had been incinerated, his insurance company had been happy to pay for him to stay in a hotel, pending their investigation into the fire and what had caused it. This situation had dragged on for some time as they argued against his claim, until eventually they had withdrawn their support on the grounds that his policy didn't cover him for arson.

Norman didn't see it that way and intended to go on fighting them. There was no way he could afford to carry on paying the hotel bill himself, however, and he now resided in a room above a pub. It wasn't ideal, but it included a cooked breakfast every morning, and in exchange for helping out behind the bar occasionally, the landlord and his wife had reduced his rent to just a few pounds a night.

On top of that, he had discovered a hidden talent for singing, and with his raw, soulful tones he had become a big hit singing karaoke on a Friday night. However, there was a downside; being in such close vicinity to a ready supply of beer and lager was doing nothing for his already over-sized waistline. The jeans he was wearing were struggling to meet in the middle, and would surely have failed without the belt that was straining to hold everything together. A white

T-shirt that hadn't seen an iron in years and Norman's tatty but much-loved denim jacket completed his ensemble.

He was waiting in the bar when Slater arrived. It was almost eight p.m.

'Have you looked in a mirror lately?' he asked, as soon as his friend appeared.

'Haven't had time,' said Slater.

'Well, prepare yourself for a shock,' said Norman, 'because the good-looking young guy I used to work with is starting to look like an advert for the disadvantages of being homeless. In fact, I know plenty of homeless people who look a whole lot better than you.'

'Yeah, thanks for that. I came here to have my spirits raised, not get kicked in the teeth. Can I get you a beer?'

'You're so late we haven't got time for that,' said Norman.

'What? Where are we going?' asked Slater.

'Have you eaten lately?'

'Not for hours.' Slater's stomach let out a loud rumble. 'Are you taking me for a meal?'

'Yeah, sort of,' said Norman, noting the look of anticipation written all over Slater's face.

'Where?' said Slater. 'Indian or Chinese?' He thought for a moment and looked down at his clothes. 'Do I need to get cleaned up?' he asked.

'No, definitely not,' said Norman, looking the dishevelled Slater up and down. 'I reckon you'll blend in just fine. Come on, let's go.'

He led the way out to the car park, plipped the locks on his car, and they climbed in.

'So where is this place?' asked Slater.

'We'll be there in just a few minutes,' said Norman. He looked at Slater's puzzled face. 'This is gonna be something quite new for you. Trust me, the food is fantastic. I think you'll love it. You can tell me all your worries when we get there, and I promise you, by the time you get home you'll realise it's not as bad as you think.'

They drove out of town for barely ten minutes, Norman successfully stonewalling all of Slater's questions about where they were going, until he swung the car off the road and into a lay-by that disappeared behind some trees.

Slater gave Norman a questioning look, but Norman just smiled.

The lay-by curved away from the road for a short distance and then ran parallel to it. It was basically a collection of pot holes connected by uneven tarmac, and it took more skill than Norman was prepared to invest to negotiate a smooth passage. Consequently, they rolled and rocked their way along, and Slater began to look slightly queasy. In the fading evening light, up ahead to the left, a large, battered van could be made out. A small chimney poked from the roof and smoke could be seen pouring from it.

'What the hell is that?' asked Slater.

'Mobile Chinese kitchen,' said Norman. 'Trust me, this guy is one hell of a cook.'

'That van looks like a health hazard. Is it even roadworthy?'

'Will you stop complaining? Just close your eyes and you won't notice.'

'Is it legal?' asked Slater.

'I wouldn't know,' said Norman, 'and as long as the food's awesome, I don't care.'

'But I might get food poisoning.'

'Jeez, listen to you! Will you just stop complaining and enjoy the food? Have I ever asked you to eat crappy food?'

'Well, no, I guess not,' admitted Slater.

'Right, and I'm not going to now. Shenzi makes the best Singapore noodles I have ever tasted, and his steamed dumplings are out of this world.'

'Well, if you say so,' said Slater, doubtfully. 'It's just a pity we have to get seasick on the way.'

'Oh, come on,' said Norman. 'Surely that's enough complaining for now! I suppose there is one positive thing about it though. At least it's taken your mind off that case for a while.'

He smiled happily as he stopped the car just behind the van and led them around the back of the van. A light had been rigged on that side of the van, facing away from the road, and a serving hatch could be seen about halfway down.

'Hi, Shenzi,' said Norman, as an ancient, wizened Chinese face appeared at the hatch. 'How are you today?'

Shenzi's face lit up when he saw Norman. 'Ah! Mister Norm. It's good to see you. How are you today, my friend?'

'I'm feeling good,' said Norman, 'but I'll be even better when you serve up my favourite food.'

'And your friend?' asked Shenzi, looking past Norman at Slater.

'Oh, yeah, he'll have the same.'

Slater nodded uncertainly. 'Yeah, why not?' he said.

'You go take a seat,' said Shenzi. 'I'll bring your food over when it's ready. You want a beer?'

'Make that two,' said Norman.

Shenzi slapped two bottles of beer on the counter, deftly flicked off the tops, and pushed them across to Norman, who picked them up and headed off towards the front of the van where a couple of sets of plastic patio tables and chairs were set up.

'Surely he's not licensed to sell beers, is he?' asked Slater.

'Are you off duty?' asked Norman, as he pulled out a chair at one of the tables and sat down.

'Of course I am,' said Slater, taking a seat opposite Norman.

'So what do you care if he's got a licence? And in any case, did you see me pay for the beers?'

'I haven't seen you pay for the food yet,' said Slater.

'Well, when I do, you'll see the price is slightly inflated,' said Norman. 'That's because he gives away the beer. I don't think you need a licence to give beer away, do you?'

'And this was your advice, was it?'

'I may have made the odd suggestion. Anyway, can we stop worrying about Shenzi and how he operates his business? Why don't you tell me about this case?'

Norman listened as Slater related the whole story from start to finish, going through all the evidence they had uncovered. The only time he stopped talking was when Shenzi arrived with a tray full of dishes, which he quickly arranged all around their table.

'And there's one more thing I haven't mentioned yet,' said Slater. 'I think it's probably why Becksy got murdered but we'll know soon enough.'

Then he told Norman all about Goodnews's decision to approach Interpol.

'She's done what?' yelled Norman. It was the first time he had actually stopped eating since their food had arrived. 'Jesus, we'll have that crazy Russian guy back over here any time now.'

'He might already be here,' said Slater.

'You think he topped Ian Becks?'

'It has to be a possibility, don't you think?' asked Slater.

'Why not go after Goodnews?' Norman shook his head in frustration.

'I was thinking about that,' said Slater. 'Maybe it's just the case that a forensics guy sends out a warning without attracting the flak that would go with murdering a senior officer.'

'You think you're next?'

'I'm assuming they don't necessarily know you've quit,' said Slater. 'So there's a good chance they think we're both behind it.'

'I hope not,' said Norman. 'I quite like living in a pub. I wouldn't want to see it burned down.'

Slater looked sideways at Norman. 'Yeah, I can see your waistline likes living in a pub too.'

'Yeah, whatever,' said Norman, dismissively. 'What about Becks being on the take? That has to be some sort of joke, right?'

'I was there in the morning and there was no pile of cash. Steve Biddeford goes in the afternoon and there's a huge pile of it.'

'And you're quite sure you didn't miss it?' asked Norman.

Slater began to protest.

'Yeah, I know,' interrupted Norman, 'but I have to ask. You were there when one of your mates got blown up. Don't tell me you're so special you weren't affected by it, because I can see in your face that you have been. Is it possible you could have missed it?'

'No,' said Slater, adamantly. 'From what she told me, they found the cash in one of the desk drawers. I went through them all that morning. I *know* it wasn't there.'

'So, someone's planted the stuff to make him look crooked,' said Norman. 'There can be no other explanation. You don't think Steve Biddeford—'

'No,' said Slater. 'He might be an idiot at times, but he wouldn't do anything like this.'

'What about this courier thing?' asked Norman. 'How can the guy be inside on CCTV but swear he never went inside. And how can he be literally on his bike, on the way home, when we can see he's inside going down to the basement?'

'He can't be lying,' said Slater. 'We put his registration number into the ANPR system. He was caught on camera speeding into Winchester at 18.26. I reckon he could just about do that if he was speeding all the way, but there's no way he could have done it if he had still been inside the building like we think he was.'

'Has the station CCTV tape been tampered with?' asked Norman.

'I don't think so,' said Slater. 'But I'm going to have to check. There has to be an explanation.'

'Of course there does,' said Norman. 'But assuming the CCTV's okay and your courier guy is genuine, there's only one conclusion that works, right?'

'Well, if there is, I'm too bloody tired to see what it is.'

'There has to be a second courier,' said Norman, with a wink and a smile.

Slater looked across at Norman. It was plain from his expression he was wondering why he hadn't thought of that himself, but Norman just chuckled.

As they finished their food, Norman looked Slater over appraisingly. His friend looked utterly exhausted. 'I think you need to get home and catch up on some sleep,' he said.

'Yeah, you're probably right,' said Slater. 'Thanks for lending an ear. I feel a lot better already.'

'No problem,' said Norman. 'You know what they say about a problem shared and all that. You know where I am any time you feel the need.'

CHAPTER FOURTEEN

Slater was in bed by midnight but he couldn't sleep. Maybe he was just too tired and had gone past the point where he could sleep, or maybe it was the idea Norm had suggested about there being two couriers. Whatever it was, it kept him tossing and turning until gone three a.m., at which point he abandoned all ideas of sleep and decided instead to get up and do something useful.

It was four a.m. when Slater pulled into the car park at Tinton Police Station. He could see Goodnews's car was still parked in the same place it had been for the last forty-six hours, and he wondered how on earth she managed to still function with almost no sleep. He looked up at her office window as he climbed from his car. There were no lights on. Perhaps she had pulled out the camp bed after all.

He walked in through the back doors and into reception to sign the log.

'What the bloody hell are you doing here?'

'Sandy,' said Slater. 'I can always guarantee a pleasant greeting when you're on duty.'

'You're supposed to be at home getting your beauty sleep,' said Sandy Mollinson. 'And looking at you, I'd say you've had nowhere near enough.'

'And I love you too,' said Slater, blowing him a kiss.

'You can't function properly without sleep,' said Mollinson. 'Or are you and Goodnews competing to see which one of you has the least sense?'

'Is she around?' asked Slater.

Mollinson grinned. 'Ha! I heard you'd had a bit of a bust-up. Trying to avoid her, are you?'

Slater rolled his eyes. 'Yes, we did have words, but right now we have a big case to solve, so no, I'm not avoiding her. I'm just wondering how she manages to keep going without sleep.'

'She's upstairs in her pit now,' said Mollinson. 'Apparently she has a camp bed up there, although how the hell she can get comfortable enough to sleep on it baffles me. My instructions are she's not to be disturbed unless another bomb goes off.'

'That suits me,' said Slater. 'I'm going to watch some videos.'

'If you're hoping to watch some of that seedy stuff that was brought in the other week, you're too late. It's all been boxed up and sent off to Winchester.'

'Oh balls,' said Slater, feigning disappointment. 'I guess I'll have to make do with the CCTV footage from the night Becksy died.'

'I thought that had been done?' said Mollinson.

'We're missing something. How else can a courier be in two places at once?'

'Magic?' Mollinson suggested.

* * *

Slater made his way to the tech suite. It was true Steve Biddeford had already been through the footage from inside the reception area, but he really felt the need to go through it again. Goodnews was right, Biddeford had missed things on CCTV before. Slater just hoped he hadn't done it again.

He figured he would probably be wasting his time looking at anything after 18.30. He would start with the reception area from 18.00 to 18.30 when it seemed everything had happened. Then he would take a look at the outside views. He could worry about looking for any later activity afterwards.

He settled into his chair, opened his notepad, pressed play, and watched. Half an hour later he pressed stop. He looked at his notepad. He'd more or less noted down what Steve Biddeford had said earlier, but with one or two additional notes he'd highlighted with an asterisk.

The first note he'd written was: *Grimm is a complete arse. It's no wonder Tom Sanders didn't see much of what was going on in the room.*

The second read: *courier red leathers too.* This had struck him as important, although he wasn't sure why yet. He wondered how many bikers actually wore red leathers. In his experience, most of them wore black. He felt red leathers would be expensive and he was pretty sure the only person he'd ever seen wearing red was Ian Becks, and yet here was a courier wearing the same. Did couriers earn that much? Maybe up in London but out here in the sticks? It seemed unlikely. No, this seemed to be too much of a coincidence to be ignored.

The third note read: *Becks knows courier.* Slater was quite sure, from the way Becks had greeted the courier, that he was not only expecting him to arrive, but he had known him as a friend. From their body language, Slater felt quite sure that Becks hadn't asked the courier to carry the package down because it was heavy. They now knew it was an envelope full of documents, and that certainly *was* what it looked like, so Becks wouldn't have needed anyone to carry it for him. In his opinion, Becks had taken the courier down to his lab for some other reason and Slater thought he knew what it was. Becks was immensely proud of his work and the way he ran his lab (some would even say he was big-headed about it). What if this courier was a friend and Becks had just been unable to resist showing off?

I seem to have found more questions than answers, thought Slater, as he searched for the footage from the outside cameras. He found the timestamp he was looking for and settled down again, pencil poised over his notepad.

On the screen, timestamped at 18.09, a motorcycle pulled up outside the station. Ignoring the double yellow lines and the notice telling him to park around the back, the rider stood his bike up on its stand, took a package from the pannier, and carried it up the steps towards the front doors. Slater knew it was supposed to be a manuscript, but even so he noted that the package was the right size to be documents, or maybe a thick technical report, the sort of thing Becks would probably have considered light reading.

The courier walked to the top of the steps and then disappeared from view. Less than a minute later he reappeared, walking down the steps. He walked to his bike, climbed on board, started it, kicked it off the stand, and roared away. Slater stopped the tape, rewound it, and watched it again. He watched it for a third time, scratching his head and paying particular attention to the timestamp as well as looking for anything that would suggest there was a technical problem with the footage.

He went back to the footage from the reception area and watched it again, then he walked out of the tech suite and back down the steps to reception.

'Sandy,' he said. 'Tell me if I'm wrong, but there's no way the timestamp could be wrong on one of the CCTV tapes is there?'

'They all run at the same time and use the same source for a timestamp,' said Mollinson. 'So the time can be wrong, but it will be wrong on every single tape. They're all in sync time-wise.'

'That's what I thought.' Slater walked across the reception and went out through the front doors and down the steps. He turned and looked up at the CCTV camera positioned above the doorway. He studied it for a minute or two, then walked back up the steps right up to the doors and looked up at the camera again, paying particular attention to the angle at which it was positioned. He took a couple of steps back and looked up for a third time.

'Shit!' he said. 'Shit, shit, shit!' He ran back through the doors into reception.

* * *

Mollinson yawned expansively as he watched Slater rush in through the doors.

'Are you busy?' Slater asked him.

Mollinson made a big deal out of looking around the room to make sure there was no one there, then he turned to Slater. 'Not especially. Why?'

'Can you watch the CCTV from out the front for a minute? I want to know when you can see me.'

Mollinson looked doubtful and raised a single eyebrow. 'Really?'

'Just humour me,' said Slater. 'It'll only take you a minute, and you've just said you're not busy.'

'Well, make it quick. We're in enough shit over the front desk security without you taking me away from it.'

Mollinson walked through the open doorway into the back office, where there was a monitor watching the front of the building. He stood and watched as the back of Slater's head appeared, followed by the rest of his body as he walked away. Then he turned and waved at the camera and began to walk towards it. He disappeared from view and Mollinson watched to see if Slater reappeared. When he didn't, Mollinson expected to hear the warning beep as the front doors opened. It was a good minute before he heard the sound.

'So, what did you see?' asked Slater when he was back inside.

'Some idiot waving at me,' said Mollinson.

'Is that all? You didn't see me giving you two fingers?'

'No, just waving.'

'Thanks, Sandy. That's just what I thought.' Slater made his way to the doors at the back of reception and pushed his way through.

Mollinson shook his head in disgust. 'Time-waster,' he called to Slater as he disappeared through the door. 'I've got better things to do, you know.'

CHAPTER FIFTEEN

It was just after six a.m. as the door swung shut behind Slater. Mollinson yawned yet again and headed into the back office. There was just time to make another brew before his shift ended at seven a.m. But before he could switch on the kettle, he was alerted by a warning beep as the front door opened. He walked back to his counter. The door was about half-way open and a little old lady was peering rather tentatively around it. She seemed to be unsure if she should come in or not.

'Can I help you?' asked Mollinson. He walked from behind the counter, made his way across to the door, and swung it open for her.

She gave him an uncertain smile. 'Oh dear,' she said. 'I'm sure you must be busy, and I don't want to waste your time.'

'Now why would you think you're wasting my time?' he asked. 'You must have something on your mind, or you wouldn't be here.' Gently, he took her arm. 'Come on inside, love,' he said, leading her through the door. 'It's much warmer in here than it is out there.'

'It's probably nothing,' she said, anxiously. 'He'll probably say I'm making a fuss about nothing.'

'You come and sit down,' said Mollinson, leading her across to his counter. 'I was just going to make myself a cup of tea. Why don't I make us both one, and then you can tell me what's worrying you.'

'But I don't want to be a bother,' she said.

'It's no bother,' he assured her, as he settled her into one of the chairs behind the counter. 'I was going to have to sit on my own and drink my tea. Now I've got someone to chat to. What's your name?'

'Iris,' she said. 'Iris Chandler.'

'Right, Iris. You get comfy while I put the kettle on.'

* * *

Slater settled back in front of the tech suite monitor and took a sip from the biggest cup of strong, black coffee he could find. He pressed play and watched the footage from outside again and then again.

When he had finished, he read through the notes he had made, then he went back to the footage from inside reception and made some more notes. Then he found the footage from the camera focused on the gates to the car park at the back of the building. There wasn't a lot more to add to his notes from this camera, but he thought it was enough to complete the picture and confirm his suspicions. Just to be sure, he read through all his notes one last time. Now he thought he was starting to make sense of what had happened in reception yesterday afternoon when the package had been delivered, and he felt pleased with himself. Sometimes the answer was right under your nose, but you had to go over and over the evidence before you could see it. On this occasion, his tenacity had definitely been rewarded.

His thoughts were interrupted by an annoying buzz from the phone next to him. He grabbed the handset.

'It's Sandy,' said the voice in his ear. 'I have someone down here I think you might want to talk to.'

'Who? What about?'

'Her name's Iris Chandler,' said Mollinson. 'She's just come in to report her husband missing.'

'I haven't got time to get involved with a missing person, Sandy,' he said, in exasperation. 'Why would you think that?'

'Because her husband works for the contract cleaners who clean this place. She hasn't seen him since he went to work on Monday afternoon.'

'And?' asked Slater.

'And he was supposed to be coming here.'

'What, and you think—'

'Of course, it might be completely unrelated,' said Mollinson. 'I mean it's not my place to tell you what to do, but I think it's a bit of a coincidence, don't you?'

Slater thought for a few moments. 'No. You're right,' he said. 'I've got so tied up with this CCTV I'm not thinking straight. I'll be right down.'

CHAPTER SIXTEEN

It was seven a.m., half an hour until the morning briefing. Slater was in the canteen. He had just settled down with a plate of bacon and eggs. He always tried to sit with his back to the wall so he was facing the room and could always see who was heading his way. He couldn't miss Goodnews when she walked in. Not for the first time, he wondered how she managed to look so good first thing in the morning. He knew for a fact she could only have snatched four or five hours' sleep in the last forty-eight hours, on a camp bed in her office, and yet she looked as fresh as a daisy.

Absently, he ran a hand over his face. The bags under his own eyes felt as if they were reaching down to his chin, yet there was no sign of tiredness about her. Even her clothes looked immaculate, with not a single crease in sight. He watched as she gathered a tray, collected her own breakfast, and turned to look for somewhere to sit. She saw him and began to head his way, and, for a moment, he hoped she wouldn't come and sit with him. Then he immediately felt guilty for being so childish.

'Morning,' she said, with a smile. 'D'you mind if I join you?'

'Of course,' he said. 'Help yourself.'

She sat down opposite him, with her back to the room, and began to unload her tray onto the table.

'Did you get much sleep?' he asked, for want of something to say.

'On a camp bed?' she said, with a wry smile. 'Och, you have to be joking. I suppose it's better than nothing but I wouldn't recommend it. What about you?'

'I probably managed about two hours in between the tossing and turning,' he said.

'That's not good. The idea was for you to get a decent night's sleep.'

'Yeah, but I couldn't sleep. I kept thinking about what that motorcycle courier guy told me. I knew we had to be missing something, so I gave up trying to sleep and came back in here. I've been watching CCTV footage for the last couple of hours.'

'I thought you were looking pleased with yourself,' she said.

Slater felt himself blushing. 'I haven't written it all up yet,' he said, 'so I'll give you the quick version. The thing is, I couldn't figure out how the courier could insist he never entered the building when we've clearly got him on CCTV. Or, at least, we thought we had him on CCTV.'

He paused to take a mouthful of breakfast. Goodnews was staring intently at his face, following his train of thought.

'Well, come on,' she said. 'You've obviously found something. Let's hear it.'

* * *

'Right, listen up everyone,' Goodnews said to the assembled team. 'We still don't have access to the forensics lab yet, but I'm told we should be able to get in there later today. I'm also promised a report from the pathologist any time now. You're probably thinking that means we're not getting anywhere, but in fact, we've had a major breakthrough thanks to DS Slater. I'll let him explain it to you.'

She nodded at Slater, and he took her place at the front of the room.

'Okay,' he said. 'We know from the CCTV footage that Ian Becks came up from his lab, signed the log book, and was then met by a courier. On that basis we figured the courier was a key figure and needed tracing. Lucky for us, he had parked his bike out front and we had a lovely shot of his registration number, making him easy to track down.

'I went to speak to him yesterday afternoon. It turns out he had collected a package from P&P Publishing in Winchester with instructions to deliver it to Ian Becks, who would be waiting to go home and might even meet him outside. They even handed me a job sheet with Ian's signature to prove the package had been delivered. This is great so far, but then it all starts to go a bit pear-shaped. You see, we've got the courier on CCTV coming into the building and meeting Ian. The problem is, the courier I spoke to swears blind he never came into the building. He says Ian was waiting outside the front doors for him.'

Slater stopped and looked around. He certainly had their attention.

'He must be lying,' said a voice.

'That thought did cross my mind too,' said Slater. 'But even when I told him we had him on CCTV he stuck to his story. What's more, he has a witness to say he was back in Winchester by six thirty, and he's caught on an ANPR camera entering Winchester just before then. There's no way he could have been there at that time if he was down in the basement with Ian when we think he was.'

Now there were puzzled faces staring back at him.

'So how does that work, then?' asked Steve Biddeford.

'Well,' said Slater. 'What if there were two couriers?'

'But I saw the footage of him arriving,' said Biddeford. 'That's where I got his registration number from.'

'I know that,' said Slater.

'Are you saying I missed something obvious?' Biddeford sounded defensive, and Slater knew he was thinking back to a year ago when he had missed something important on CCTV for a case.

'I'm not saying that at all,' said Slater. 'You didn't look any further because we only asked you to find the registration number. At the time, we hadn't spoken to the courier so we didn't see any need to search the footage for anything else. It was only after I had spoken to him I realised there might be more to it than we first thought.'

'So what have you got that makes you think there were two couriers?' asked Goodnews, obviously keen to keep the briefing from developing into a slanging match between Biddeford and Slater.

'I've watched footage from reception, the front of the building, and the rear car park,' he said. 'Watching each one in isolation, it's not immediately obvious what's going on, but when you put them together, this is what happens.'

Using a hand switch, he started a video playing.

'At 18.03, a courier drives into the rear car park. As he should, he parks his bike, walks out of the car park, and heads around to the front of the building. Things to bear in mind: one, he doesn't take his crash helmet off. Two, he's not carrying anything. Three, he's wearing red leathers.

'At 18.09, another courier arrives. This one is too lazy to park at the back and walk round, so he parks out front, ignoring the double yellow lines and the notice asking him to park around the back. He immediately takes his crash helmet off and can easily be identified as Justin Wells from ASprint couriers. As he walks up the steps to the front door, you can see he's wearing black leathers and he has a package under his arm.

'Now, at this point he disappears from view because the camera out front doesn't actually cover the front door. It's set at such an angle that half a dozen people can stand on that top step and be out of view. Less than a minute later, Justin comes back into view, walking down the steps. You can clearly see he is no longer carrying a package. He puts on his crash helmet, jumps on his bike, and roars away.'

He stopped the video while he found the next piece of footage.

'So where's the first courier?' asked a voice.

'Here,' said Slater, clicking his switch and looking up at the screen. 'At 18.11, the front door opens and a courier walks in carrying a package.' He paused the video. 'Anyone notice anything about this guy compared to the one we've just been watching?'

'He's wearing his crash helmet,' said someone.

'Which he never takes off, all the time he's in there,' added Slater.

'He's wearing red leathers,' said another voice.

'Exactly. Justin was wearing black leathers and no crash helmet, and now, suddenly, he's wearing red leathers and a crash helmet.'

'It's two different people,' said Biddeford. 'But how did they do that? The timestamp must be wrong.'

'Apparently the timestamp is universal,' said Slater. 'All the tapes are in perfect sync. When Justin collected the package from Winchester, it was a rush job. Someone had cocked-up in the publisher's dispatch department, and they had almost left it too late. Justin was none too pleased to get a job that late in the day, so he was in a hurry. He was told the person waiting for the package was also in a hurry and would probably be waiting outside, and would be easily identifiable by his red motorcycle leathers.'

'According to Justin, when he got here there was a guy waiting at the top of the steps in red leathers. He carried the package up the steps, the guy signed for it, and Justin left. It was the perfect delivery for him, he didn't even have to go inside the building!'

'What about a description for this guy at the top of the steps?' asked Biddeford.

Slater gave him a little smile. 'He was wearing a crash helmet with a dark visor,' he said.

'So he meets the courier on the top step, out of view of CCTV, signs for the package and then takes it in to deliver it to Ian?' asked Biddeford.

'That's what I think, yeah,' said Slater, nodding his head.

'But why? If it was a bomb, why go anywhere near it when the real courier could have delivered it?'

Goodnews had come to stand alongside Slater. 'That's one question we need to address,' she said. 'Along with a few others, like who is this man?'

'What happened to him anyway?' asked Biddeford. 'Where did he go?'

'Footage from the camera focused on the rear car park shows him coming through the barrier at the far end of the car park, casually walking over to his bike, climbing on, and riding away. He was as cool as a cucumber. Anyone seeing him out there would have thought he was just a courier doing his job. And, of course, by this time he was wearing Becksy's crash helmet.'

'What happened to his own crash helmet?' asked Biddeford.

'He disappears from view for a few seconds and reappears carrying it,' said Slater. 'My guess is he opened the fire exit just long enough to place it outside.'

'So that's another bloody camera not set up right,' said Goodnews. 'It should catch those doors as well.'

'One thing I will say,' said Slater. 'When Becksy meets this guy in reception, I'm sure he knows him. His body language is totally open, like he trusted the guy. And then he leads him down towards the basement. I'm sure he wouldn't do that unless he knew the guy.'

'So there's another question,' said Goodnews. 'If the guy knew Ian, why was he keeping his crash helmet on? Was it just to hide his face from the camera, or was it because he wasn't actually who Ian thought he was.'

There was a rumble of conversation through the room.

'A couple more things before you go,' said Goodnews. 'First, there's a slight possibility this has got something to do with a case from a few months ago when former DS Norman got kidnapped. You may recall there was some involvement from a couple of Serbian gangsters. It's possible

I've inadvertently stirred them up and this is some sort of payback for that. I'm not convinced it *is* that, but it has to be considered, so just be aware of the possibility we could come across some dangerous people during this investigation.

'Also, we have a missing person I would like you to bear in mind. He might, or might not, be relevant to this case, but as he was a cleaner who worked here, and he disappeared the night Ian died, I would like you all to make a note of his details and keep an eye out for him or the van he was driving when he disappeared. Details of all this stuff are attached to today's worksheets.'

* * *

'That's really good work, figuring out there were two couriers,' Goodnews told Slater when everyone had left.

'Thank you,' said Slater, 'although I'm not sure I haven't just stirred up the waters and made them even muddier.'

'My dad used to love fishing,' she said. 'Sometimes he would take me with him. He used to tell me that when the waters got muddied it meant there was a fish close by. Maybe you've just shown us where our fish is.'

'I dunno about that,' he said. 'Yesterday we had no leads and now we seem to have possibilities popping up all over the shop. If it's a fish you're looking for, we now have a shoal to choose from.'

'It's better to have some leads rather than none,' she reminded him.

'How come you didn't tell them about all the dosh and evidence you found at Becksy's flat?' he asked.

'I've told Steve Biddeford that it goes no further until we've had a chance to check it out.'

'Yesterday you were convinced he was bent.'

'I said I *thought* it looked like it,' she said, 'but, believe it or not, I don't want it to be true any more than you do. Apart from the fact Ian can't defend himself, can you imagine what will happen if it was found to be true? Every single case he's been involved in over the last three years could be subject to review. It doesn't bear thinking about.'

'You didn't have to mention about the Interpol thing,' he said, sheepishly.

'Of course I did,' she said. 'What if I'm wrong and they *are* involved and I didn't warn anyone?'

'D'you think they are?'

'I still honestly think it's unlikely, but I can't ignore the possibility.'

'I'm sorry about the way I behaved yesterday,' Slater said. 'I said some things I shouldn't have.'

'When I thought about it afterwards,' she said, 'I actually thought you probably had every right to be angry. I should have warned you and Norman. As for anything you might have said, well, it's water under the bridge now. If we're going to solve this case we need to be on the same side, so how about we draw a line under that, and move on. Deal?'

She held her hand out. Slater wasn't really sure how he felt about the situation, but she was right about them having to be on the same side. He looked her in the eye, took her hand, and shook it.

'Deal,' he said.

'I'm not interrupting anything, am I?' asked a voice from the doorway. It was Eddie Brent from the fire service.

'No, come on in,' said Goodnews, spinning round to face the new arrival. 'I hope you've come to tell me I can get into the forensics lab at last.'

'I have indeed,' said Brent.

'What can you tell us?' she asked.

'I've got my report here,' he said, raising his hand to show them a sheaf of papers. 'I can take you down there and run through it before I go, if you like.'

'That sounds like a good idea.'

The phone began to ring and Slater grabbed it and raised it to his ear, listening for a moment. It was Eamon Murphy, the forensic pathologist.

'That was Eamon,' Slater said, as he replaced the receiver. 'He's got something he thinks we need to see. He says it's urgent.'

'Bugger,' said Goodnews. 'That sounds ominous. I wanted you to come downstairs and hear this report.'

'Why don't I go and see Eamon while you go down to the lab?' he said. 'It'll save time.'

'Good idea,' she said. 'We can catch up when you get back.'

CHAPTER SEVENTEEN

Tinton officers were lucky enough to have a mortuary that met the necessary standards tucked away beneath Tinton Hospital. Rumour suggested it would be downgraded after the next round of cuts, and possibly even the entire hospital would be closed, but that decision was something everyone would have to deal with when it happened. For the moment, it was case of carry on as usual.

After a rocky start, Dr Eamon Murphy had worked very hard to convince everyone he could cut it as a forensic pathologist, and he had proved himself to be both thorough and reliable. He wasn't the quickest, but that was because he liked to make sure he got it right. As far as Slater was concerned, that was how it should be, and Murphy had quickly become someone he felt he could rely on to give him the facts without frills.

'What's so urgent then, Eamon?' asked Slater, once the greetings were out of the way. 'I thought it was going to be a pretty straightforward case of man killed by bomb blast.'

'Yes, that's what I thought too,' said Murphy. 'Until I opened him up.'

Slater winced. He found dealing with a dead body bad enough, but the thought of opening someone up and removing their organs always turned his stomach over.

'You're not going to make me look at his insides, are you?' he asked.

Murphy smiled sympathetically. 'That won't be necessary,' he said. 'I can tell you without showing you.'

'In that case, I shouldn't need a sick bag.'

'That's true,' said Murphy, 'but I think you're in for a surprise. When the body was brought in here, it was easy to see it had been caught in a blast. There were severe burns to the top of the face and top of the head, and most of the hair was gone. The fire service guys assured me the body had been blown backwards into a wall which had lots of shelves, and that the contents of those shelves had then come down and buried him.

'Bearing in mind those shelves held lots of books, specimen jars and other quite heavy objects, it would have been reasonable to expect to find severe bruising to the back of the body from the impact with the wall and shelves, and bruising to the front from the objects raining down from the shelves.'

Murphy stopped to take a mouthful of tea.

'Are you telling me you found something else?' asked Slater.

'I'm telling you I didn't find any significant bruising,' said Murphy. 'Almost none at all, in fact.'

'But how could that happen?'

'You know enough about these things to know bruises are caused by blood leaking from damaged capillaries, right?' asked Murphy.

Slater nodded.

'And you know blood pools in the lower regions of a dead body.'

'I'm not with you,' said Slater.

'Bear with me and all will become clear. I believe the original theory suggested Ian was working at his desk when the device blew up in front of him, is that right?'

'Yeah,' said Slater. 'But why do you say, "the original theory"? Are you suggesting something else?'

'Let's say you were working at your desk,' said Murphy, 'and this thing explodes on the desk in front of you. It's a fiery blast so it's going to burn you pretty badly, but where do you think the burns would be worst?'

'On my face,' said Slater, using his hands to indicate how the blast would come at him. 'It would come from just below my chest, so it would hit my chin first, I suppose.'

'Exactly,' said Murphy. 'It would be on an upward trajectory. It would hit your chin and under your neck, go up your nose, scorch your eyes, remove your eyebrows, and melt any hair above your forehead at the front. However, the burns on this body would indicate the top of his head took the brunt of the blast. Burns to the face were much less than those to the top of his head, and there were no burns to the neck.'

'So the bomb went off above his head? But how would that work? It would have to be suspended in mid-air?'

Murphy smiled. 'It's a puzzle, isn't it? So I thought I should check with the experts. The bomb guys assure me the device was on the desk, as we all assumed, when it detonated.'

'So what are we saying?' asked Slater. 'Was he kneeling on the floor or something?'

'If he'd been on the floor, it's doubtful he would have been thrown backwards into the wall. The desk would have deflected most of the blast over his head,' said Murphy. 'But what if he was slumped on the desk, with his head resting on his arms?'

'You mean he fell asleep?' asked Slater.

'Mmm, well, not exactly. Blood doesn't pool in sleeping bodies.'

'What? You mean he was already dead?' cried Slater.

'It's not cut and dried,' said Murphy. 'I still need to do a bit more work, but that's what I think. If he had been alive, he would have breathed in the hot gases from the blast. His lungs would have been cooked, but they were as clean as a whistle. There was no sign of any damage from hot gases.

'When the body was found, it was lying on its back, which has definitely made it harder to prove, but from the way liver mortis had set in I would say the body was dead before it ended up on its back. Also, rigor mortis was way more advanced than I would have expected if he had been killed by the bomb. I think he was probably killed two to three hours before that, and the body was then positioned in the chair with the head resting on the arms. That's why the top of the head took the blast, and why the wounds aren't consistent with what I would have expected.'

'Bloody hell,' said Slater. 'I wasn't expecting anything like that!'

'I'm sorry if I'm confusing the issue,' said Murphy.

'Don't worry about that. It is what it is. You can only do your job and tell us what you find. Do you know how he was killed?'

'I'm not going to speculate. I haven't found anything conclusive, like a blow to the head with a blunt instrument. It appears he suffered some sort of respiratory failure, just why, I'm not sure, and I'm not going to guess. I'm waiting for the toxicology results, maybe there will be something in there.'

'Just so I'm clear,' said Slater, 'are you saying this is fact or just your best guess? I mean if you can't find conclusive proof he was dead before the bomb went off, we're up shit creek without a paddle, right?'

'The fact his lungs weren't scorched proves he was dead. I'd stake my reputation on that,' said Murphy. 'But because this is so important I've asked for a second opinion. Another forensic pathologist will be here later today to go over my findings and offer his own opinion. We should have the tox report back by then as well.'

'You'll keep me informed, yeah?' asked Slater.

'Of course,' said Murphy. 'You'll be the first one to know.'

'I'd better go and tell my boss the good news.' Slater smiled wryly. 'She's not gonna like this one little bit.'

'Tell her I'm sorry if it doesn't fit in with her theory.'

'I'll do that,' said Slater. 'But don't be surprised if she doesn't accept your apology. This is just the latest in a long line of unexpected surprises.'

CHAPTER EIGHTEEN

By the time Slater got back to the police station, Eddie Brent had delivered his report to Goodnews and left. He found her down in the wrecked forensics lab.

'It's a bit of a mess,' he said.

Goodnews sighed, resignedly. 'That's an understatement,' she said. 'After all that arguing I had to do with the chief constable to keep it open, now it looks as if someone's given him a good excuse to change his mind and close it down.'

'You're kidding me,' said Slater. 'He won't do that, will he?'

'It'll cost a fortune to put this right,' she said, looking around. 'We've lost our star forensic scientist, and there's a possibility he might have been compromised. I was doing well up until now, maybe even pushing my luck and getting a bit too big for my boots. Would you miss an opportunity like this to put me in my place?'

'But it's hardly your fault, is it?'

'It's on my watch,' she said, with a shrug. 'So as far as the CC is concerned, it *must* be my fault.'

Slater felt a certain amount of sympathy for her, but he had always thought this was the sort of thing that was likely to happen when you sat yourself in the hot seat; sooner or later, you would get your arse burned.

'Anyway,' she said, 'enough about my problems. Let me run you through what they think happened in here.'

She pointed to the desk where Ian Becks used to sit. 'You can see from the huge scorch mark where it went off. They reckon it was an incendiary device designed to cause a fire rather than bring the building down. It was triggered by a pay-as-you-go mobile phone. They found melted bits of it scattered around. Fortunately, the CO_2 extinguishers put the fire out pretty quickly so the main damage is restricted to the immediate vicinity of Ian's desk.'

'That's a pretty specific target, then,' said Slater.

'It looks that way. It wasn't a huge blast but it would have hit him right in the face and was enough to send him back into that wall behind. That brought everything down on top of him off those shelves.'

She pointed at what was left of the shelves. The contents were now in a huge pile on the floor.

'The poor bugger was buried under all that lot. If they hadn't heard his mobile phone ringing when you called him, they might not have found him for hours. They say it's not the sort of device that's normally used to kill people. If he hadn't been sat right in front of it there's a good chance he would still be alive.'

'Actually he wouldn't,' said Slater. 'Eamon reckons he was dead before the bomb went off.'

Goodnews looked stunned. 'If it wasn't the bomb that killed him, what the hell was it?' she asked, incredulous.

'He's not sure yet. There's nothing physical he can point to as being a definite cause of death, but the damage sustained by his body isn't consistent with him working at his desk when it went off. If he *had* been alive, his lungs would have been scorched from breathing in the hot blast, but they're squeaky clean. There's also a problem with liver mortis and rigor mortis. The timing just isn't right.

'He thinks Ian was killed a couple of hours earlier and the body was placed in the chair at the desk so it would look like he had been working there. He didn't say as much, but I got the impression he thinks something will show up in the toxicology report.'

'Could he be wrong?' she asked.

'He seems pretty confident to me, but just to be sure he's got another pathologist coming down to check out his findings.'

'That means he's not sure then.'

'I think it's just Eamon being thorough,' Slater said. 'He wouldn't have told us if he wasn't pretty sure of himself. He's just covering his arse because he knows it's not what anyone expected.'

'So, if we assume he's right,' said Goodnews, 'Ian was dead before seven p.m.—'

'Which puts our mystery fake courier right in the frame,' added Slater.

'But what's the incendiary for?' she asked. 'If there was something he wanted destroyed, why not do it while he's there? I mean, if it was records or something, he could have just taken them away and destroyed them at will.'

'Perhaps it had nothing to do with that,' said Slater. 'Maybe it was simply all about destroying Becksy. You know, destroy the face, destroy the person.'

'That makes it a very personal sort of murder. How would that fit with your Serbian mafia theory?'

'It doesn't rule them out,' he protested. 'These are clever and devious people. They could easily stage a murder to look like anything you want if they thought it would throw us off the scent.'

'I'm still not convinced,' she said, 'but I suppose you're right, we can't dismiss it completely.'

The doors creaked open and a PC popped his head around it. 'Bloody hell,' he said, when he saw the extent of the damage.

'Yeah,' said Slater, grimly. 'Normal service is unlikely to be resumed anytime soon.'

The PC looked suitably glum.

'I hope you didn't come down here just to gawp at the damage,' said Goodnews.

'No, ma'am,' he said. 'Sorry. Sergeant Sanders said to tell you they think they've found the van.'

Goodnews and Slater exchanged puzzled looks.

'Van?' said Slater. 'What van?'

'The missing one that you asked everyone to look out for, the missing cleaner's van,' said the PC.

'Blimey, yes,' said Slater. 'I'd nearly forgotten all about that. I'll be right up.'

The PC headed back upstairs.

'I assume you want me to deal with it?' asked Slater.

'Aye, please,' Goodnews said. 'Take Biddeford with you if you like.'

'Do I have to?' he asked, as he started towards the doors.

'Yes. You need to talk to each other. This case is getting more complicated by the hour, and we have a very small team to work with. If we're going to solve it, I need everyone working together. That means you two as well. I don't care how you do it, just make sure it works, alright?'

'I suppose when you put it like that, I don't have much choice, do I?'

'None at all,' she said. 'And be careful. If you have the slightest suspicion about that van, you stay away until we get the bomb squad in.'

That stopped Slater in his tracks. 'You don't think that's likely, do you?'

'I certainly bloody hope not,' she said, 'but with this case, who can tell?'

CHAPTER NINETEEN

'The boss thinks we need to talk,' said Slater. 'She's concerned we spend too much time at loggerheads and it'll interfere with the investigation.'

'Perhaps if you both trusted me bit more and didn't keep checking up on me, it would help,' said Biddeford, eyes on the road ahead as he drove. 'I mean why were you checking that CCTV footage again? I'd already done it.'

Slater had to tread a little carefully here. He didn't want Biddeford to find out Goodnews had asked him to check it again. There was no need for him to know that, because that wasn't why he *had* checked it in the end.

'I thought I had explained that,' he said, patiently. 'When I spoke to the courier, he was adamant he hadn't been inside the building. Even when I told him we had him on CCTV he wouldn't change his story. I would have asked you to check it, but I couldn't sleep thinking about it so I decided as I was awake I might just as well come in and do it myself. I'm sure you would have done the same.'

'So you weren't just checking up on me?' asked Biddeford.

Slater sighed. 'I can't make you believe me, Steve,' he said. 'It's down to you, mate. It's the same with this idea you have that I'm trying to hold you back all the time. You seem to think I've got some grudge against you because of something that happened months and months ago. I let go of that a long, long time ago. You're the one who's keeping that flame burning, not me.'

Biddeford said nothing for a few moments, then he took a quick glance at Slater. 'But you have checked me out, right?' he asked.

'I've had to, once or twice,' said Slater. 'You know yourself there are bits of this job you're brilliant at and bits that you hate. We're all the same. I hate going to post-mortems and I hate telling people they've lost a family member, but it's part of the job, and you have to give it one hundred percent even when you hate doing it. If you're honest, you'll admit you don't always do that. You tend to rush through the stuff you don't like and that's when someone has to check up on you.'

Biddeford's face reddened, and Slater could see he was struggling to know what to say next.

'You make me sound like a right wanker,' he said, eventually.

'You know that's not true,' said Slater. 'In my opinion, you can be a bloody good copper when you're on your game. It's just those slack moments that let you down.'

'Christ, how bad am I?' asked Biddeford. 'Is this why Goodnews won't recommend me for DS?'

'Actually, she'd love to,' said Slater. 'But she can't all the time you're making silly mistakes. Cut those out and you'll make it easily.'

Out of the corner of his eye, he was sure he saw Biddeford sit up a little straighter, and lift his head a little higher.

'This must be the place,' said Slater, as they turned a corner and saw the blue flashing lights up ahead.

The van was hidden down a narrow alleyway that led to a disused factory at the far end of an old industrial site. The alleyway was lined with chain-link fencing, so the van was clearly visible, but with half the other units empty it was no wonder no one had reported it sooner.

'Good hiding place,' said Biddeford, as he climbed from the car. 'Out in the open where there's no one to see it. Clever.'

The van was parked with the passenger side hard against the fence. Even so, there were only a couple of feet to spare on the driver's side.

'Goodnews thinks we need to be careful in case it's a booby trap,' said Slater.

'She's getting a bit carried away, isn't she?' said Biddeford. 'This is Tinton, not bloody Afghanistan.'

'But we *have* just had our forensics lab firebombed,' Slater reminded him.

'Yeah, but even so. Is it really likely?'

'Probably not,' agreed Slater. 'But we'll humour her and take it slowly, okay?'

'Fair enough,' said Biddeford. 'Shall we do it?'

Slater nodded and they walked slowly and carefully towards the back of the van.

They got to within about three yards of it when there was suddenly a loud booming noise from the van. Biddeford threw himself to the ground. Slater felt his heart skip several beats but nothing else happened. Noisily, he released the breath he had been holding. He looked down at Biddeford, who was still lying face down with his hands over his head.

'Nice reflexes,' said Slater, with a smirk, 'but I think you can get up now. If it was a bomb, it was a very gentle one.'

Biddeford climbed sheepishly to his feet. 'You can laugh,' he said, brushing himself down, 'but it would have been you who got your head blown off, not me.'

'At this range we would both be goners,' said Slater, 'no matter how good your reflexes are.'

'I suppose you have a point,' admitted Biddeford. 'But what the bloody hell was it?'

Slater peered through the back window. 'I think we've found our missing man. He was just letting us know he's in there.'

Biddeford joined Slater and squinted through the window.

A small figure lay in the back of the van. A black hood had been pulled over his head and he was tied up with what appeared to be several yards of rope wound round and round his chest and arms. His feet were tied together, but he had sufficient room to kick out at the side of the van, hence the booming noise.

'Well, one thing's for sure,' said Biddeford. 'He's not related to Harry Houdini, is he?'

'The poor old bloke's been in there for the best part of two days,' said Slater. 'We're probably lucky we haven't got another dead body on our hands. You'd better call an ambulance while I see if I can get him out of there.'

Half an hour later, a very tearful and painfully stiff Joe Chandler was whisked off to hospital in an ambulance. The paramedics had been highly impressed with his resilience. Apart from dehydration, and some pretty severe cramp, he didn't appear to have suffered any major physical trauma. What effect it would have on him psychologically remained to be seen.

Unsurprisingly, he hadn't been able to tell the two detectives much, and Slater hadn't wanted to push him too hard. It seemed he knew very little and had seen nothing.

'What do you think?' asked Biddeford. 'Is his disappearance really relevant to Becksy's death?'

'I can't see it to be honest,' said Slater. 'If we're to assume this fake courier guy killed him and then rode off into the sunset having set a bomb to destroy the lab, where does the cleaner come into it?'

'Perhaps we're missing something.'

'I've got a nagging feeling you're right,' said Slater. 'But I'm buggered if I can think what it might be.'

'So what do we do now?'

'We can't ignore the possibility this is important. I'd like you to drive me back to the station and then get up to the hospital and see if you can get any sense out of old Joe. If he *is* part of it, I've got a feeling he won't be able to help us much. This courier guy is way too careful to show his face or say much, but we have to try.'

'I'll give it a go,' said Biddeford. 'You never know, we might get lucky.'

CHAPTER TWENTY

Biddeford dropped Slater at the back gate and headed off to the hospital. Slater made his way through the pedestrian gate and headed across the car park. As he walked, he thought about what he might have for lunch; it was well after one o'clock and he was starving. But before he had got even halfway to the back doors, his mobile phone began to jangle in his pocket.

Really? Do you have to ring now? he thought as he fumbled in his pocket. He didn't recognise the number showing on the screen, but then he handed out his card all over the place . . .

'Sergeant Slater, this is Bethan Becks. You said to call if I thought of anything that might help.'

'Hi, Bethan,' he said. 'Have you remembered something?'

'It's not that I've remembered something. But something's happened.'

'What is it? Are you alright?'

'I'm a bit shocked to be honest,' she said. 'I've been sent a letter. It's from Ian. He must have posted it the day he died.'

'Where are you?' he asked.

'I've just got home. The postman must have come while I was out.'

'Alright, Bethan,' he said, sounding a lot calmer than he felt. 'I want you to try and not get too many fingerprints on the letter. I'm going to head over there now. I'll be with you just as soon as I can.'

He ended the call and headed towards his car. Lunch would have to wait; this might be important. At the very least, it might tell them if anything had been bothering Ian that day. As he walked, he found Goodnews's number and pressed call. She answered as he climbed into his car.

'How did you get on?' she asked.

'Oh, we found him,' he told her. 'He's a bit sore and very upset, but other than that he seems to be okay.'

'Did he tell you anything?'

'Not yet. Steve's gone over to the hospital to see if he can get him to talk once they've sorted him out.'

'Where are you now?' she asked.

'I've just had a call from Bethan Becks. She's had a letter from Ian. It was posted the day he died.'

'Oh aye? That might be interesting. You'd better head on over there and see what's what.'

'That's what I thought,' he said. 'I'll catch up with you later.'

* * *

When Bethan Becks' front door swung open, Slater was rather taken aback to find a man standing facing him. He was casually dressed in jeans and a T-shirt, but even so, he managed to make Slater feel scruffy in his own shirt, jeans and faded jacket.

'You must be DS Slater,' said the man. He held his hand out and Slater shook it. 'I'm Jimmy Huston,' he said. 'I'm Bethan's boyfriend. She called me when she got the letter. I had the day off work so I came straight over. It was me that suggested she should call you.'

'Oh, right,' said Slater. 'Thanks. You did the right thing.'

'Come on in,' said Huston, stepping back to let Slater through and pointing towards the lounge. 'Beth's through there.' He lowered his voice. 'She's been pretty upset by this whole terrible business, and now this letter's arrived and set her right back.'

'I know how upset she is,' said Slater, stopping next to him. 'I was the one who had to tell her about it.'

'Oh, yeah, sorry, of course you were,' said Huston. 'That must be a horrible job, telling people things like that.'

'Yeah, there are better things to have to do.' Slater headed towards the lounge.

'I'm just making some tea,' said Huston. 'Can I get you one?'

'Please, that would be great. White, no sugar, thanks,' said Slater over his shoulder.

Huston nodded and went off to the kitchen.

Beth was sitting on a settee, the letter lying on a coffee table in front of her. She had obviously been crying and looked desperately unhappy, but managed a small smile of recognition as he came into the room.

'How are you, Beth?' he asked.

'I was just about holding it together,' she said, glancing down at the letter, 'until this arrived. It can't be right. It's just all wrong.'

'Can I read it?' he asked, gently.

'Of course.'

He took a pair of latex gloves from his pocket, pulled them on, and then carefully picked up the letter. There were just a handful of lines so it didn't take long to read. When he had finished, he glanced at Beth, but she had a faraway look in her eyes as if she was unaware he was there. Not quite able to take in what he had read, he went through the letter again.

'You're quite sure it's Ian's handwriting?' he asked.

'Oh yes,' she said. 'He was never a tidy writer.'

Slater had read enough of Ian Becks' reports to know that for a fact. 'Did you know he was thinking about doing this?'

'Why he would he want to do such a thing?' she said. 'He was just getting his life together. He had his book deal and he had just met someone. He had everything to live for. Why would he kill himself? And what does it mean when he

102

says he can't live with what he's done any longer? I just don't understand.'

Slater thought about the cash that had been found in Becks' flat, and for the first time he felt a shadow of doubt, but he would need convincing before he shared that with Bethan.

'Can you think of anything he's done that might make him think this way?' he asked.

'As far as I know, the only thing he's ever regretted is marrying me,' she said. 'But he knew I didn't hold that against him. We were still good friends. We'd moved on from that.'

Huston appeared, carrying a tray. 'Here you go, love,' he said, handing a cup to Bethan. 'Drink this, it'll make you feel better.'

He handed Slater a cup and then sat down next to Bethan.

'I need to use the loo,' she said, getting to her feet. 'Excuse me a minute.'

'It's a bad business, isn't it?' Huston asked Slater, as Bethan left the room. 'It just goes to show you never really know what people are thinking deep inside. I guess everyone has at least one skeleton in the closet.'

Slater heard what Huston said, but he wasn't going to get into *that* conversation right now. He was studying the handwriting on the letter. It looked like Becks' untidy scrawl, but he felt there was something not quite right about it, although he couldn't have said what it was.

'How well did you know Ian, Mr Huston?' he asked.

'We came from the same town,' he said. 'I vaguely knew Ian through my brother back then, but more recently when I started dating Bethan I met him and got to know him a bit.'

'How long ago was that?' asked Slater.

'About six months ago.'

'What did you think of Ian?'

'It was a shame about him and Beth,' said Huston. 'But he seemed to be a nice guy, even if he was confused about who he was. Having said that, he seemed to be getting his head together, you know? Becoming the real Ian. And when

I found out he was writing a novel, well, I work for a publishing company. I thought I might be able to help him, so I persuaded them to take a look at it for him.'

'Was that the manuscript that was delivered to him the day he died?'

'Yes, I believe that's right. It's not my department, but I believe they had suggested some revisions and stuff that he needed to put right, and then there was a good chance they might take it further.'

Just then, Bethan came back into the room. Slater jumped to his feet; something was nagging away in his head and he needed to go.

'I'm going to take this letter back to the station with me,' he said. 'I'll get some tests done.'

He said his goodbyes and Huston showed him to the front door.

'These tests. You don't think it's fake, do you?' asked Huston, quietly, as he opened the door for Slater. 'Only Bethan's convinced it's Ian's handwriting.'

Slater stared at Huston. There was something about the man he didn't like.

'It's procedure,' he said. 'Boring stuff, but it has to be done.'

* * *

As Slater climbed into his car and started back towards Tinton, he reflected on the letter he had in his pocket. He still wasn't convinced Ian Becks was crooked. He couldn't deny the letter made it seem a more credible idea, but there were enough questions to maintain the element of doubt. For a start, why would someone like Becksy turn against everything he stood for? What was it about the letter that made him suspicious? And wasn't a bomb a rather extreme and untidy way of committing suicide? And if the bomb hadn't been the cause of death, then why had it been planted in the first place? And by whom?

CHAPTER TWENTY-ONE

It was late afternoon by the time Slater managed to get back and find Goodnews. She was sitting at her desk, looking distracted and almost distraught. Slater had never seen her like this before, and he wondered if perhaps she had been given some bad news. Maybe someone close to her had died.

'Are you alright?' he asked. 'Only I can come back later if you've just had some bad news or something.'

She suddenly seemed to be aware he was standing in front of her. 'What?'

'Have you had some bad news?'

'Bad news? You can't begin to imagine,' she said. 'I hope you've come to give me some good news. I could do with a lifeline right now.'

Carefully, he placed the letter down in front of her. She quickly read it and then slowly read it a second time.

'So that's it, then,' she said. 'He was crooked, and he couldn't live with himself any longer.'

'Really?' said Slater in dismay. 'I know you'd like a quick result, but that's ridiculous!'

She frowned up at him.

'Have you forgotten what the pathologist said?' he asked. 'He reckons Ian was dead before the bomb went off.

And the bomb guy said it was detonated by a mobile phone. Have you ever heard of a dead man making a telephone call?'

'I suppose there is that,' she said.

'What do you mean "you suppose there is that"?' Slater said, his voice awash with irony.

'These things can easily be scheduled with a computer,' Goodnews said. 'Anyway, you don't have all the facts.'

'What's that supposed to mean?'

'I had a call from Interpol while you were out. Remember that fingerprint I had Ian send over to them?'

Slater nodded.

'Well, the bloody thing's disappeared, vanished without trace.'

'Yeah, but we've got a hard copy here,' said Slater. He looked at her face. 'We *have* still got the hard copy, haven't we?'

'Not any more,' she said. 'I've been down there checking. It's not in the filing cabinet where it should be, and we don't even have a copy on the bloody computer system anymore.'

'But it must be on the central database,' he said.

She shook her head. 'Oh no. It appears some bugger's hacked the system and deleted it.'

'And you think Becksy—' began Slater.

'I don't think he hacked the system, but I think he vaporised the bloody original hard copy the night he cremated himself,' she said. 'I suspect it was on the desk right where the incendiary went off. Our one chance of tracing that bastard and it's gone up in smoke.'

'Oh shit!' said Slater.

'Oh shit, is right, and deep shit is what I'm now in, right up to my neck.'

'Have you told the CC?'

'I still have that pleasure to come,' Goodnews said. 'I was just hoping you might come back with some miracle I could offer to deflect his attention, you know?'

'Christ, I'm sorry, boss,' he said. 'I wish I could help, but miracles aren't really my thing.'

She gave him a sad smile. 'You know, there are times when I feel we're fighting against each other, but even when I think you must hate me, I know when it comes to it, you'd be there sticking up for me. That sort of loyalty is hard to find.'

For a moment, Slater was embarrassed and didn't quite know what to say. 'Even *you* can't be all bad,' he joked. 'And I have to admit, there are one or two things you've changed for the better.'

She managed a half smile. 'Only one or two?'

'Well, alright, quite a few things,' he admitted. 'But I don't want you to think you're doing too well.'

'Ha! I think the CC will make sure I know I'm not,' she said, ruefully. She looked up at the clock. It was just before five p.m. 'Will you do me a favour?'

'Sure. What is it?'

'Can you go and get two coffees while I phone him?'

'You mean can I clear off and give you some privacy?' Slater said with a smile.

'Something like that, yes,' she said. 'I wouldn't be surprised if I'm no longer your boss when you get back.'

'Don't talk bollocks,' he said. 'He's not going to do that. He can't afford to lose someone like you.'

'Don't be too sure about that. He's been known to wield the hatchet for far less.'

'Cobblers,' said Slater. 'I'll get the coffees; you call the old man. How long do you want me to take?'

'Ten minutes should be long enough,' she said, glumly.

'Right, ten minutes it is,' he said, heading for the door.

* * *

When Slater got back to her office ten minutes later, she was nowhere to be seen, and he wondered what had happened. He put the coffees down and looked around, as if that would give him some kind of clue. Then she quickly slipped through the door and closed it behind her.

'Just needed to powder my nose,' she explained. As she sat down behind her desk, she glanced up at him. It was obvious she had been crying.

'He didn't take it too well, then?' he asked.

'About as well as I expected. At least he hasn't sacked me. Yet. But it was a close thing, and there's not much chance of meeting his expectations quick enough to save the situation.'

She let out a huge sigh and placed her head in her hands.

'What's happened to that positive attitude you're always telling me about?' he asked.

'Aye. I know. I really shouldn't let anyone see me like this.'

'Do you want me to go?'

'No,' she said. 'Don't you dare. I need someone to help me figure out what the hell's really going on here, and I think you're the best hope I have.'

Slater felt a small glow of pride. It never did any harm to have your ego massaged, after all. 'What have you got in mind?' he asked.

'I'm beginning to think there's more to this case than first meets the eye,' she said. 'Some things just don't add up, so I think the two of us need to go through what we know and see if we can make sense of it.'

'Okay,' he said. 'I'm happy to do that, but can I make a suggestion?'

'Aye, go ahead.'

'How about we adjourn to the pub? I missed lunch and I could do with a good meal and, if you don't mind me saying, you look like you could do with a drink.'

'You know what? I haven't eaten since breakfast either and I'm bloody starving, so sod it, why not?' she said. 'Come on, I'll treat you to dinner.'

* * *

The pub was only a couple of hundred yards from the police station, so they left their cars in the car park and walked.

There was a chilly wind blowing, and by the time they got to the pub, the pale-skinned Goodnews had cheeks that glowed a healthy pink. During the short walk, they had chatted about nothing in particular, and that seemed to have enabled her to relax. She was much more like the Goodnews Slater knew by the time they were stood at the bar.

'Right,' said Goodnews. 'Shall we set up a tab?'

'How long are you thinking of staying? he asked.

'How long is a piece of string? I've got no reason to rush home, have you?'

'Well, no, I suppose not.'

'Well then, we'll stay here as long as we're making progress. Is that okay with you?'

'Yeah, I suppose that's okay,' said Slater. 'As long as we don't end up drinking too much.'

'That's settled then,' she said.

The barman came over to take their order.

'Can we start a tab?' she asked. 'Only we'll be here for a while and we'd like to order some food as well.'

'Sure,' he said, obviously recognising them both as police officers from previous visits. 'What can I get you?'

'I'll have a double whisky with loads of ice,' she said, 'and a fruit juice for my friend here who's worried about drinking too much.'

'Whoa. Hang on minute,' protested Slater. 'That's not what I said at all. I'll have a pint of lager, please.'

The barman smiled and went to get their drinks while they studied a menu.

'Are you sure you can handle it?' Goodnews teased Slater. 'Only I understand you have trouble holding your drink.'

Slater sighed. She was referring to an incident a while ago, when Slater had got drunk and his partner DC Naomi Darling had ended up taking him home. She had stayed the night at his house, and next morning he wasn't quite sure if anything had happened between them. In the event, nothing had happened, but at the time Goodnews had been horrified to think he might have taken advantage of his much younger partner. It had taken all Darling's persuasive powers to convince her nothing had happened.

Their drinks arrived and they ordered their food, then she led them across to a corner table.

'You're never going to let me forget that night, are you?' he asked, as they sat down.

'Wouldn't dream of it,' she said, with a wicked smile. 'It's always handy to have something I can use when I need to be persuasive.'

'Isn't that called blackmail?' he asked.

Her smile widened even more. 'Aye. I believe it is.'

'You've cheered up all of a sudden,' he said.

'Aye, I have that,' she agreed. 'It's getting away from the job. Sometimes you live it and breathe it twenty-four seven, and if you don't have anything outside to take your mind off it, it takes over completely. You live alone, you must know what I mean. This is like a night out.'

Slater knew well enough what she meant about the job becoming all consuming, but he wasn't convinced spending the evening talking about an investigation constituted a night out. He thought perhaps Goodnews must be seriously lonely, but he didn't think it would be wise to say so.

'Well, yeah,' he agreed, 'if you're not careful, the job *does* take over your whole life.' His thoughts flitted to Cindy, his last girlfriend, and he felt glum suddenly. His dedication to his work had pushed her away and when she *had* come back, she'd chosen the morning DC Darling was there. And of course Darling had been wearing precious little when she had opened the front door. And then, of course, he had shouted, 'Put some toast on for me, Darling,' down from upstairs while Cindy stood on the doorstep. He'd tried to explain it away to her but she'd had none of it and he hadn't heard from her again.

'Anyway, what's happening with Darling?' he asked, pushing Cindy out of his head.

'Nothing, at the moment,' Goodnews said. 'Unfortunately for her, she's going to have to wait. I'm not having that idiot

Grimm demanding everyone's attention while we've got such an important case to deal with.'

'But the poor kid's suspended,' he said. 'It hardly seems fair to keep her suspended.'

'Your "poor kid" beat the crap out of a suspect in front of a witness,' she said. 'He may never be able to father any children because of what she did to him. She's probably going to be charged with grievous bodily harm. At least all the time she's suspended she still has a job and a salary.'

'You think they'll kick her out?'

'I don't think they'll have a choice. It doesn't matter which way you look at it, you just can't have a police officer behaving that way.'

'If only I hadn't been in hospital,' he said. 'Maybe I could have done something.'

'Trust me, you wouldn't have stopped her,' she said. 'She hunted the guy down when she was supposed to have been off duty. Are you telling me you spend your evenings with her too, and you would have been there to stop her?'

'No, of course I don't,' he said. 'I just find it so hard to believe. I mean, there's nothing of her, and that guy's twice the size of me!'

'Aye, it's pretty scary to think she could do that. Sadly, she's become another black mark for me. I was the one who put her forward for the fast-track programme. She should have been taking her DS exams now, not being suspended from duty. The CC says it brings my judgement into question.'

They sipped their drinks in silence for a few moments.

'Right,' said Goodnews. 'That's enough talk about an inquiry that's out of our hands. Let's talk about the one we're trying to solve. Or at least, the one we're trying to solve until the chief constable takes it off us and calls in some smug arsehole from Winchester.'

'Is that what he threatened?'

'That was just one of many threats he made,' she said, grimly. 'He used to see me as a shining light, but right now, after all the recent happenings, I think I'm just a dying ember.'

'It can't be that bad,' said Slater, encouragingly.

'Oh, it can. Even if we solve this without any more cock-ups, it's brought to light so many other issues I think I'll be lucky to survive.'

'He can't blame you for everything.'

'Oh, sure he can,' she said. 'Darling was my protégé. The piss-poor security at Tinton has to be down to me, because I did the review. The forensics lab I fought tooth and nail to save will cost a fortune to repair, so that's not likely to happen, and he'll say if it had been closed, like he wanted, this would never have happened. Then there's the question of a forensic expert who may have been crooked. That could mean every case we've closed in the last three years could be reopened. And now there's the fingerprint that seems to have vanished into thin air. He's even blaming me for the fact the database may have been hacked.'

She gave him a sad little smile. 'Shall I go on? Do I need to?'

Slater found it hard to argue with her assessment. When you added it all together, it was a pretty damaging list for anyone to try and put right. But that didn't mean they had to throw the towel in.

'Okay,' he admitted. 'When you put it like that, it doesn't look too good.'

Goodnews laughed quietly. 'You're quite the master of understatement, do you know that?'

'I can't believe you're going to throw the towel in,' he said. 'From what I've seen, you're a lot better than that. I think you should try to ignore all that other stuff and focus on this case. That's what we came here for, right?'

Goodnews sighed. 'Aye, I suppose you're right. Are you sure you don't want to leave the sinking ship?'

He frowned at her. 'Piss off.'

She tried to look shocked, but didn't really succeed. 'You can't speak to me like that! I'm your senior officer,' she said, in mock outrage.

'I think you'll find we're off duty,' he said. 'At least I am.'

'I'm never off duty.'

'You should try it some time. It's that time you spend with people called friends. Friends are all equal in rank, and are allowed to be frank with each other and, speaking as a friend, I'm telling you to stop talking like that.'

She looked doubtful, as if she had never considered such a possibility, but before she could speak, Slater was off again.

'Do you really think I'd be here if I didn't want to help?' he said.

'And you see me as a friend?' she asked.

'Why not?'

'But we seem to spend a lot of time arguing.'

'So we don't agree about everything,' he said, 'but we still get the job done, don't we?'

She nodded. 'Aye, I suppose we do,' she admitted.

'Well, in my opinion that's the sign of a healthy relationship,' he said. 'And anyway, it's not just about helping you. Ian Becks was a good bloke. If I don't do everything I can to help solve this case, I'd be letting him down. And another thing — feeling sorry for yourself has never solved anything for anyone, and it won't help you now, so can you please stop it?'

She sat back and her mouth dropped open. 'Well, that's told me, hasn't it?' she said.

'Like I said, friends are supposed to be able to speak frankly to each other. Don't you agree?'

'I'm not sure I've ever looked at it like that,' she said. 'As your boss I'm supposed to keep a distance between us.'

'Well, have you ever thought that maybe part of your problem is that the distance you maintain is much greater than it needs to be?' he asked.

'Bloody hell. What are you, the police psychologist all of a sudden?'

'Look, I'm just trying to help. If you don't want me to, I can quite easily go home.'

'But why would you want to help me?'

'Because I care,' Slater said. 'It's what friends do. Now, are we going to discuss this case or not?'

Goodness looked rather stunned by what he had said. 'I think I need another drink, first,' she said.

* * *

'Right,' said Slater, their drinks replenished, 'let's get started.' He had decided it might be better if he led the conversation and, to his surprise, Goodnews didn't seem to have a problem with that.

'We know a courier arrived on the night Ian died and delivered a parcel to someone stood on the front steps that he thought was Ian, but we now know wasn't. Let's call this bloke Mystery Man, for want of something better. Mystery Man signs for the parcel and then takes it inside to reception where he meets Ian Becks. Becks appears to know the guy and takes him through the back doors, presumably to his lab.'

'First question,' said Goodnews. 'Why would he do that?'

'My best guess so far,' said Slater, 'is he wanted to show off. He was really proud of his job and the way he ran things. This was a chance to show someone from outside and impress them.'

'Next obvious question. Who is Mystery Man?'

'Could be he was someone Ian had met at the gay bar?' suggested Slater. 'Then again, he could be someone sent from Serbia.'

'But he wouldn't know someone from Serbia, would he?'

'You've got me there,' said Slater, 'so let's go with the gay friend theory.'

'Okay,' she said. 'Go on.'

'Mystery Man comes back upstairs, and because he's wearing Ian's crash helmet and red leathers, the duty sergeant assumes that's who it is and the guy walks out unchallenged.'

He took a drink from his pint before he continued. 'The next thing we know is the explosion. An incendiary device goes off in the forensics lab. It causes damage, but not that much when you think the entire place could have been reduced to rubble and the entire building brought down on top of it.'

'So why not do that?' asked Goodnews. 'Why not bring the whole lot down? It would have made sure we didn't find the body, wouldn't it?'

'Yeah,' agreed Slater. 'I was stumped by that one, but then we didn't know about the fingerprint going missing before. What if the whole point of the fire was simply to destroy that fingerprint?'

'You seem to be forgetting the suicide note,' she said.

'Just bear with me for now. I'm not convinced that's for real.'

'But we know he was crooked. It all adds up,' she argued.

'I don't believe that, either,' said Slater, adamantly. 'What about if someone was trying to frame him?'

'Where on earth has that come from?' asked Goodnews.

'Just let me run with this for a minute. Let's suppose this Slick Tony, the Serbian gangster guy, is behind this. You asked Ian to send a fingerprint to Interpol, right? Now, we know he had at least one mole in there, who is supposed to have been removed, but suppose there's another one? As soon as the fingerprint appears, the mole tells his boss. They know it's Ian Becks who sent the enquiry, so they need to stop him.

'They intercept a package to Ian Becks and make the delivery themselves. Ian takes the guy down to the lab, where the guy bumps him off, finds the hard copy of the print, and plants a device to destroy the evidence and Ian's body at the same time. They also steal some evidence from the lab and plant it at Ian's flat, along with some serious cash to make him look bent.'

'What about the suicide note? Where does that come in?'

'Maybe Mystery Man forced him to write the note before he died. Then they use it to back up the idea he was guilty about being crooked.'

'It sounds good,' she said, 'until you start poking at it, and then holes start to appear. I think you're making the evidence fit your theory about Serbian gangsters.'

'What holes?' he said.

'Well, first you say he's met someone at the gay bar, and now you want him to be a Serbian gangster. Then there's the suicide note. You think it's a fake of some sort, but there's no proof. We can get it analysed by a handwriting expert, but I wouldn't hold out too much hope. Then there's the matter of our kidnapped cleaner. Where does he fit in?'

Slater knew she had a point. He had seen the holes appearing as he had been explaining it to her.

'Yeah. Okay, so I haven't figured it all out yet,' he admitted.

'And I still don't understand why they would use such a tiny bomb,' continued Goodnews. 'Yes, it was enough to start a small fire, but it was never going to be enough to destroy the body.'

'Look, it's a theory,' he said. 'I admit I don't know where all the pieces fit yet, but what did we have before?'

'It's a good try,' she said. 'But you know as well as me, it doesn't really fly, does it?'

'I admit we have some pieces that don't seem to fit, but we're still waiting for the toxicology report and we haven't heard from the cleaner yet. What he has to say might make all the difference.'

Their conversation was interrupted by the arrival of their food. A massive steak and chips for Goodnews and a curry for Slater.

'Right,' she said to Slater. 'That's it now. No more talk about this case until tomorrow. Let's just enjoy our food. I don't know about you, but I'm bloody starving.'

Slater marvelled at the size of the steak on her plate. 'You're never going to eat all that, are you?' he said, staring at it. 'It's so big it's overhanging the plate.'

'Just watch me,' she said. 'I eat like this all the time at home. This is just a snack.'

She began to carve into her steak and took a huge mouthful. Slater took a discreet look at her slim figure.

'I can't see where you put it all,' he said, dipping into his much smaller curry. 'If I ate like that I'd end up as big as Norman.'

'I put lots of energy into everything I do,' she said. 'I'll soon burn this off.'

She took another huge mouthful, and sat back to enjoy it. Slater watched her out of the corner of his eye and remembered when she had first arrived at Tinton. They had worked a case together, and he recalled how she had impressed him with her fitness, easily keeping up with him when they were chasing a suspect. He had been the one left gasping for breath, while she hardly seemed to have any problem. Then a wistful look crossed his face as he remembered something else that had happened on that case. She caught him watching her and saw the look on his face.

'Come on,' she said. 'What are you thinking about?'

'Nothing special,' he said guiltily. 'I was just remembering how you outran me when you first came here.'

'Oh aye,' she said. 'I try to keep myself fit. Anytime you want a rematch, just let me know.'

'No, it's okay, I'll pass on that if you don't mind,' he said.

Slater looked at her again. She seemed to be positively glowing with vitality now, as if all her worries had somehow been lifted from her shoulders. Then again, it could have been the amount of whisky she had consumed.

'I seem to recall something else that happened when we were working on that case,' she said.

'Oh no,' he said. 'Not again. This is something else you're never going to let me forget, isn't it?'

'It's not every day a DI gets grabbed by a DS and kissed,' she said, a wicked grin firmly back in place on her face.

Slater squirmed with embarrassment. 'Look, I'm sorry, okay,' he said. 'The guy was walking straight towards us. He would have recognised me for sure. I had to do something.'

'So you say,' she teased.

'It was one of those spur-of-the-moment things, driven by desperation,' he said.

'Driven by desperation,' she said, pretending to be appalled. 'Is that what you tell all the women you kiss?'

'I didn't mean it like that, and you know it. If you must know, I thought it was a bit of inspired, out-of-the-box thinking.'

She threw her head back and laughed out loud. 'Oh, it was out-of-the-box, alright,' she agreed. 'I've read all the manuals on avoiding detection when following a suspect, and I can assure you, grabbing your DI and sticking your tongue down her throat doesn't appear anywhere.'

'I didn't use my bloody tongue,' he said, testily. 'I've said it about a hundred times before, but I'll say it again anyway. I'm sorry I kissed you, alright? I'll make sure it never happens again.'

'Oh, I don't want you to apologise,' she said.

'You made enough fuss at the time.'

'That was because you took me by surprise. I didn't know what was happening.'

'I didn't exactly have time to explain, did I?' he said, exasperated.

'Och, I know that,' she said, before looking coyly at him. 'Anyway, I don't think I've ever said I didn't enjoy it.' She got to her feet and collected their glasses.

Slater's mouth had dropped open.

'Didn't your mother ever tell you to keep your mouth shut when you're eating?' she asked, then indicated his glass. 'I take it you want another drink?'

Slater managed to close his mouth, but he still couldn't speak.

'I'll take that as a "yes", then,' she said, and made her way over to the bar.

Shit, thought Slater, realising he really couldn't read her at all. *Is she flirting with me, is it just the drink talking, or am I getting this all wrong?* Things could get seriously bloody awkward if she was flirting with him. But she wouldn't, would she? No, of course not. If anything happened between them it would stop any further progress up that slippery career pole, and she wouldn't want that.

'I think we'll be needing to order a taxi to get us home,' she said when she came back with the drinks. 'We're both well over the limit now. It wouldn't look good if we got caught, would it?'

She sat down and started looking absently around the pub, as if she'd never been inside one before.

'It's alright for me, I'm only ten minutes away,' he said. 'But you live thirty miles away. It'll cost you a fortune.'

'I'll walk back to the office and get out the camp bed,' she said.

'You can't sleep on that bloody thing again,' he said. Then, without a second thought, he added, 'Why don't you come back to my place?'

She snapped her head back to look straight at him. He couldn't tell if she was horrified or delighted by the idea.

Oh crap. That was stupid of me. Why did I say that?

'I mean I've got a spare room,' he said, quickly. 'I didn't mean to suggest we should, err, you know. Well, that's not that I meant. I just mean my spare bed must be more comfortable than your camp bed.'

She tried to look horrified, but her face soon broke into a grin, and then she started laughing. 'That's very sweet of you,' she said. 'But I don't think I could impose on you like that.'

He breathed a sigh of relief, but his mouth didn't seem to be connected to his thoughts any more.

'Don't be silly, it's no trouble,' he said. 'I had that room decorated months ago, and it's a new bed, too, never been slept in. I've been waiting for someone to try it out.'

CHAPTER TWENTY-TWO

Goodnews was sitting in her office, gazing out of the window behind her desk. She wasn't looking at anything in particular, just staring into space, wondering what the hell was happening to her life. Normally, nothing was ever done without her taking the time to assess the likely outcome. She was always in full control and things ran like clockwork, but just lately it seemed a lot of things were happening over which she had no control, and last night she had even become reckless and let her guard down — something she never did. It seemed everything was beginning to fall apart.

She normally worked with an open-door policy, but this morning the door was closed. A sudden knock interrupted her thoughts; she had asked Slater to come up and see her. Reluctantly, she slowly swung her chair round to face the door.

'Come in,' she called.

The door opened slightly and he poked his head through. 'You wanted to see me?'

'Yes,' she said. 'Come in and shut the door.'

She watched him as he did as she asked and walked across to her desk. She looked up at him from behind the desk. For once, she didn't feel quite as confident as she normally was, and she suddenly realised she was using the desk as a barrier between them. As if to prove to herself just how rattled she was, she found she was fiddling nervously with a pencil on her desk.

'Is this about last night?' he asked.

She looked away for a moment and her cheeks flushed. 'I thought we had agreed nothing happened last night,' she said. 'It was just two colleagues having a couple of drinks while they discussed a case.'

She watched as he pursed his lips. He was clearly irritated.

'I think you'll find *you* agreed that,' he said. 'I don't recall being asked what I thought.'

'Look,' she said, realising she probably sounded rather desperate, 'if anyone was to find out, it would be the end of my career.'

'Well, no one's going to find out anything from me,' he said.

She thought for a second. 'Everyone found out about Darling being at your house that night,' she pointed out.

'I think you'll find that was a bit different. That night *I* was the one who had had too much to drink. She did me a favour and took me home. Anyway, nothing happened when Darling stayed over and you know that.'

'It took a lot of denying from both of you, though, didn't it?'

'I can't help it if people have suspicious minds,' he said.

'Well, I don't want to have to deny anything, okay?'

'You've already made that crystal clear,' said Slater, testily. 'But, like I told you a hundred times already, I know how to be discreet. I won't tell a soul.'

Goodnews placed her elbows on her desk and put her head in her hands. 'Less than a week ago, my life was going just how I wanted, and I had everything under control,' she said. 'But now, well, I don't know. It's like I'm driving a car downhill, but the steering's gone, and there are no brakes . . .'

'Well, don't blame me,' said Slater. 'All I did was offer you my spare bed for the night.'

She thought about what he was saying, then she looked up. 'No, you're right,' she said. 'It's not your fault and, if I'm honest, last night was just what I needed. For a few hours, I forgot all about the chief constable and his demands.'

'Ah, right. So that's what this is about. What's he done now?'

'He's just called to tell me there's no turning back from the decision to close the forensics lab.'

'Crap,' said Slater. 'That's a big blow, but at least you knew it could happen.'

'Aye,' she said, 'but if that goes, so does one of my best arguments for closing another station and moving all the staff over here. Without the lab, Tinton becomes the favourite to close.'

'Ah, right,' he said. 'Is that for real?'

'Aye. And what with our non-existent security, and a suicide on the premises, I don't think we've got a hope in hell of surviving.'

'Suicide?' said Slater. 'What suicide?'

'That's another decision he's made,' Goodnews said. 'I've been instructed to accept Ian Becks' death was suicide and close the inquiry.'

'But what about all the other evidence?' asked Slater, in dismay. 'What about the pathology report? What about the fact a dead man can't make a phone call to trigger the bomb? We can't stop now!'

'I don't have any choice. If I don't close the case, I'll be removed from my job and someone else will close it.'

'Give us until the end of the week,' he said. 'You know as well as I do this wasn't suicide. We can prove it; we just need a bit more time.'

She looked up at his face and could see how desperately disappointed he was. 'I'm sorry, but my hands are tied. I understand how you feel but we don't have any more time. I have to reassign everyone today and wind it up.'

'But it's not all up-to-date yet,' he said. 'You can't just abandon an investigation half-finished. Someone will have to finish it off, right?'

'Well, yes, of course,' she said.

'Well, I could do that, couldn't I?'

Goodnews thought about it. He was right to say she wasn't convinced it was suicide, and she had actually argued that point with the CC, but he had been adamant she had to accept it was suicide, close the case, and move on. He had also made it quite clear what would happen to her if she ignored his instructions. Then she had an idea that made her sit up straight. *Yes*, she thought, *there* is *a way we can get a couple more days out of this.*

'Okay,' she said, suddenly feeling in control again. 'I need to know you understand it's not my choice to close this case.'

'Well, yeah, of course I do,' said Slater. 'It's just the chief constable trying to put you in your place. I can see that.'

'Right. I just needed to know you understand my position here.'

'Oh come on, be fair,' he said. 'I'm not a complete idiot.'

She gave him a little smile. Her first one of the morning. 'Right, here's what's going to happen. I'm going to call a halt to the investigation and reassign everyone, but obviously I need someone to wrap everything up and close the investigation properly. That someone will be you. I suggest you might find more peace and quiet, and fewer distractions, if you take it home and do it. What do you think?'

Slater didn't need to think for long. 'So let me get this straight,' he said. 'You want me to work from home, where no one else knows what I'm doing. So, if I wanted to go out and speak to someone just to make sure they were happy with their statement, that would be okay.'

'You're a conscientious DS,' she said. 'I trust you to do the job without having to keep tabs on you all the time. I think you know what I'm saying. Just remember you're on your own.'

This seemed to cheer him up. 'How long have I got?' he asked.

'I can hide it until the end of the week without a problem,' she said.

Now he didn't look quite so happy. 'But it's already Thursday morning,' he said. 'That means I've only got two and a half days!'

'If you can find me something I can use to prove it definitely was murder, I'll go and stand toe-to-toe with my boss and he'll have to back down,' she said. 'But until then, this is the best I can do.'

'This sounds like mission impossible,' he said. 'Shouldn't we be sending for Tom Cruise?'

'I'm putting my neck on the line here for you,' she said, 'but, of course, if you think it's beyond your capabilities . . .'

She had guessed this would be the right one of his buttons to push, and sure enough, she was correct.

'I'll do it,' he said, indignantly. 'Just make sure that if I do find something, you can make a good enough argument to keep the case going.'

'Och, don't worry,' she said. 'You find a good one and I'll argue until I'm blue in the face.'

'And if it is Serbia, and we're stirring up a nest of vipers?' he asked.

'Then we'll have to deal with it, won't we?' she said, decisively.

CHAPTER TWENTY-THREE

Slater placed the pile of assorted paperwork on the back seat of his car and climbed into the driver's seat. He had worked on his own from home before, and actually quite enjoyed the freedom it would give him, although with such a tight deadline it would have been handy to have some sort of help.

He had just started his car when his mobile phone began to ring.

'I was trying to get hold of you last night,' said Norman's voice in his ear. 'Did you have your phone switched off? I left a message on your landline, but you didn't call back.'

'Ah, yeah,' he said. 'Err, I was a bit busy, you know how it is.'

'If you had your phone switched off it means you were off duty for once,' said Norman. 'What was it, a hot date?'

Slater blushed. 'Something like that,' he admitted.

'So, who was the lucky lady? Anyone I know?'

'What did you want, Norm?' asked Slater, hoping to deflect Norman's train of thought. 'Only I'm driving.'

'Okay,' said Norman. 'If you don't want to tell me, that's fine, you keep your secret.'

'So what's so important you were trying to track me down?' asked Slater.

'I just wondered if you might wanna come and see Shenzi tonight.'

'I would, Norm, but I'm really up to my neck at the moment. I'm going to be working twenty-four hours a day for a couple of days.'

'No shit,' said Norman. 'Whatever happened to duty rosters?'

'This is a bit of a special case.'

'I thought you were working on Becksy's case?'

'Yeah, I am,' said Slater. 'But Goodnews has pissed off the chief constable, and now I'm having to work on my own from home.'

'How the hell does that work?' asked Norman. 'I thought she could do no wrong.'

'It's complicated. That was then, and this is now. It's office politics and all that crap.'

'You sound like you're in the shit,' said Norman. 'You want some help?'

Slater thought for a moment. Norman wasn't police any more so using him would be right out of order, but then again, this whole situation with the chief constable was right out of order.

'Can you spare a couple of hours?' he asked.

Norman laughed. 'Hey, look, I'm retired with nothing to do at the moment. I can spare a couple of weeks! Where are you?'

'I'm just heading for home. It's my office for the next two and a half days.'

'Gimme half an hour and I'll be there,' said Norman.

Slater tossed his mobile phone onto the passenger seat, started his car, and zoomed out of the car park. With any luck, he would have enough time to remove all traces of Goodnews from his house before Norman got there.

CHAPTER TWENTY-FOUR

Slater had already told Norman about the case, but things had moved on since then, so Norman had insisted Slater start again from scratch and tell him everything they knew.

They had just finished watching the CCTV footage from the three different cameras.

'So I was right about there being two couriers,' said Norman, 'but in my head I figured they would have been working together. You reckon they weren't. Are you quite sure this guy from ASprint isn't bullshitting you? I mean, I can see it looks like he didn't know, but maybe they planned it the way it happened.'

'Well, he convinced me he was for real,' said Slater, 'but even so, I did consider the possibility it had been planned—'

'But you didn't go for it,' finished Norman.

'The thing is, it relies too much on chance to have been planned by the two of them. What if the traffic had been bad and the courier was delayed? What if Becksy had gone outside and been waiting when the real courier arrived? What if he hadn't waited? It's not as if it was urgent — the parcel could easily have been left at the front desk for him to collect next morning.'

'Yeah, I see what you mean,' said Norman. 'But even if you say it was just the guy who came into reception who planned it, doesn't chance come into it just the same?'

Slater thought about it. He could see what Norm meant, and he couldn't really argue with it, but he was still convinced Justin Wells had been telling him the truth.

'We can come back to that,' said Norman. 'Tell me why you think Slick Tony and his Russian hitman have to be behind this.'

'That's easy,' said Slater. 'What are the chances Becksy sends a fingerprint query to Interpol about the big man, and then within a week Becksy gets incinerated and the hard evidence goes with him?'

'But didn't you say it was Goodnews who had the bright idea of stirring up the shit through Interpol?' asked Norman. 'So why haven't they tried to kill her?'

'Maybe she's next,' said Slater. 'And maybe we're on the hit list as well.'

'That doesn't work for me,' said Norman. 'If they were going after both of them, why wait? Wouldn't they have done them quick? This way, Goodnews knows they're coming for her, right?'

'She doesn't believe they will,' said Slater.

'Well, for once, I agree with her,' said Norman. 'And I don't see us as targets either.'

'How can you be so sure?'

'I can't be sure, but something about this doesn't add up for me. You said yourself you thought it was weird they would go to all the trouble of murdering Ian and then frame him as well, and I agree with you. Remember when they came after us? They could easily have killed both of us, but they didn't. What did that Russian guy tell you?'

'You mean the one who was pointing a gun at me?' asked Slater.

'Yeah, he pointed it at you but he didn't pull the trigger, did he? Likewise, he turned my home into an open fire, but he watched me for several nights and didn't make a move until he was sure I wasn't going to be in there. That's my point, remember? So what did he say?'

'He said killing us wasn't worth all the hassle it would create for them,' recalled Slater. 'They figured the UK police force wouldn't have the cash to make a big deal out of a warning, but they would be obliged to find the money if a police officer was murdered.'

'Exactly,' said Norman. 'So they're not going to go after a DCI, are they? And why would they kill Ian Becks? It has to be a whole lot less hassle in the long run if they frame him and destroy his credibility, hasn't it?'

'I can buy that,' said Slater. 'But there's just one little problem with that idea. They *did* kill him, didn't they?'

'But did they?' argued Norman. 'Let's look at this again. Okay, we know there was an explosion, and we know Ian's dead body was found afterwards, but didn't the pathologist say he was dead before the bomb went off?'

'Yeah, you're right,' said Slater. 'I'm looking at this through blinkers, aren't I? I'm so sure they're to blame, I'm ignoring the facts.'

'Okay,' said Norman. 'So let's have a look at some of the facts again, now you've lost the blinkers.'

Slater felt rather stupid that he had needed his ex-partner to step in and sweep the fog from his eyes.

'Here's something you need to consider before you decide it's all about the bomb,' said Norman. 'I've seen the work of bombers up in London. Even if you only want to kill one person, you don't use a piddly little incendiary device. They're meant for starting fires, not killing people.'

Slater nodded unhappily. He should have been thinking like this from the start, but as soon as he had found out about the Interpol connection he'd only had eyes for one theory.

'Don't look so glum,' said Norman. 'So you've been focused on one suspect and it's swayed your thinking. We all do it from time to time. The important thing is now you've got the blinkers off you can look at everything with fresh eyes. Let me put some suggestions to you. If he was dead a

129

couple of hours before the explosion, doesn't that point the finger at the mystery guy in the red leathers?'

'Yeah, of course it does,' agreed Slater, 'but that doesn't mean he wasn't sent from Serbia.'

'I'm not saying it doesn't,' said Norman. 'But it doesn't mean he *was* sent from there either.'

Slater pulled a face but he knew Norman was speaking sense.

'You're keeping an open mind, Dave, remember?'

Slater managed a smile. 'Yeah, I know, I'm just tired, but I don't have time to be, you know?'

'Maybe you should have had an early night instead of going on that hot date.'

Slater blushed. 'Yeah, yeah,' he said, 'whatever.'

Norman waited to see if Slater was going to elaborate, but he waited in vain.

'Okay,' he said, eventually. 'What about the cleaner who was kidnapped?'

'Yeah, that seems too much of a coincidence,' agreed Slater, 'but I can't see where it fits in and we haven't spoken to him yet. Steve Biddeford was hoping to talk to him this morning, but that was before the shit hit the fan. I don't know if he actually did, and I can't ask him without telling him what I'm doing.'

'Maybe you need to go to the hospital yourself,' said Norman.

Slater sighed. His face spoke volumes.

'Yeah, I know. It's gonna be real hard trying to do all this on your own. I know I'm not authorised, and I shouldn't be anywhere near a police inquiry, but how about I help out? I've got no badge so I can't interview anyone, but I can sit down and go through all the evidence if you want.'

Slater considered Norman's offer.

'Look, I know it goes against the rules,' said Norman.

'No, bugger the rules,' said Slater. 'Everything about this situation goes against the bloody rules.'

Norman beamed a big smile. 'So we're good then, yeah?'

'Yeah, we're good,' said Slater. 'The old team's back in business, even if it is unofficial.'

'Now that's fighting talk,' said Norman, 'and I like the sound of it. Have you got your laptop here as well?'

Slater pointed to a laptop bag on his settee. 'It's over there. I've changed my login details but I'll write them down for you.'

'I don't suppose you have a whiteboard?' asked Norman, optimistically.

Slater laughed. 'Jesus, you don't want much, do you, Norm?'

'I thought that was probably asking too much.'

'Just hang on a minute,' said Slater. 'I may not have a whiteboard, but I do have walls.' He pointed to the walls around them.

'You've just had a decorator in,' said Norman. 'You don't wanna spoil your newly painted walls.'

'He hasn't done this room yet. You can stick sheets of paper to the walls. I've got some tape that peels off easy. I've used it before. It's not perfect but it works.'

'Well, if you're sure,' said Norman, uncertainly.

'We owe it to Becksy, so yes, I'm sure,' said Slater, decisively.

'Go to the hospital and see your little old man. By the time you get back I'll have the evidence up on the wall so we can see what we've got and where the gaps are.'

'One thing,' said Slater. 'The only one who knows what I'm doing is Goodnews—'

'She's okay with this?' asked a surprised Norman.

'It was her idea,' said Slater.

'Really? Wow! What have you been doing to sweeten her up so much?'

Slater felt his face reddening, so he turned away and pretended to be hunting for his car keys. 'The thing is,' he said, as he searched, 'she might phone me. She'll probably use my mobile number, but if she can't get hold of me she might call here on the landline.'

'I gotcha,' said Norman, with a wry smile. 'She wouldn't be too happy if I answered the phone, right?'

'Right.'

'Don't worry, I won't touch it. I don't have anything to say to her anyway.'

'I'll catch you later,' said Slater.

'I have to leave at seven, just for a couple of hours,' said Norman, 'but I'll come back after that.'

'I should be back before then.'

'If not, you can bring me up to speed later,' said Norman.

CHAPTER TWENTY-FIVE

It was six p.m. Slater had had a frustrating time at the hospital. Joe Chandler had been well enough to talk to him and had gone into great detail about how frightened he had been and how he'd thought he was going to die, but in terms of evidence, he had nothing to offer. All Slater learned was that it was a man who had abducted old Joe. He had sneaked up behind him and offered to cut the old man's throat should he wish to argue in any way whatsoever. Naturally, poor old Joe had done as he was told, which basically amounted to being tied up and forced to wear a hood.

Slater climbed into his car and slapped the steering wheel in frustration. It was an interview that had been necessary, but ultimately it had been a waste of time, and he had precious little of that. His mobile phone started to ring.

'Where are you?' Goodnews asked. 'I thought you'd be at home so I tried your landline.'

'I'm at the hospital. I've been talking to Joe Chandler, the kidnapped cleaner.'

'Did he have anything to offer?' she asked, optimistically.

'Lots of information about how scared he was, but sod all that's any help to us.'

'You'd have kicked yourself if you hadn't spoken to him and he knew something.'

'Yeah, I know,' he agreed. 'It's just a bit frustrating to know it was a waste of time, especially when there's so little of it.'

'Well, this might cheer you up,' she said. 'Eamon Murphy just called. He's got that toxicology report we're waiting for. He was going to bring it over, but I said you'd pick it up.'

'That's handy,' said Slater. 'I'm in just the right place. Did he say why it's taken so long?'

'I'll let him tell you that himself,' she said.

'That sounds intriguing. Don't I even get a hint?'

'Not from me,' she said, 'but I can tell you you'll like it.'

'I'd better go then.'

'Right,' she said. 'Well, as the CC has decided we have no case to investigate I'm going to go home for a change. If you need me for anything, just call.'

Slater climbed back out of his car, plipped the locks, slipped his phone into his pocket, and headed back across the car park.

* * *

'I seem to recall Ian used to take great delight in finding things that changed the course of your investigations,' said Eamon Murphy when Slater got to his office.

'Yeah,' remembered Slater, fondly. 'For him it was like scoring the winning goal in the cup final. It was as if it proved we really couldn't manage without him.'

'Well, it might be my turn to do the same, with Ian's involvement from beyond the grave, as it were.'

'Come on, Eamon. We've waited long enough for this report already.'

'Sorry about that, but I had to make sense of the report before I could pass it on to you.'

'Don't keep me in suspense,' Slater pleaded.

'I wasn't sure what we would find in his blood, but I guessed there would be something,' said Murphy. 'You will recall it's my belief he was dead before the bomb exploded, through respiratory failure, but I'd been unable to pinpoint why. When my colleague arrived to check my work he agreed with my findings and he suggested what it was. The toxicology report proved he was right. There was an enormous amount of morphine in his blood. That's what caused his respiratory failure.'

'Morphine?' echoed Slater. 'Are you telling me he overdosed on morphine?'

Murphy smiled. 'Now that's an interesting question. Did he commit suicide or was he murdered? I think it's safe to say we were supposed to believe he overdosed, but we're not that silly, are we?'

'You're losing me, Eamon,' said Slater. 'I haven't had much sleep this week, so you'll have to tell me, not ask me.'

'Okay. Let me make it easy for you. There were no traces of morphine in his stomach contents so the only way it could have been administered would have been with a needle, but I found no trace of any needle marks when I first examined the body. To be fair, I wasn't looking specifically for needle marks, but a fresh one should have been pretty easy to spot. It actually took two of us most of this afternoon to locate it.'

Slater sighed. He wondered why these people had to go around the houses with their explanations. Why couldn't they keep it simple?

'Did he inject himself, or not?' he asked.

'If you were going to inject yourself with a powerful painkiller, where would you stick the needle?' asked Murphy.

Slater shaped his right hand as if he was holding a syringe. He made to inject the invisible syringe into his left arm.

'In my left arm, I suppose,' he said, 'or maybe in one of my thighs.'

'Exactly,' said Murphy. 'Ian Becks was a leftie, but the principle's the same. You would expect him to inject his right arm or a thigh. It shouldn't be hard to spot that needle mark, but I couldn't find one in any of the obvious places, and nor could my colleague, so we started to look everywhere.'

'You found it, right?' asked Slater.

'We did, eventually. In the back of his neck. It was above the hairline, and we very nearly missed it.'

Slater shaped his hand again and raised it to the back of his neck. 'You're kidding me,' he said. 'It's hardly a natural thing to do, is it? And why try to hide it anyway? Ian would know you do bloods and stomach contents. He wouldn't be fooling anyone, and he would know that.'

'That's what I thought,' agreed Murphy. 'It only makes sense if—'

'Someone else injected it,' finished Slater.

'That's what I think, and my colleague is prepared to put pen to paper and agree with my conclusion.'

'I knew he hadn't topped himself,' said Slater, excitement bright in his eyes.

'I'm no expert,' said Murphy, 'but he certainly didn't seem to be on the brink last time I spoke to him.'

'It made no sense,' agreed Slater. 'His life was just coming together. He had everything to live for.'

* * *

Slater had stopped for fish and chips and eaten them at a leisurely pace in his car, so it was approaching eight p.m. by the time got home. He knew Norman would be long gone, but even so, he was surprised to find his little house in total darkness; Norm wasn't usually conscientious about conserving energy by switching lights off.

He unlocked the front door, walked in, and pushed it closed behind him. Then he switched on the light.

'Ah, good evening at last,' said an unexpected, accented voice.

Startled by the sudden voice, Slater froze momentarily with his back to the room. Then a grim feeling of realisation began to take hold. He was sure he knew that voice.

Holy shit, thought Slater, *this is it. They've come for me!*

Slowly, carefully, he turned to face the owner of the voice. As he took in the grinning face of the man sitting in his favourite armchair, a sinking feeling began to creep into his mind, but he wasn't about to give up without a fight.

'You?' he said. 'What are you doing here?'

'That's such a stupid question, don't you think?' said the Russian, cheerfully. 'I thought you would be pleased to see me.'

Slater's blood slowly began to run cold when he realised the Russian was holding all the cards, just like the last time they had met. At least this time the pistol wasn't in the man's hand pointed straight at him, but it lay on the arm of the chair, within easy reach of his right hand.

'I'm disappointed to see you haven't improved your security since the last time we met,' said the Russian, his slow, clipped tones giving him an icy authority. 'But then I suppose it's just like the motor mechanic who looks after everyone else's car but neglects his own.'

'I'm disappointed to see you haven't improved your manners,' Slater retorted, sounding much braver than he felt.

'Oh, you mean the pistol?' asked the Russian. 'I'm sorry if it offends you, but I find it's a very effective way of establishing authority. But trust me, as long as you stay where you are, the pistol will stay where it is.'

This news didn't exactly make Slater relax, but he recalled the last time they had met when the Russian could very easily have blown his head off if he had so wished. He had made the same promise back then and kept it, so he chose to take him at face value. And, anyway, he really was in no position to argue.

'Why would I be pleased to see you?' he asked. 'You've just murdered one of my friends.'

'Oh please,' said the Russian. 'Do you really think we would be so stupid? What possible reason would we have for doing such a thing.'

'We have evidence, a fingerprint—'

'I think not,' corrected the Russian. 'I'm sure you must be aware by now that no such fingerprint exists.'

'Ha! So it *was* you lot.'

'Oh yes. Of course we have removed your "evidence". I will even admit we removed some additional evidence from your forensics lab and planted it, along with some cash, in your friend's flat to undermine his position and destroy his credibility. These things I admit we have done, but you're an intelligent man, Mr Slater. Surely you are asking yourself why we would have done these things if we had intended to murder him?'

This thought had occurred to Slater, but he wasn't going to admit it now. 'So you admit you stole evidence from our lab?'

'It wasn't difficult,' said the Russian. 'We even planted a small incendiary device as a further diversion.'

'But that's what killed Becksy.'

The Russian shook his head and tut-tutted. 'Really, Mr Slater,' he said. 'Is that the best you can do? How disappointing. Do I really look that stupid? We both know Mr Becks was dead long before our little fire starter was detonated.'

'How could you know that?'

'I know a lot more than you can imagine. Security in your police station is almost as bad as it is here. I believe that's down to your lady friend, the lovely DCI Goodnews.'

Slater ignored the reference to Goodnews. He was much more interested in what happened the night Becks died. 'How do you know Becks was already dead?' he asked.

The Russian sighed. 'Come, come, Mr Slater. You're supposed to be the detective here. Do I really have to do all your work for you?'

'You've broken into my house,' said Slater, 'and, not for the first time, you have a gun pointed at me. On top of that, you want me to believe you haven't committed a crime which all our evidence suggests you have done. So why not humour me and tell me why I should believe you?'

'I've already told you we had no reason to kill Mr Becks,' said the Russian. 'Perhaps you should look at your evidence again and start to believe what you actually see, and not what you want to see.'

Slater was confused.

'I had to do something to pass the time after Mr Norman left, so I had a look through your case file,' explained the Russian. 'You already know the mystery courier in the red leathers killed Mr Becks, you just don't know why.'

'I think he was working for you,' said Slater, 'and I'm going to find the link that proves it.'

The Russian laughed out loud and shook his head at Slater. 'I hate to disappoint you, but you won't find that link, because it doesn't exist. You really need to take off those blinkers that only allow you to see Serbia as your answer. Where is our motive? Isn't that what you look for?'

'Your motive is the fingerprint.'

'But we both know that particular motive doesn't exist now. If there is no fingerprint, then by definition that cannot be a motive.'

Slater said nothing but studied the Russian's implacable face. It didn't tell him anything. This guy was so cool he gave absolutely nothing away. He wondered if it was possible he might actually be telling the truth.

'I was rather hoping you were going to bring DCI Goodnews back with you, like last night,' said the Russian. 'I would so like to meet her. I wonder what your chief constable would say if he knew about your relationship.'

Despite the seriousness of the situation Slater could feel his face redden. 'There is no relationship,' he said.

The Russian smiled, indulgently. 'Discretion,' he said. 'I like that. Such an important quality to have.'

'There's nothing to be discreet about,' snapped Slater.

'I beg to differ.'

'You can differ all you like. You're barking up the wrong tree. There is no relationship.'

'As you wish.' The Russian's smile made it obvious he didn't believe him.

'For a start, it's none of your bloody business,' said Slater, 'and I certainly don't care what you think.'

'Ah, but I can see you so obviously do,' said the Russian, his grin becoming wider and wider. He let Slater stew angrily for a few seconds before he continued. 'But I have to agree,' he said. 'Your love life really is none of my business. However, I would hate to see your career ruined by an ill-advised relationship with a senior officer. Let's hope the chief doesn't get to hear about it, for the sake of both your careers.'

'Is that a threat?'

The Russian smiled again. He obviously enjoyed getting under Slater's skin. 'I'd prefer to see it as good advice.'

'Piss off,' said Slater, angrily. 'I don't need your bloody advice.'

The Russian shrugged amiably. 'As you wish. But I'm sure you'll find your friend Mr Norman would agree with me. How is he by the way? Such a pity he retired; you made such a good team.'

'That would never have happened if it wasn't for you torching his flat,' said Slater.

The Russian waved a dismissive hand. 'DCI Goodnews was going to happen anyway,' he said, 'and she would still have forced him out. It may have taken her a little longer without my intervention, but she would have achieved her goal eventually.'

He smiled at Slater again. Slater glowered back.

'Anyway, I didn't come here to talk about these things,' he said. 'I understand you have very little time before this investigation is closed. Unlike you, it seems your chief constable is prepared to accept we're not involved, and instead he's prepared to accept a suicide verdict to stop you wasting any more time on us. But we both know it wasn't suicide, don't we?'

'How do you know all this?' asked Slater.

The Russian smiled his indulgent smile again. 'How I know is unimportant. I've come here to help you catch your friend's murderer before it's too late, but you won't do that if you waste any more time going after us. You already know who did this. Don't waste any more time on us, you'll prove nothing. Find your mystery man, he's the real killer.'

'I suppose you'll be telling me you know his motive next,' said Slater, indignantly.

The Russian chuckled. 'I think I've given you more than enough help already, don't you?'

He took hold of the pistol and eased himself from his armchair. Slater's heart seemed to miss several beats and his stomach lurched violently. He stepped back involuntarily and raised his hands.

'Please, relax,' said the Russian. 'I like you, Mr Slater. You have principles, you understand discretion, and you are devoted to your job. These are excellent qualities in any man.'

'I'm supposed to feel grateful, am I?' growled Slater.

'We may be on opposite sides of the fence, Mr Slater, but even so, I can recognise you as a fundamentally good man. Your choice of girlfriend may be unwise, but then, none of us are perfect, are we?'

Slater's face reddened even more.

'My point is why on earth would I want to shoot a good man for no good reason?' The Russian smiled, yet again, and then waved the gun to indicate what he wanted Slater to do. 'Please, come and sit in this chair.'

At the sudden movement of the gun, Slater suddenly became unsteady on his feet and wobbled. The Russian tightened his grip on the gun and straightened his aim.

'Now please, there's no need to be a hero,' he said. 'I may not want to shoot you, but I will if you give me reason to.'

'Don't panic,' said Slater, trying to maintain some sort of composure. 'I'm not feeling heroic tonight. Guns tend to have that effect on me for some reason.'

Facing each other, they shuffled around the room until they had exchanged places, and Slater sank into the chair. He was actually quite relieved to be sitting down. His legs now seemed to be made of jelly and he was no longer in full control of them.

'I'm going to say goodbye now,' said the Russian. 'Please stay where you are for five minutes.'

He walked across to the front door and pulled it open. Before he left, he stopped on the threshold and turned.

'Remember,' he said, 'it's often the oldest skeleton in the closet that rattles loudest.'

Then he turned and walked out, pulling the door closed behind him.

Slater was no coward, but the stress of facing a menacing man with a gun had taken its toll. As he tried to get up and give chase, he discovered he no longer had any control of his legs and they immediately gave way beneath him, leaving him in an untidy heap on the floor.

'Oh bollocks,' he muttered, as he lay there waiting for his heart to stop racing. 'I hate bloody guns.'

After a couple of minutes, he was pretty sure his legs would now work normally, and although his heart was still beating pretty fast, at least he could now count the beats. He knew he really should get up off the floor and do something, but he didn't. He just lay there.

CHAPTER TWENTY-SIX

It was nine p.m. when Norman let himself into Slater's house.

'It's only me,' he called, as he opened the door and walked in. 'I took your spare key. I hope you don't mi—'

He left the sentence unfinished as he did a quick double take. Slater was still lying on his back on the floor, where he had been since the Russian left. Norman rushed across to his friend and knelt down by his side.

'Dave! Dave! Are you okay?' Gently, he patted Slater's cheek.

Slater opened one eye and looked at him.

'Are you hurt?' asked Norman, alarmed.

'My pride is severely dented, but physically I'm fine,' said Slater.

'What happened? What are you doing on the floor?'

'Honestly?' asked Slater, still on his back. 'I'm so pissed off I just couldn't be arsed to get up.'

'You'll be fine,' said Norman. 'We just need to step back, see what we've missed and we'll solve this case just like we've solved others before.'

Slater sighed, a big, heavy sigh. 'I've had enough of this shit, Norm. This is the second time I've had some arsehole point a bloody gun at me, and what do I have to fight back with? Bugger all, that's what. How can we be expected to fight crime when the bloody criminals have all the weapons? And if we do fight back, we get accused of police brutality! How does that bloody work? It's just not worth it anymore.'

'Wait, wait, wait,' said a shocked Norman. 'What's this about a gun? Who's been pointing a gun at you? What the hell's happened?'

'Do you remember the Russian guy?' asked Slater.

'How can I forget the guy who turned my flat into a fireball? What? You're kidding me, right? Has he been here?'

Slater gave him a rueful look.

'Have you called it in?' asked Norman. 'You have, haven't you?'

'What's the bloody point, Norm? The guy's like a ghost. He'll be long gone and he never leaves a trace, does he?'

'Jeez, you really are pissed off, aren't you? I thought you'd got over all that negative stuff.'

Slater looked glum. 'Yeah, so did I. Will you help me up?'

Norman stood up, gave Slater a hand and pulled him to his feet, where he wobbled unsteadily.

'You'd better sit down a minute,' said Norman, guiding him back into the armchair. 'Can I get you a cup of tea?'

Slater leaned forward and scrubbed his face with his hands. 'There are some beers in the fridge,' he said. 'Grab a couple and I'll tell you what you've missed.'

* * *

'Jeez, I'm sorry you've been through that again,' said Norman, when Slater had finished relating his story. 'Maybe if I'd stayed here—'

'He waited until you went out, Norm,' said Slater. 'It was me he wanted to see. And it's not your fault, you've got nothing to be sorry for.'

'This all down to Goodnews,' said Norman. 'If she hadn't stirred up the shit—'

'He didn't come here to kill me, Norm. I wouldn't be talking to you now if that was his intention.'

'D'you think he's telling the truth?'

'Now that's the million-dollar question, but I'm not dead, am I?'

'So you do believe him,' said Norman.

'Ever since I knew about the fingerprint, I was convinced it had to be them,' said Slater. 'But, like the guy said, if the fingerprint was the motive and it doesn't exist anymore, then neither does the motive.'

'Yeah, but he would say that, wouldn't he?' argued Norman. 'It's just as likely he's doing this to throw you off the scent. You've only got two days, right? So if he sends you off in another direction it could take you those two days to realise it.'

'Oh, I know that,' said Slater. 'But what if he *is* telling the truth and we don't follow it up? We're damned if we do, and we're damned if we don't.'

'So what do we know that backs up his argument?'

'Becksy was dead before the explosion,' said Slater, 'and we know the Mystery Man in the red leathers went down to the lab with him, and was there at, or very close to, the time he died.'

'Well, that's it then,' said Norman. 'We focus on that guy. Maybe it will lead us back to the Russian and his friends anyway.'

'He says it won't.'

'We can judge that for ourselves, when the time comes. Do we know anything about this guy?'

'The only clue we have that might help is that when Ian saw him on the CCTV footage, he seemed to know him.'

'So we start with friends and family,' said Norman. 'I have to admit, I don't trust this Russian guy.'

'I wouldn't trust him as far as I can throw him,' said Slater, 'but he seems to know a whole lot of stuff that he's right about.'

'You have to wonder how he knows all that,' said Norman. 'It's not all in the file, is it? I mean, how does he know what the chief constable thinks?'

'Yeah, it's almost as if he's directing operations himself, isn't it?' suggested Slater.

'That doesn't bear thinking about,' said Norman. 'We know they've got someone inside at Interpol, but d'you think they've got someone in their pocket here as well? Jesus, that would have to be someone pretty high up to know what the CC's thinking, don't you think? It would need to be a DCI or someone like that.'

They both knew what Norman was implying, but Slater wasn't going to get into that conversation. 'Let's not go down that road, Norm,' he said.

Before either of them could say anything else, his land-line began to ring.

'Who the hell is that, at this time of night?' asked Norman.

The phone continued to ring but Slater made no attempt to get up and answer it.

'Are you gonna get that?'

'No, bugger it, I can't be arsed. If it's important they'll leave a message.'

The answer machine kicked in and they heard his voice telling the caller to leave a message after the beep. Then the machine did beep and they heard a voice. Slater immediately regretted his decision to ignore the call.

'Hi, it's Marion,' said the voice of DCI Marion Goodnews. 'I'm sorry I missed you. I just called to apologise for what I said this morning, and to thank you for last night. I really did have a lovely time. You made me forget all about work for a few hours, and that's something I haven't done for a long time. It was just what I needed. Thanks again.'

Norman looked enquiringly at Slater but said nothing. Not for the first time that day, Slater felt his face redden.

'Look,' he said, flustered. 'She had a load of shit from the CC, she was pretty down, and we went for a drink after work. I just tried to cheer her up. That's all there was to it.'

'But you both ended up back here,' said Norman.

'She'd had a lot to drink. I couldn't let her drive home,' explained Slater, sounding desperate. 'It's not what you think.'

Norman held up his hands. 'Hey, what I think doesn't matter. It's none of my business what you do with your boss in your spare time. I just hope you realise what you're doing, that's all.'

Slater's face reddened even more, but now he was angry. First the Russian was telling him how to run his personal life and now his best friend was having a go.

'It's no different to me and you going out for a pint and me letting you sleep here because you've had too much to drink,' he said, angrily.

'Don't start getting arsey with me,' said Norman. 'I'm just a friend looking out for you. I just think you need to remember what we were saying a couple of minutes ago about someone being in the Russian guy's pocket.'

'Look, I know you don't like her,' said Slater, 'but I can tell you one thing for sure — she's not in anyone's pocket. Anyway, she's been running this investigation so it's not as if she needs to pick my brains for information.'

'Wasn't it Shakespeare who said something about protesting too much?' asked Norman, innocently.

Slater was smarting, but he was also trying hard to make sure this didn't get out of hand. 'We're not going to fall out over this, are we?' he asked.

'There's no reason why we should, is there?'

'Not as long as you remember it's my life.'

'Look, I'm sorry,' said Norman. 'I'm probably the last person who should be giving out advice about relationships after the car crash my life became. I just don't want to see you get hurt.'

'Jesus, Norm, she just used my spare room for a night, that's all. She was having a bad day and I took her for a drink. I'd have done the same for you.'

'Just don't ask me to be best man, that's all,' said Norman. 'That would be a step too far.'

'Oh, for f—' Slater just caught Norman's cheeky grin before the word escaped his lips. 'Oh, ha, ha, very funny.'

'Come on,' said Norman, amicably. 'We've got better things to do, right?'

'You're right,' Slater agreed, knowing Norman only had his best interests at heart. 'We can argue about my life's choices another time. We should focus on what we do best.'

'Okay. So where do you think we should go from here?'

'Right now I'm shattered,' said Slater, climbing to his feet. 'I think I should go to bed and get a few hours' sleep.'

'Yeah,' said Norman. 'I think that's a good idea. You look like you haven't slept for days.'

'What about you?' asked Slater. 'Are you coming up?'

'It's very sweet of you to offer,' said Norman, the cheeky grin all over his face again, 'but I really don't want to share with you.'

'Yeah, right. You know very well what I mean. Don't tell me you don't sleep these days.'

'Oh, don't worry about me. I'm wide awake,' said Norman. 'That's another thing about being retired — you get the chance to sleep whenever you want. I've caught up on all that sleep I used to miss out on and then some. If it's okay with you, I'll sit down here and go through this file again. Then I might use your laptop and do some digging around online.'

'Sure. Fill your boots,' said Slater. 'When you get tired, you know there's a spare bed, right?'

'What time are we starting in the morning?' asked Norman.

'I'm going to set my alarm for six.'

'I'll be there.'

Slater climbed slowly up the stairs and struggled out of his clothes. He was dead on his feet as he climbed into bed. As his head hit the pillow he caught a faint whiff of perfume and for a moment he was confused, but only for a moment.

CHAPTER TWENTY-SEVEN

When Slater came down the next morning, his lounge walls were adorned with assorted sheets of paper, some with photographs attached and some linked by lengths of red string.

'I take it you've been up all night?' he asked.

'Too right I have,' said Norman. 'It's like I was Frankenstein's monster and I just got that electric shock. I really didn't realise how much I missed all this.'

'So, what have you learned?'

'I've been wondering how your friend the Russian could have known Becksy died a couple of hours before the bomb went off. There are three possibilities. He could have read it in the file while he was waiting for you last night, someone could have told him, or he was there and saw what happened.'

'But you think he was there?' asked Slater.

'I do, yes,' said Norman. 'Or if he wasn't there in person, he had someone working for him.'

'What makes you so sure?'

'You said he told you he knew it wasn't suicide. Now, how could he know that, and why would he care? I mean a suicide verdict clears them of a murder charge, so what difference does it make to him?'

Slater stared at Norman's patchwork of papers on his wall.

'So who was watch—' he began. 'Oh, hang on. The cleaner was abducted, wasn't he?'

'Right,' said Norman. 'It's an easy switch to make, and there's not too much risk. Who's gonna take any notice of a cleaner down in the basement? Who's even going to see him, unless they go down there?'

'Christ, we should have been onto that sooner. I knew it was important,' said Slater. 'It was never going to be a bloody coincidence, was it?'

'We can worry about what you should have done another time,' said Norman. 'Right now we need to try and figure out what he saw.'

'Well, let's make an assumption for a minute,' said Slater. 'Let's accept the Russian's telling the truth and they did put a fake cleaner into the basement. He waits for Becksy to leave, then he goes into the lab, finds the fingerprint, removes it and sets up the incendiary device. He was quick, but even so, before he can escape, Becksy comes back down to the lab, this time with the mystery rider.'

'Right,' said Norman, picking up the thread. 'So he hides somewhere in the lab and he watches as Becksy gets bumped off. Then, somehow, he manages to find an escape route and he legs it as quick as he can, and who can blame him? This should have been a nice easy job. He was just supposed to nick some evidence and set a firebomb. No one told him anything about getting involved in murder.'

'This is starting to make the Russian's story sound even more credible,' said Slater.

'Yeah, tell me about it,' said Norman. 'Much as I hate to admit it, I think we have to take a chance and do what he suggested.'

'I need to eat first,' said Slater, heading for the kitchen.

'There's something else about all this that worries me,' said Norman, following in Slater's wake. 'Why is the chief constable so keen to believe it's a suicide?'

'He's trying to put Goodnews in her place,' said Slater. 'She's got too big for her boots. This is his chance to show her who's boss.'

'I don't buy that,' said Norman. 'From what you were telling me, she's in enough shit with Darling being suspended and the non-existent security at Tinton. He can easily enough stamp on her for all that if he wants to. A murder in a police station is a big deal because it looks bad on everyone, all the way to the top.'

'Yeah,' agreed Slater, opening and closing cupboards, 'a murder does look bad, but if it's an employee committing suicide, it's a whole new ball game. In this scenario, the dead guy was supposed to be in the building so it becomes much easier to gloss over the lapses in security. To anyone looking in from the outside, it suggests no one got in who shouldn't have.'

'I hope you're right,' said Norman, leaning against the kitchen doorpost.

'So do I,' said Slater, 'because, if the CC is bent, then we're all in trouble. Anyway, we don't have time to worry about that. We're already running out of time.'

'Yeah, you're right,' said Norman. 'But it would be interesting to take a closer look, don't you think?'

'Maybe later,' said Slater, having finished his search. 'Right, do you fancy cereal, or would you prefer cereal?'

'Cupboards bare again?'

'Afraid so.'

'I guess I'll have cereal then. You have got milk, haven't you?'

'That's one thing I have got,' said Slater, swinging open the fridge door to demonstrate. He busied himself making two bowls of cereal and passed one to Norman.

'Thanks. So tell me again what his parting words were last night.'

Slater watched him take a huge spoonful of cereal before he answered. 'He said "it's often the oldest skeleton in the closet that rattles loudest".'

Norman chewed thoughtfully. 'Any idea what that refers to?'

'I can only think he means there's something from Becksy's past,' said Slater.

'You don't think it's about him being gay, do you? I mean he wasn't exactly shouting it from the rooftops.'

'It's a possibility,' said Slater. 'But he said the "oldest skeleton". My hunch is he was referring to something from way back when.'

'D'you think Bethan might be able to help out with that?'

'It wouldn't hurt to ask, although now I think about it, she did mention something about bullying at his old school.'

'I can imagine a geek like him would have been a perfect target for school bullies,' said Norman.

'That's exactly what I thought,' admitted Slater, 'but I didn't see how it could be relevant to his murder.'

'I agree it seems unlikely, but it would be somewhere to start. Did she tell you which school it was?'

'Yeah, I wrote it down in my notebook. It's not local though. It's out Winchester way, I think.'

'I'll give them a call later,' said Norman. 'You never know, they could have some information that would help.'

* * *

'Hello, Bethan,' said Slater, when she opened her front door. 'I'm sorry to be here again.'

'I hope you haven't come to try and convince me about this stupid suicide idea,' she said, angrily. 'I've never heard anything so absurd in all my life.'

'Oh. You've been told about that.' He was thinking fast. He wondered who had decided to tell her. It would have been good if whoever it was had thought to tell him. Should he tell her the truth?

'It's ridiculous,' she said.

Slater made his decision. 'Yes,' he said, 'I quite agree. And so does the pathologist.'

'I'm sorry?' she said. 'But I thought—'

'Can I come in, Beth? It's a bit public out here.'

She studied him, her face a picture of suspicion.

'I'm on your side, Beth,' he pleaded. 'Ian was a good mate as well as a colleague.'

She seemed to relax, and then stepped back to let him in. 'He used to talk about you,' she said. 'He thought the three of you made a good team, him, you and the other guy who got kidnapped.'

'Norman,' said Slater.

'That's the one. Ian said he was always good for making everyone laugh.'

Slater smiled at the memory. 'Oh, we had plenty of laughs,' he said, fondly. 'We got some good results too.'

'Come and sit down and tell me about the pathologist,' she said.

He followed her through to the lounge and sat down. 'I won't bore you with the fine detail,' he said. 'The long and the short of it is Ian's blood was full of morphine. When they eventually found the needle mark from the injection, it was quite clear it would have been difficult for him to have injected himself, and why would he hide it anyway? The conclusion has to be someone murdered him.'

She sat perfectly still for few moments and said nothing.

'We also have reason to believe his death may be related to an event from his past,' he continued. 'Do you have any idea what this might be?'

'I honestly have no idea,' she said. 'As far as I know, there are no major events in his past. Jimmy's got quite close to Ian, maybe he knows something.'

'Is he here?' asked Slater.

'No, he's back at work now I've got myself a bit more together.'

'He seems like a nice guy.'

'Yes, he is,' she agreed. 'He's been my rock through this.'

'How did you meet him?'

'It was quite strange really,' she said. 'He came to our wedding reception. It turns out they were at the same school, but Ian hadn't seen Jimmy for years because he had left the area. But he had come back, and somehow he had found out about the wedding. He wasn't invited, he just turned up, but Ian felt as he'd made the effort we couldn't turn him away, so we let him stay.'

'So, did they resume their friendship?' asked Slater.

'That was the funny thing,' she said. 'He disappeared again, and we didn't see him for a long time. Then, when Ian and I divorced, he came back on the scene, and the rest, as they say, is history.'

'That was good timing on his part,' said Slater, but the inference was lost on her. 'He was telling me he works for Ian's publishing company.'

'Yes,' she said. 'It was his idea Ian should submit his manuscript. He was very supportive, he even put in a good word with his bosses.'

'He doesn't deal with that sort of thing himself, then?'

'Oh no,' she said. 'He runs the mailing room. Dispatching letters and parcels, stuff like that.'

Like a bloodhound picking up a scent, Slater felt a sudden rush of adrenaline, but he kept his excitement in check and remained calm.

'Well, thanks for talking to me,' he said, 'but I'm going to have to get going. And don't worry, I won't settle for a suicide verdict, I promise.'

He knew he shouldn't make such promises, and he regretted it as soon as he'd said it, but it was too late now, he couldn't take his words back. He would just have to make sure he didn't let her down.

* * *

He climbed into his car and drove away from Bethan Becks' house, but as soon as he had gone round the first corner, he pulled over and called Norman.

'There's someone I need you to check out,' he told Norman. 'His name's Jimmy Huston.'

He spelt the name out and Norman read it back to him.

'Who's he?' asked Norman.

'He's Bethan Becks' boyfriend.'

'Ah, right, yeah, of course. So what's he done to arouse your suspicions?'

'He works for P&P Publishing.'

'Now there's a coincidence,' said Norman.

'It gets better,' said Slater. 'He works in the mailing room. In fact, he runs it.'

'Oh my,' said Norman. 'Now that *is* interesting. Does he deliver manuscripts?'

'Ha! That would be too easy,' said Slater, 'but he must know something about the couriers they use. Funny he didn't mention it when I spoke to him before.'

'Did you ask Bethan about that?'

'I didn't want to ask too much and spook her. If she gets suspicious and starts asking him questions he might do a runner. I'd like you to see if you can find any ammo I can use when I talk to him again.'

'Okay,' said Norman. 'I'll warm up your trusty laptop and see if I can dig anything up you can add to the armoury.'

'Did you get hold of the school?' asked Slater.

'I did, but the secretary made it clear they're not too keen on talking to me. However, I'm sure if a nice detective sergeant was to arrive waving a warrant card, he wouldn't have too much trouble getting past her. She seemed genuinely saddened to hear about the death of an old pupil, I just made the mistake of telling her I'm not a policeman. I think she jumped to the conclusion that meant I must be a journalist sniffing around for a bit of scandal.'

'You're losing your touch,' said Slater.

'Yeah, it's weird,' admitted Norman. 'I must have told thousands of little white lies over the years to help get the job done, and yet these days I seem to find it difficult to even think of one when I need it. I must have become more honest now I've retired.'

'That's a worrying idea,' said Slater.

He heard Norman chuckle over the line. 'If it's worrying you, think how I feel.'

Slater laughed out loud. 'What's the address of that school?' he asked, 'I might as well get over there now.'

'I'll text it to you,' said Norman. 'Have fun now, and mind you don't get lippy and end up being put into detention.'

Less than a minute later, Slater's phone beeped. He opened the message and read it. He thought he knew vaguely where this school was, but just to make sure he didn't waste any time, he tapped the address into his car's satnav.

'Right,' he said to himself, as he put the car into gear and pulled away. 'Let's see if we can find any skeletons to rattle.'

CHAPTER TWENTY-EIGHT

Slater parked in the car park of Radletts School, looked at the front of the old building, and shivered involuntarily. He was two years older than Ian Becks, but whereas he couldn't wait to escape at the earliest opportunity, Becks had stayed on another two years in the sixth form. So he figured Becks must have left school about five years later, which would have been around nineteen or twenty years ago. As he opened his car door, he wondered what chance there was that any of the teachers from back then would still be here. Was this going to be a wild goose chase?

As he pushed open the doors and walked into the school, Slater began to get that same old feeling he used to get all those years ago when he was a schoolboy. The school he went to back then was housed in a similar building to this one. It even seemed to smell the same. He almost expected the head-master to come out and shout at him at any minute. Then he realised that was ridiculous. He was nearly forty years old, for goodness' sake.

To his relief, the headmaster didn't come out and shout at him. In fact, there didn't appear to be anyone anywhere to *do* any shouting. He could see no signs to direct him any-where, so he stopped and listened for evidence of life. All he could hear was a faint tap tap sound, not unlike the sound of someone using an old typewriter. The sound seemed to be coming from a corridor to his left, so he followed it until he found the source.

The door to the room bore the words *School Secretary*. The door was closed, but there was a hatch in the wall with two small sliding-glass windows. He walked to the hatch and peered inside. A kindly looking woman, who Slater guessed must be in her mid-fifties, was efficiently tapping away at an old typewriter. She was engrossed in her work and didn't notice him until he knocked on one of the windows. She looked up, acknowledged him with a warm smile, rose from her desk, and walked across to the window. She slid one of the two windows open.

'Good morning,' she said. 'How can I help you?'

Slater had to bend down to see her face as he spoke to her. As he spoke, he showed his warrant card.

'I'm DS Slater from Tinton Police. We're investigating the death of an old pupil and I wondered if there was anyone here who might be able to help us.'

'I'm Mrs Spencer, the school secretary. I'm afraid the teachers are on strike today, so there's hardly anyone here,' she said. 'Why don't you come into my office? It'll be much easier than stooping to see me through that window.'

He opened the door and walked into her office. It was very neat and orderly, with another desk on the opposite side of the room from the one she had been sitting at.

'Can you tell me who the pupil was and when he was a student here?' she asked.

'His name was Ian Becks. I believe he was a student from around 1989 until 1996.'

'Goodness, that is a long time ago. I don't think any of the teachers from back then are still here.'

Slater's heart sank. 'Oh, that's a pity,' he said. 'Ian was a colleague. We believe his death may be related to an event from his youth. We were hoping someone here might have been able to help.'

'Well, you may be in luck,' she said. 'It just so happens I am the one constant in this place. I've been school secretary since 1986. Obviously I didn't know the boys as well as a teacher would, but even so, I might be able to help.'

She walked across to the second desk, pulled out a chair and sat down. 'What was the boy's name again?' she asked, as she fired up the computer in front of her.

'Ian Becks.'

'I feel I should know that name.'

'You might have seen it in the newspaper,' said Slater. 'He was a forensic scientist. He died in the forensics lab in the basement at Tinton Police Station.'

'No, that's not it,' she said, as her fingers flicked across the keyboard. 'There must be something in here . . .'

'How come you still use a typewriter when you've got the computer?' he asked.

'I prefer it for writing letters. It's no good for doing circulars and things like that, but when it's a one-off letter I just think it produces a better finished product. I've got nothing against computers, I just like a good, old-fashioned typewriter.'

Slater watched as she studied her computer screen for a moment, pressed a couple of keys, and then he saw her face break into a broad smile.

'Ah. Here we are,' she said. 'No wonder I remembered the name. He went on to get a First at Oxford.'

'That sounds like him,' said Slater.

'When I first started to put all this information onto a database, the others told me I was mad and I was wasting my time,' she said, 'but I knew it would come in useful. I've got all the school reports on here for every pupil from 1980 onwards, and where I know what they went on to achieve, I've got that too. If you want to know how many of our kids went on to Oxford or Cambridge on any given year I've only got to push a button and I can tell you.'

Slater wasn't as impressed with the database as Mrs Spencer obviously was. He had been hoping for a bit more than which university Becksy went to. He already knew that.

'Can you tell me anything else about him?'

'Oh yes,' she said. 'I've got his school reports for every year he was here. Let's have a look and see if there's anything that might interest you.'

'Don't let me hold you up,' he said, thinking that her idea of what was interesting might be quite different to his. 'Why don't I sit and read the reports? Then you can get on with your letter.'

'Is that allowed?' she asked. 'With all this data protection malarkey, don't you need a warrant or something?'

Inwardly, Slater sighed. If she was going to insist, this was going to be damned hard work.

'Well, I could go back to Tinton and tell my boss you're holding up a possible murder inquiry until we get a warrant,' he said. 'But I'm sure you don't really want me to do that.'

'Murder inquiry?' she said. 'You didn't say anything about a murder.'

'It's a possible murder inquiry. We're not sure yet, but obviously the quicker we get on the better it will be.'

'Oh, well, when you put it like that,' she said. 'I suppose it wouldn't hurt. And Mr Becks is dead, isn't he?'

'I'm afraid he is, and you'd be helping his wife if we can get this settled quickly.'

'Oh yes, poor thing.' She stood up from her chair and stepped aside. 'Here you are, Sergeant. If there's anything you need, just call, I'm only across the room.'

'Thank you, Mrs Spencer,' he said. 'I really appreciate your help.'

He slid into her vacant seat and began to delve into Ian Becks' schooldays. He didn't know what he was looking for, so he figured the sensible thing would be to start from the beginning. It seems Becks was just an average kid when he first arrived at the school. His year one report was certainly nothing to write home about. In fact, Slater thought he could remember getting a better report himself, and he had hated every minute.

Year two was much the same, and then, in year three, results seemed to pick up. Something had changed. Becks had become a model student. This improvement was maintained for the rest of his time at the school, finishing with his acceptance into Oxford. Slater wondered what had happened between the year two results and those for year three. Perhaps he should look again at that year three report. As he read through it again, he realised he had somehow missed the summary first time around, but this time he read it word for word, and that's where he found the answer.

Since Ian has been removed from the bad influences he had previously associated with, his performance has improved dramatically.

Slater read the summary again. He wondered how he might find out who those bad influences were.

'Is there a school summary report for each year?' he asked Mrs Spencer.

'If you come back out to the home page, you'll find a link to all the annual reports. Are you looking for any year in particular?'

'1991 and 1992.'

'I can remember 1992,' she said. 'It was a bad year. A pupil died in an accident right at the start of the school year. It took months for everyone to get over it.'

Slater did as he had been instructed and found the link to the school year summaries. He clicked on 1992 and began to read. When he had finished, he read through it again, making notes in his notebook as he went. Then he clicked on the 1991 link and read the summary for that year, adding more notes as he went. After twenty minutes, he pushed back his seat and stood up.

'Thank you for your help, Mrs Spencer,' he said. 'I really do appreciate it.'

'Have you found anything that will help?' she asked.

'Possibly. There are one or two things that might be of interest. We won't know how helpful they are until we follow them up.'

'If there's anything else I can do, please let me know, won't you?' she said.

'Of course,' he said. 'I'll leave you in peace now.'

* * *

'You're not going to believe this,' said Slater five minutes later, when Norman answered his phone.

'I take it you found the missing skeleton,' said Norman.

'Can you believe our favourite geek wasn't always a geek? It turns out Ian Becks wasn't the *victim* of bullies at school. He was one of the bullies.'

There was silence for a few seconds.

'You're kidding me, right?' asked Norman. 'He couldn't hurt a fly.'

'Ah, he couldn't now,' agreed Slater, 'but back at the beginning of the nineties he and two cronies were the scourge of their school. Apparently there was one kid in their class who they nearly drove nuts, and they even picked on kids a year or two older!'

'Wow! It just goes to show you never know what's in someone's past,' said Norman. 'Do you think it's relevant to his death?'

'Listen to this, and see what you think,' said Slater. 'For the first two years at that school, Ian was very average, but then, in year three, he's separated from his fellow thugs and he becomes a model student.'

'So they were a bad influence,' said Norman. 'Lots of kids team up with the wrong friends. It happens all the time.'

'Yeah,' agreed Slater, 'but wait until you hear this bit. At the beginning of what would have been year three for Ian, one of the kids at the school was riding his bike along the canal path when he was hit on the head by a brick dropped on him from a bridge above. He fell in the river and drowned.'

'Holy shit,' said Norman.

'According to the headmaster at the time, it was believed by many people that Becks and his cronies were to blame, although nothing was ever proved.'

'Jesus, that would certainly be something you'd never stop feeling guilty about,' said Norman.

'That only works if he committed suicide,' said Slater, 'and we know he didn't.'

'Yeah, but what if someone made him write it in an attempt to make it look like suicide?'

'What, you mean seeking revenge?' asked Slater.

'Why not?'

Slater thought about it. It had to be a possibility. The same idea had crossed his own mind before Norman had mentioned it. 'We're getting ahead of ourselves here. We'd need to prove there was someone left to seek revenge before we go too far down that road.'

'I take it you have some names?' asked Norman.

'Two cronies, one victim who survived the bullying, and a kid who was killed, possibly by the bullies.'

'Let's have 'em, then,' said Norman.

'Did you find anything on Jimmy Huston?' asked Slater.

'Nothing worth getting excited about so far. I'll tell you when you get back. You are coming back?'

'I'll be about half an hour or so.

'Okay, gimme those names and I'll make a start.'

CHAPTER TWENTY-NINE

Slater parked his car and rushed into his house.

'Hi, honey, I'm home,' he called, as he opened the front door.

'If you think I'm going to rush over and give you a kiss, you've got another think coming,' said Norman.

'You mean you haven't got lunch ready and done the ironing?' asked Slater, trying to sound disappointed.

'I would have, but I couldn't find the maid's outfit.'

'Damn. I should have shown you where I hide it.'

'Are you going to carry on arsing about, or do you want to know what I've found?' asked Norman.

'Okay, what have we got?' asked Slater, heading for the kitchen. 'I guess it must be good.'

'Well, I figured we wouldn't have time to try and access old police files so I had a look online to see if I could find any old news stories about the kid who was knocked off his bike. It was a long time ago, so I didn't expect to find too much, but I did manage to find the kid's name. He was called Adam Radford.

'I did a search to see if he had any brothers or sisters. It turns out he had an older brother. His name's James. All I know for sure so far is that he didn't go to the same school.'

'What do you mean, the only thing you know for sure?' asked Slater.

'The guy leaves school and then within five years, he seems to disappear. I can't find any trace of him anywhere, but there's no death certificate so I figure he must still be alive. Maybe he changed his name for some reason. I'm gonna look into that after I've checked out the living victim. He might be worth talking to.'

'Okay, you stay on that,' said Slater. 'I'll see if I can trace these other two bullies on my old personal laptop.'

'Yeah, who woulda thought? Becksy the bully. It just doesn't seem possible, does it?'

'It's all there in his school reports,' said Slater. 'It even looks as if he was the ringleader. Apparently they spoke to his parents about it in the first year, but it didn't seem to make much difference.'

'Can I hear the sounds of a skeleton beginning to rattle, or are we being sent on a wild goose chase?' asked Norman.

'Yeah, you have to wonder, don't you?' admitted Slater, 'but there's only one way we're going to find out. What gets me is how the hell did that bloody Russian know about this?'

'Is there anything they don't know? They seemed to know everything there was to know about us two the last time we crossed paths.'

'It's pretty scary when you think about it,' said Slater as he started up his old laptop.

Norman shrugged. 'I guess it's probably best not to think about it, then.'

That was the last thing either of them said for the best part of an hour. Eventually, Slater got up, stretched, and went off to the kitchen. A few minutes later, he reappeared with two mugs of tea.

'Watcha got so far, then?' he asked, as he placed a mug in front of Norman.

'Well, this guy Malcolm Jennings, the one they used to pick on, is still around. They might have bullied him, but it doesn't seem to have had any lasting effects. He's a dentist working in Winchester. He's got his own practice, so he must be doing alright.'

'What about the missing brother?'

'I'm not quite there yet,' said Norman. 'Give me another hour on that one. Have you found anything?'

'I've been looking at fellow thug number one. He's called Terry Jones, or at least that's what he *was* called.'

'Don't tell me he's changed his name as well,' said Norman.

'Oh no,' said Slater. 'His name *was*, because he no longer is.'

'What's that supposed to mean?'

'It means he's dead.'

'How did that happen?'

'It's a bit vague,' said Slater. 'All it says on the death certificate is cardiac arrest.'

'He's a bit young to die from natural causes.'

'There must be dozens of reasons why someone's heart would stop, and it doesn't have to be age related.'

'Yeah, I suppose that's true, enough,' agreed Norman. 'When did it happen?'

'Just about three months ago.'

'Oh well, I suppose on the positive side that means there's one less person to interview,' said Norman. 'What about bully number two?'

'I haven't got to him yet. I just needed a break for a few minutes.'

'I read somewhere you should take a break every half hour,' said Norman, patting his rather generous girth. 'Apparently it stops you getting fat. Personally I think that's a load of crap, but what do I know? One thing's for sure, I'd never get anything done if I stopped that often.'

Slater put his head back and poured the last of his tea into his mouth. 'I think you're supposed to get up and move around when you stop. That's what helps fight the fat. It's better for your heart as well.'

'Yeah, right, thank you for your unwelcome advice, Dr Slater,' said Norman.

'Just getting my own back for the unwelcome advice about my private life.'

Norman smiled. 'Touché.'

'Let's crack on,' said Slater. 'We need to find out if this is a waste of time, and we need to find out pretty quick.'

Half an hour later, Slater let out a whistle. 'Listen to this,' he called across to Norman. 'This is bully number two, aka John Willand. Apparently he's suffered from depression since his late teens. He disappeared off the radar five years ago, but resurfaced six weeks ago. It's believed he had been living rough around this area for all that time he was missing.'

'So where did he resurface?' asked Norman.

'Winchester.'

'Do you have an address?'

'It's too late for that,' said Slater. 'Apparently he was a junkie. He overdosed six weeks ago.'

'Jesus,' said Norman. 'What was his poison, heroin?'

'It seems that was his drug of choice,' said Slater. 'I'm going to call Winchester Police. Apparently they found the body. Maybe they can shed some light on what exactly happened.'

'You sound like you think this is important,' said Norman.

'Three bullies die in the space of three months? What do you think? If there's anything suspicious about this guy's death, then I'm convinced.'

'Much as I hate that Russian arsehole, I think even I might be persuaded by that,' said Norman.

Slater took his mobile phone and went into the kitchen. Ten minutes later he was back. 'If you were a heroin addict, would you inject morphine?' he asked Norman.

'I doubt I would be able to get hold of the stuff,' said Norman. 'It's not something that's readily available out on the street, is it? I'm no expert, but as I understand it morphine is strictly regulated. Also heroin is about three times stronger, isn't it? I guess you would need to use a heck of a lot more morphine to get the same hit. It seems to me heroin would be the easier option if only because of availability.'

'Right,' said Slater, 'but if you *could* get hold of the stuff?'

'Have you ever met an addict who would turn down the chance of a hit? Some of these guys would inject snake venom if you told 'em it would make 'em high.'

'Yeah, that's what they decided at Winchester. According to their theory, the guy stole some morphine from the hospital and took the whole lot in one hit. The thing is, the hospital hasn't had any stolen.'

'So now what?' asked Norman.

'Death by overdose, case closed.'

'That sounds plain lazy to me.'

'That's exactly what it is,' said Slater, grimly. 'The guy I was speaking to seems to think a junkie's life isn't worth spending time on, so he took the easy route. He said it saved him a lot of wasted time.'

Norman shook his head in dismay. 'Jeez. And you wonder why I don't wanna come back to work with the police force.'

'It makes me ashamed to know I work with people like that,' said Slater.

'Let's not waste our breath on arseholes,' said Norman. 'I take it you think there's a good chance this guy didn't inject himself, right?'

'They reckon the syringe was still in his arm when they found him,' said Slater, 'but no one bothered to find out if the guy was right- or left-handed.'

'What about the pathologist?' asked Norman. 'I take it they did use a pathologist?'

'I could give the lab a call, I suppose. They can't possibly be any less helpful.'

Slater went back into the kitchen and soon Norman could make out his voice as he made his call.

'Now we're getting somewhere,' he said to Norman, when he finished his call. 'It seems the pathologist has got a bit more humanity about him. He says all the old needle marks were in the crook of the left elbow, with some in the left thigh. The only one in the right arm was the one that killed him. He claims he drew attention to the fact he thought it was a suspicious death because a) the guy was right-handed, and b) morphine isn't readily available and wasn't stolen from the hospital, but the investigating officer didn't seem to want to hear him.'

'I take it that would be the same DS Arsehole who you spoke to earlier.'

'Got it in one,' said Slater.

'Well, let's ignore his conclusion and draw our own,' said Norman. 'In my opinion, there's a very strong suspicion that someone injected the guy, a former school bully, with a massive overdose of morphine, right?'

'I would say so,' agreed Slater.

'And that just happens to be the way our former colleague, and one-time school bully, was killed,' said Norman.

'Exactly.'

'I think it would be fair to say this is unlikely to be a coincidence, wouldn't you?'

'Eamon says Becksy died because the morphine caused him to stop breathing,' said Slater. 'I reckon if you stopped breathing that would probably stop your heart pretty quickly too, don't you?'

'You might have a problem trying to prove that. I bet someone, somewhere, is going to say you're jumping to conclusions.'

'Yeah, well let 'em,' said Slater, 'because that's exactly what I am going to do. We don't have time to mess about trying to prove everything beyond doubt, we're just going to have to go with what looks to be the most likely scenario.'

'Oh, I'm with you,' said Norman. 'I'm just playing devil's advocate.'

'My hunch is it wouldn't be a problem, now we're moving away from the Serbian connection,' said Slater. 'But rather than take any chances, let's just keep on going as we are.'

'So, are we assuming this is probably a case of revenge?' asked Norman. 'Like perhaps someone whose younger brother was killed might seek to even the score?'

'It fits, doesn't it?' said Slater. 'It's a pretty powerful reason for wanting revenge. Just imagine how the resentment might build after all these years?'

'In that case, you're going to love what I've just found,' said Norman. 'Remember I said the dead kid, Adam Radford, had a brother called James who seemed to have disappeared? Well, he reappeared when he changed his name by deed poll.'

Slater's mind was racing. 'Bethan Becks' boyfriend is called Jimmy. It's not him, is it?'

'Aww, you've spoiled my surprise.'

'Is it him? Jimmy Huston? You're kidding me,' said Slater, the words rushing from his mouth.

'The very same,' said Norman.

'Bloody hell, the slimy bugger's been watching Becksy for months, worming his way into his life, even climbing into bed with his ex-wife.'

'And if he works in the mailing room at the publisher he would have known when that package was going to be delivered,' Norman said. 'Does he ride a motorbike?'

'I dunno,' said Slater, 'but it's not going to be hard to find out, is it?'

CHAPTER THIRTY

Slater was on his mobile phone, talking to Goodnews.

'So you're asking me to believe this Russian guy let himself into your house and waited for you to come home, just so he could tell you he's innocent?' she asked, when he had finished telling her what had happened.

'I'm not asking you to believe me, I'm telling you what happened.'

'But why would he tell you?'

'Because he feels he knows me and he trusts me,' said Slater, patiently.

'He trusts you? What the bloody hell does that mean? You're supposed to be on opposite sides!'

'Of course we are, but he says that doesn't mean he can't appreciate the other man's qualities.'

'You make it sound like you've become best mates all of a sudden,' she said, suspiciously.

'Don't be daft,' he said. 'He'd still blow my brains out if I crossed him. It's just that he thinks I would rather catch the person who killed my friend than waste time chasing after the wrong people.'

'His lot are still guilty of breaking into the lab, stealing evidence and setting a fire bomb.'

'None of which we're likely to be able to prove very easily,' said Slater.

'Or so he says,' argued Goodnews.

'Have you found any evidence down in that lab? Did we find any evidence at Becksy's place?'

'Well no,' conceded Goodnews. 'But why do you think we should believe him?'

Slater's patience was being tested. He really couldn't see why she had a problem with this.

'Because everything he says makes sense,' he said, 'and from what I've found so far, he's spot on. And he just seems to know too much to be bullshitting us. In fact, he seems to know everything we know, and a heck of a lot more. I'm beginning to think he must have someone on the inside.'

'For God's sake, don't say that,' said Goodnews. 'That really would bring the curtain down on my career.'

'I don't think it's anyone local. These people wouldn't mess around with minions. They'd want someone who knows what's going on everywhere.'

'He told you this, did he?'

'He made one or two comments of interest,' said Slater. 'But we're getting off track here. Are you going to bring this bloke in or what?'

'D'you really think this Russian guy is telling the truth?'

'I'd put money on it,' said Slater, sulkily, 'and I'd like to think you trust my judgement, but at the end of the day, it's down to you, I suppose.'

'Oh please, don't start with that sulky little boy attitude. You know I trust your judgement, it's just that it's a big call when I'm under the microscope and we're supposed to be closing the investigation.'

'Look,' said Slater, testily, 'you asked me to carry on investigating to see if I could find evidence to justify reopening the case. If this isn't good enough evidence, then I don't know what is.'

'Alright, I'll do it,' she said. 'But don't think what happened the other night has got anything to do with my decision.'

'What? I didn't think it had made any difference,' he said, the irritation loud and clear in his voice. 'And I should hope it wouldn't. Jesus, you're not going to keep on bringing that up, are you?'

'Let's just leave it, shall we? I'll go and have him brought in right now.'

'D'you need me to come in and interview him? Only I've got all the information here.'

'You'd best stay away for now,' she said.

'Look, you're going to have to find a way to make this work. You're the one who seems to be having a problem, not me.'

'It's not because of that,' Goodnews said, angrily, 'and I don't have a problem with what happened. However, I do have a problem with a certain DI Grimm hovering around every bloody corner. I'm pretty sure he's been sent to spy on me, but his pretext is that he's looking for you. At the moment there's not much he can do, but if you come in here now, he's just going to be an even bigger pain in the arse than usual and he'll bugger everything up.'

'Oh, right,' said Slater, chastened.

'I'm actually covering your arse, you ungrateful sod.'

'Sorry.'

'So you bloody should be,' she said. 'Just make sure you email me all the stuff you have on him.'

'Right,' he said. 'I'll do it now.' He ended the call and tossed his phone down. 'Bloody women.'

'What's this? A lover's tiff?' teased Norman, a wicked grin on his face.

'Not now, Norm,' he said, grumpily. 'I'm not in the mood.'

Norman chuckled quietly to himself but said nothing.

'I'm going for a shower,' said Slater.

'Well, make sure you wash that shitty mood away,' said Norman. 'And just remember, whatever your problem is with Goodnews, it's not my fault.'

Now Slater felt guilty, but he didn't say anything, he just stomped off up the stairs.

'I'm going out for an hour,' Norman called up the stairs behind him. 'I'll bring back a takeaway.'

CHAPTER THIRTY-ONE

'Has he said anything?' Goodnews asked Biddeford.

It was just past six p.m. when Jimmy Huston had been led into the interview room. Now they were watching him through the observation window. He was sitting at a table in the centre of the room, looking totally bemused.

'Only that he doesn't know what the hell's going on. He's playing the bemused innocence card.'

'He certainly looks bemused,' she said, 'but then I didn't really expect him to confess. You'd better have a quick look through these notes before we start the interview, just so you know where we're coming from.'

She handed Biddeford a sheaf of papers she had printed from Slater's emails and waited as he skimmed through them. After a couple of minutes, he handed them back.

'Okay?' she asked.

'Looks like some good work to me,' he said.

'Aye. Now let's see what your man has to say about it all.'

Before she could move, the door swung open and DI Grimm walked in, carrying a cup of coffee.

'Going to interview a suspect?' he asked.

'Yes, I am,' said Goodnews.

'Mind if I watch?'

Goodnews couldn't think of any plausible reason to say no. 'I suppose that will be alright,' she said, grudgingly.

'Oh good,' he said, pulling a chair up to the observation window and settling down. 'I've got a ringside seat and a cup coffee. All I need now is some popcorn.'

He gave her one of his false, grimace-like smiles. She gave him an equally fake one back and then led Biddeford out of the observation room and into the interview room. They settled at the table and she introduced herself and Biddeford, and then explained to Huston that he was here voluntarily, that this wasn't a formal interview, and that it wouldn't be recorded.

'Did you understand all that?' she asked.

'I told Sergeant Slater I'll do anything I can to help,' he said. 'It wasn't necessary to send your goons over to my workplace. What's everyone there going to think?'

'I would imagine they'll think you've come to help us by answering a few questions,' she replied, evenly. 'Just like you said you would.'

'A telephone call would have been enough if you wanted to talk to me. All you had to do was ask and I would have come over.'

'If you're so keen to help, perhaps you can start by telling me where you were on Monday evening between the hours of five and eight?' asked Goodnews.

'I was at a managers' meeting at work from just before five until gone eight,' said Huston, without hesitation, 'and then I went home to Bethan's. I got there at about eight forty-five. You can ask her; she'll tell you the same.'

'Oh, we will ask her, don't worry,' she said. 'In fact, DC Biddeford will go and arrange for someone to do that right now.'

Biddeford left the room. As he closed the door, Goodnews spoke again.

'Tell me about your relationship with Ian Becks.'

And Huston did. He told her more or less exactly what he had told Slater. He even told the same story about attending the Becks' wedding without an invitation. Goodnews was disappointed there were no discrepancies she could seize upon, but she wasn't really surprised. She knew this murder had been well planned, so she didn't expect Huston to be an easy nut to crack.

Biddeford had returned while Huston was speaking and he resumed his position riding shotgun. Almost as soon as Huston had finished speaking, there was a knock on the door. Biddeford opened it and was handed a slip of paper. As he closed the door he read it. The scribbled lines told him P&P Publishing had confirmed the managers' meeting and Bethan Becks had confirmed what time he had arrived at her house. He pulled a face, folded the paper, walked across the room and handed it to Goodnews. She read the note, looked up at him, and then read it again. Then she screwed it up and tossed it into the waste bin. If Biddeford was surprised, he didn't show it.

'Do you ride a motorcycle, Mr Huston?'

'Yes, I do.'

'What sort is it?'

'It's a Yamaha.'

'You're sure it's not a Suzuki?'

'I think I know which motorcycle I own,' said Huston.

'So you must have a crash helmet?' she asked.

'Only a fool rides without one.'

'Can you describe it for me?'

'It's like millions of others,' he said. 'Black, full face, with a tinted visor.'

Goodnews was getting irritated. This wasn't going how she had expected. Maybe if she took a different direction with the questions.

'Why did you change your name, Mr Huston? What was wrong with Radford as a surname?'

Huston looked both shocked and perplexed by her question.

'I'm sorry?' he said. 'I've not changed my name! I was born Jimmy Huston, and I still am Jimmy Huston.'

'But, according to the records, you changed your name from Radford to Huston by deed poll two years ago.'

'Is this some sort of bizarre game?' asked Huston. 'I've just told you I have not changed my name. I've always been Jimmy Huston. Ask Bethan. When I gatecrashed their wedding, I was Jimmy Huston, and that was six years ago. I don't know where you get your information from but it's complete rubbish.'

Goodnews looked to Biddeford for help, but he was fumbling through the paperwork in front of him, trying to make some sense of what was happening. He looked back at her and shrugged. It didn't make sense to him, either.

'I think maybe we'll take a little break now,' said Goodnews, shakily.

'No, I don't think so,' said Huston, glaring at her. 'I know my rights. Even though you sent your storm troopers to collect me, I came here voluntarily. I'm not under arrest, so I can leave whenever I want. I don't think you *are* going to arrest me, are you?'

The last sentence was more of a challenge than a question.

Goodnews held his eye, but she felt distinctly embarrassed, and she said nothing. Biddeford had suddenly found something to study up on the ceiling.

'No,' said Huston, pushing his chair back and rising to his feet. 'I didn't think so. I'm exercising my rights and I'm leaving. If you need my help, you know where to find me, but if all you're going to do is waste my time with stupid, meaningless drivel, please don't bother.'

He marched across to the door, flung it open and marched from the room.

Goodnews was struggling to keep her composure. She would happily have strangled someone right now, but with Grimm watching, she needed to keep control. She took a few deep breaths and stood up. Cautiously, Biddeford did the same. He looked at her, but he didn't need to be a genius to work out she wasn't in the mood for warm smiles. Her normally pale cheeks were a vivid red, her lips had almost disappeared, and her pale green eyes seemed to glow with an inner fury.

'Throw that rubbish in the bin,' she said, curtly, indicating their notes, and then she stomped angrily from the room.

Biddeford thought it might be wise to give her some space right now, so he stayed where he was until she had left the room. When she had gone, he gathered up the notes from the table and threw them into the bin. He was immensely grateful that he hadn't been the one to prepare them, and, consequently, wouldn't be the one getting his balls chewed off in the very near future.

* * *

To get back from the interview room, Goodnews had to walk past the observation room. The door was open and, to her dismay, Grimm was leaning against the doorframe, a broad grin creasing his face. As she approached, he spoke.

'Well, I thought that went really well,' he said. 'And you got it done so fast. It's not every day I get the chance to watch one of the force's rising stars in action, but I have to say, it's been very educational. Any advice you'd like to pass on?'

'Yes. Fuck off,' she said, as she passed.

His grin became even wider as he turned to watch her march down the corridor away from him.

'Is that one "f" or two?' he asked. 'Only I need to get it right when I write my report for the CC.'

She had already figured out he was there as a spy, but somehow hearing him say it made it even worse.

CHAPTER THIRTY-TWO

It was seven thirty. Slater and Norman had just finished their meal and were thinking about getting back to work when the doorbell rang. Slater walked across and swung the door open. Goodnews was on the step, her face a picture of barely controlled rage. Unfortunately, it was a picture Slater was a bit slow to recognise.

'Oh. I wasn't expecting you,' he said. 'Is there a problem?''

'Is there a problem? I'll say there's bloody problem,' she snarled. She was breathing hard.

'Ah,' he said, finally catching her mood. 'Is it something I've done?'

'Yes, it bloody well is. I've never been so humiliated in my life. And to make it worse, DI bloody Grimm was observing, and he's going to be reporting back to the chief constable.'

'Oh,' said Slater.

'Is that all you're going to say? Bloody oh, and bloody ah? I trusted you and you've made me look a fool. I want an explanation.'

Slater still had no idea what exactly it was he had or hadn't done, so he was momentarily at a loss to know what to say. Instead, he watched open-mouthed as she spat her words at him. He half expected her to start breathing fire at the same time. Then, suddenly, she barged her way past him into the house, tossing her bag onto the nearest armchair. The first thing she saw was Norman, trying his best to become invisible but failing miserably.

'What's he doing here?' she demanded.

Slater tried to offer an explanation, but she was in no mood to listen. 'Err, well, I thought I could do with a hand—' he began.

'Is that your laptop he's using?'

'I was out on the road, and we thought it would be—'

'But he's not a police officer, is he?' she roared. 'Any evidence you find would be inadmissible, not that it matters when all you come up with is rubbish anyway.'

'It's only inadmissible if anyone knows,' said Slater.

'Oh, great,' she said. 'Not content with making a fool of me, now you want me to break the bloody law and hide the fact, is that it?'

Norman stood up, and began to put on his jacket.

'Where do you think you're going?' she demanded.

'I don't think that's any of your business,' he said, stiffly. 'Like you already pointed out, I'm not a police officer, so I don't have to listen to any more of your crap.'

He headed across the room and stopped by the front door. 'I'm going out for a couple of hours, Dave,' he said, pulling the door open. 'I'll speak to you later.'

He walked out, pulling the door closed behind him.

'Whatever your problem is, there's no need to take it out on him,' said Slater. 'It's not his fault.'

'He shouldn't even be helping you,' she said.

'Yes, you're quite right, he shouldn't be helping me, but the truth is I shouldn't need his help, should I? And I shouldn't have to creep about working from home like this. This should be a proper murder inquiry with everyone working on it. There's no way Becks committed suicide, and we all know it. But because the chief constable has said "jump" and you don't have big enough balls to challenge him, there's a very good chance someone's going to get away with murder!'

He didn't think she could have got any angrier, but he seemed to have just moved her up a notch.

'How dare you?' she demanded.

'What? You're not exactly going toe-to-toe with him like you said you would, are you?'

'Oh, right, let's just hold it there a minute. If I'd confronted him with this stuff about Jimmy Huston and got him to reopen the inquiry, and then it had all gone pear-shaped, how would that have made me look? Oh no, hang on a minute. Let's forget what would have happened, because it really *has* happened and he's going to know anyway. That bastard Grimm sat and watched the whole thing. He can't wait to get back and report.'

'Oh, for God's sake,' he said. 'It's not always about your damned career. How about you do what's right for the victim instead of what's right for your precious career, just this once? Becksy wasn't just some random bloke, he was one of us!' He realised he was shouting at her now.

'Yes,' she said. 'I know that, but Jimmy Huston didn't kill him. He couldn't have. He has an alibi.'

'Yeah, but alibis can be broken—' began Slater, but she wasn't interested in his suggestions.

'He's got twelve bloody witnesses who are all willing to swear he was at a meeting until well after Ian Becks died,' she shouted. 'How are we going to break that?'

'Ah.' It was all he could think of to say.

'There you go again with your bloody ahs and ohs again,' she said. 'I wonder what you're going to say when I tell you the best bit.'

'Best bit?' he said. 'What do you mean best bit?'

She had been slowly advancing and was right in front of him now. 'When I asked him why he had changed his name, do you know what he told me?'

Slater didn't know, and he thought he probably wasn't required to guess.

'He told me was born Jimmy Huston, and that he's always been Jimmy Huston, and he was still Jimmy Huston when he first met Bethan Becks six years ago. He's even got a passport that was issued eight years ago in the name of Jimmy Huston. How do you explain that, eh?'

She barely paused long enough for him to speak before continuing.

'Lost for words now, aren't you?' She was leaning forward, her face creased with anger as she spat the words right in his face. 'How do you think I felt when he told me? You see, it doesn't matter how big my balls are when I'm given useless information like that, does it?'

Slater's mouth opened once or twice, but he couldn't actually think of anything sensible to say. 'There must be some mistake,' was the best he could manage.

'Oh there's been a whole bagful of bloody mistakes,' she said, 'and it looks like I'm the one who's made them all. I made a mistake in trusting you, I made a mistake in thinking you were a competent detective, and I made my biggest mistake of all the other bloody night when I let you—'

'Just hold it right there,' roared Slater. 'I've had enough of this. If I've made a mistake I'm sorry. It happens. I never said I was perfect, I'm just human, right? And as for the other night, I seem to remember you were the one who came to me. You were the one in tears looking for comfort and I gave it. If anyone made a mistake, it was me.'

'I don't remember you turning me away,' she said.

'No, I didn't,' he admitted, 'but, I'm not perfect, I was just being human. I'll tell you something else — I don't regret being human or making mistakes. It's better than spending all my time trying to prove to everyone how bloody perfect I am.'

'I had to sit there and let Huston go,' she said. 'Just after he had totally humiliated me in front of DI sodding Grimm. And that's all down to you not doing your bloody job properly, you stupid arse.'

'You're more worried about what Grimm thinks than about the fact we sent you after the wrong bloke, aren't you?' said Slater. 'Don't you have anything else in your life apart from your career? No wonder you were so desperate the other night.'

Her eyes flashed angrily and for a moment he thought she was going to slap his face, but she seemed to change her mind at the last second and turned away from him.

'Don't you start lecturing me about how to run my life,' she said. 'I don't need advice from the likes of you.'

'You were asking me for advice the other night.'

She whirled back at him again. 'Yes, and I've already told you that was a bloody big mistake,' she snapped. 'I should have known you'd try to take advantage of the situation.'

'Have you heard yourself? Because I tell you what, I've heard enough. Like I said before, you're the one who's got the problem with this. As far as I'm concerned, it changes nothing, and I haven't tried to take advantage of anything, and deep inside you know I haven't. If you regret it that much, you'd better find some way of dealing with it.'

'I've had enough of this,' she said, collecting her bag from the chair where she'd thrown it. 'I'm going. I think it would be best if I take you off this case and you take a few days' leave while I think about what I'm going to do with you.'

'What you're going to do with me?' repeated Slater, aghast. 'What? Are you going to push me out of the door just because you got carried away the other night and now you can't deal with it?'

'I think we've reached a point where it's going to be difficult to continue working together,' she said. 'Maybe it's time for you to move on.'

'Oh, right. I see,' said Slater. 'So what happened the other night is all down to me. Well, d'you know what? I've been thinking about whether I want to carry on doing this recently, and I think you're probably right, it *is* time for me to move on. But you don't need to waste any of your precious time thinking about what you're going to do about me, I'll make it easy for you. I resign.'

Goodnews hadn't bargained on this turn of events and it showed on her face. 'Now you're bluffing. You don't mean that.'

'Yes I do. As of this very minute, I resign. You can stick your job right where the sun doesn't shine.'

'You can't do that.'

'Of course, you'd like to be the one who makes that decision, wouldn't you?' he said. 'I bet sacking people makes you feel really powerful, doesn't it?'

Her face told him he probably wasn't a million miles from the truth.

'You talk utter rubbish at times,' she said.

He smiled a false smile. 'I think you've got a problem there, because although your mouth is saying those words, your face is telling me something quite different.'

'If you really want to resign I need it in writing,' she said.

'You'll get it.'

'And you'll have to work a notice period.'

'You must owe me at least a month's leave, and you said you want me out of the way. Why don't I take that leave, starting now?'

'I'm not accepting your resignation.'

'Fine. I'll just stop turning up and you'll have to sack me.'

'Now you're just being petty. I think you need those few days I suggested to cool down and think about it,' she said, not quite so sure of herself now.

'I don't think I do,' he said, 'but I'll take them anyway. Now, I think it's probably best if you go, don't you?'

CHAPTER THIRTY-THREE

It was after nine p.m. by the time Norman let himself back into Slater's house.

To his surprise, Slater was sprawled in an armchair watching football on TV, a can of lager in his hand, and two empties on the coffee table next to him.

'Hi,' he called.

Without taking his eyes from the TV, Slater grunted and raised his can to acknowledge Norman's arrival.

'Beers are in the fridge,' he said.

'Am I right in thinking the dragon's flown away?' asked Norman, as he passed through on his way to the kitchen.

'Only after she finally ran out of fire,' said Slater.

'Jeez, was she in a shit mood!' called Norman from the kitchen, as he took a can from the fridge and popped the ring pull. 'What brought all that on?'

He came back and sat on the settee. Slater still hadn't taken his eyes from the TV.

'I take it this must be a good game?' said Norman, somewhat miffed that Slater didn't appear to be listening.

'Apparently I'm incompetent and can't be trusted,' said Slater.

'What? Since when? You must be the best guy she's got there by miles.'

'But unfortunately I'm human, and being human I mess things up sometimes,' said Slater. 'And this time I messed up big time.'

'We all make mistakes,' said Norman. 'Surely it can't be that bad.'

'Jimmy Huston has an unbreakable alibi.'

'Okay, so that's not so bad.'

'Well, actually, Norm, that's not the bad bit. There's been a major cock-up. We told her Jimmy Huston had changed his name from James Radford.'

'Yeah, that's right,' said Norman.

'Ah, but it's not,' said Slater. 'He was born Jimmy Huston. He has a passport that says Jimmy Huston, and it was issued eight years ago.'

'But that can't be right,' said Norman. 'I saw it in the records for myself.'

'You can't have done, mate,' said Slater.

'I'll go and check right now, if you want.'

'No, don't worry,' said Slater. 'It doesn't matter now, anyway. We're off the case.'

'What do you mean "off the case"?'

'Well, I suppose officially you were never on it, and I'm sort of unofficially suspended,' said Slater.

'This is bullshit,' said Norman. 'She can't suspend you.'

'Well, she hasn't officially suspended me. What she actually said was she thought I should take a few days' leave while she decided what she was going to do with me.'

'Holy shit! Is she trying to push you out? What the hell's going on with you two? I thought you got on okay.'

Slater looked guilty. 'Yeah, well, we *did* get on okay. The problem is we got on a bit more than okay when she stayed the other night, and now she's regretting it, and saying it was all my fault.'

'Oh, Jesus,' said Norman. 'Is that what this is all about? I told you—'

'Norm, I don't need to hear it now, mate. I know you told me, and I probably should have listened, but I didn't, okay? Keeping on about it won't change what's happened, but it will piss me off.'

'No, you're right. I'm sorry, it won't change anything.' said Norman. 'I just don't know what to suggest. Wouldn't it be great if we could turn back the clock?'

'Actually,' said Slater, 'I don't think it would make any difference. I'm sure I would do exactly the same thing all over again. I don't regret it one little bit.'

'Jeez, spare me the gory details.'

'I'm not going to give you any details. I'm just saying if the situation occurred again . . .'

'I don't think that's likely, do you?'

'I'm making sure of it,' said Slater. 'I've resigned.'

Norman's mouth flapped open wordlessly. It was almost a full minute before he spoke. 'Now you're really talking crap,' he said. 'Being a detective is who you are. What else are you gonna do?'

'I dunno yet,' said Slater.

'Nah. You're just saying that cos you're pissed off. You'll feel differently when you've had a few hours to think about it.'

'I don't think I will, Norm. I told you the other day I'd just about had enough, didn't I? Well, now I have had enough.'

'When you act in haste, you repent at leisure,' said Norman. 'You mark my words.'

'Yeah, maybe I will,' said Slater. 'But I don't think so.'

'So what's gonna happen about this case?'

'I'm off it,' said Slater, 'so I can't do anything about it. I suppose they're going to go for the easy option and settle for suicide. It saves having to explain why the security was so crap.'

'Don't you think that stinks?' asked Norman.

'Well, of course it bloody stinks, but what can I do about it?'

'I thought Becksy wasn't just good at what he did, I thought he was also a mate.'

'He was one of the best,' agreed Slater.

'Without his help, we wouldn't have solved half the cases we did, you know.'

'Yeah, I know.'

'D'you think he would have sat back and let it go, if it was one of us that had been murdered?'

Slater sighed. Of course he knew the answer. 'What exactly is it you think I can do, Norm?' he asked.

'Well, for a start you could pull yourself together and stop feeling sorry for yourself. Try behaving like an adult.'

'What's that supposed to mean?'

'Well, look at you,' said Norman. 'Sitting there, drowning your sorrows. Why don't you admit it? What happened the other night was your fault. You should have known there was a possibility something would happen if you brought her back here. Jesus, you wanted it to happen.'

'That's a load of bollocks,' said Slater.

'Are you kidding me? Why do you think you don't regret it? You've fancied the pants off each other since she arrived, but neither of you is prepared to face up to it. Now it's happened, neither of you can deal with it.'

'You're talking crap.'

'Ask anyone down at the station,' said Norman. 'Everyone agrees you can almost see the sparks flying when you get near each other. Why do you think you two are always arguing? It's called sexual tension, my friend.'

Slater was going to protest but Norman didn't give him a chance.

'And don't tell me you don't find her attractive.'

'Have you finished?' asked Slater. 'She was the one who came to my room. How the hell does that make it my fault?'

'Can you hear yourself?' asked Norman. 'You haven't listened to a word I've said, and now you're blaming her. You're as bad as each other. I can't tell you how to sort out this mess, but I can tell you this: if you just sit back and let them tell the world Becksy committed suicide, you'll regret it for the rest of your life.'

Slater wanted to argue his case and tell Norman he was wrong about him and Goodnews, but the more he thought about Becks, the guiltier he felt about letting it go, and the less he cared about the situation with her.

'But what can I do?' he asked, rather helplessly. 'I'm off the case.'

'We still have all the case notes, don't we?' asked Norman. 'Yeah, so?'

'So let's carry on our own friggin' investigation!' snapped Norman. 'Look, I definitely found evidence that someone called James Radford changed his name to Jimmy Huston. I can see now I should have looked a lot deeper into it. If it's totally wrong, it's my cock-up, not yours.'

'It doesn't matter whose cock-up it was, Norm. As far as Goodnews is concerned, you shouldn't have been anywhere near the case in the first place.'

'But the point is, I didn't make it up. It was right there in front of my eyes,' said Norman. 'I think we need to look further into it. I also think we should see if there are any other possibilities we should look at. Maybe we should talk to the other kid they bullied, you know, the dentist guy. Maybe we need to look at the gay thing. Becksy had just recently started going to a gay bar and he'd been attacked. Why not take a closer look at that? Why not take a look at every angle we can think of?'

'What if they close the inquiry?'

'What if they do? We'll just continue with our own unofficial inquiry. If we can find a murderer, they won't have any choice about reopening it, will they? We owe it to Becksy, don't you think?'

'You know what? You're right,' said Slater. 'And what have I got to lose? The worst they can do is sack me, and what do I care? I'm going to quit anyway.'

'Go get yourself cleaned up,' said Norman. 'We might as well start right now.'

'Why do I need to get cleaned up?'

'Because we're going out for a drink. I hear that gay bar in town is quite popular, and I haven't been there yet.'

'Seriously?' asked Slater.

'Yeah, I know, it might be a waste of time,' said Norman. 'But if it is, at least we'll know.'

'Give me ten minutes,' said Slater.

CHAPTER THIRTY-FOUR

Dickie's Bar was situated in a quiet street off the high street. It had been one of the numerous public houses in Tinton that had closed in the last ten years and had been empty for a good few years until Dickie Barlow had recognised the money-making potential of opening the town's first gay bar and laying on a drag queen show every weekend. Six months on, it was a roaring success, attracting a large clientele from Tinton and the surrounding area, especially at weekends. Today was Friday, so although it was still quite busy, it was still early enough for people to hold a conversation without shouting.

Slater felt vaguely out of place as he approached the doors, but Norman had no such qualms and breezed through them like he was their most regular customer.

'I don't feel right in here,' Slater mumbled to Norman as he looked around.

'Relax,' said Norman. 'It's just a pub. Let me do the talking if you're feeling nervous. Come on, let's get a drink before people start to notice us.'

'Notice us,' echoed Slater, looking at the way everyone else was dressed. 'They can't miss us; we stick out like sore thumbs.'

When he looked back, Norman had already headed off towards the bar and he had to scuttle after him.

A neat and tidy barman wearing a wide smile, white shirt and red bow tie came over to serve them.

'Good evening, gents,' he said. 'My name's Nico. What can I get you?'

'Two halves of that Italian lager,' said Norman, pointing at the nearest beer tap. 'Quiet in here tonight, Nico,' he said, as he watched the barman pour their drinks.

'You've not been here before?' asked Nico.

'First time,' said Norman.

'You should come on a Saturday when we've got a drag act on. It's standing room only.'

'Maybe we'll give it a try.'

'I'm not sure your friend would enjoy it,' said Nico, glancing at Slater, who was still looking around. 'He doesn't look the sort who would enjoy being pressed up against a lot of gorgeous young boys.'

He placed the two glasses on the bar.

'In fact,' he said, 'if I didn't know better I'd say he might be an officer of the law.'

He had raised his voice, and Slater turned back to them suddenly.

Norman smiled. 'Yeah,' he said. 'He's not very good at this. That's why he doesn't work Vice very often.'

The barman's face fell.

'No, wait,' said Norman. 'This isn't a raid or anything like that. We're not interested in what goes on in here. We need your help with something.'

Nico was looking doubtful. 'What sort of something?' he asked.

'A friend of ours has been murdered,' said Norman. 'He used to work at Tinton Police Station. They're trying to say he committed suicide, but we don't believe he did. We're trying to prove we're right.'

'What makes you think I can help?'

Norman slipped a photo of Ian Becks in front of the barman. 'He was gay, and we believe he had been coming here. This is one of several angles we're working on. We're just trying to find out if he did come here, and if there's anyone here who can help us learn a bit more about this side of his life.'

Nico looked at the photo and then looked back up at Norman. 'Don't I need to see a badge or something?' he asked.

Slater took his warrant card from his pocket and allowed Nico to see it.

'What about you?' Nico asked Norman. 'Where's your badge?'

'I'm retired,' said Norman. 'I'm doing this because this guy was a good friend of ours.'

'He's for real,' said Slater. 'He used to be my partner until a few months ago.'

This seemed to be good enough for Nico. 'Yeah, I think I know him,' he said, 'although he hasn't been in here recently. I think he said his name was Ian, or something like that. You say he's dead? How the hell did that happen?'

'I can't tell you that,' said Slater. 'But trust me, it definitely wasn't suicide. Whoever did this knew exactly what they were doing.'

Nico was beginning to look worried.

'D'you know something?' asked Norman. 'Only your face says you do.'

'I don't know if it means anything, but a couple of the guys have been attacked by some idiot using a cricket bat or something like that.'

'Was this guy one of those who were attacked?' asked Norman.

'Yes, I believe he was.'

'Why didn't anyone report it to the police?'

Nico looked down his nose at Norman. 'Oh, come on,' he said. 'Why do you think?'

Norman knew what Nico meant, but not for the first time, he thought this just went to prove prejudice was a two-way thing.

'How can you blame them for not helping if you don't tell them you have a problem?'

Nico looked as if he might want to pursue the argument, but Slater wasn't going to go down that road.

'Look,' he said. 'We're up against a deadline here. We're trying to stop someone from getting away with murder. Did Ian have any friends in here?'

'I think he had a boyfriend,' said Nico. 'I saw them together a few times.'

'What's this boyfriend's name?' asked Norman.

'I don't know. I don't think I ever actually spoke to him.'

'Can you describe him?'

Nico nodded at Slater. 'He was about the same build and height as you, but good-looking, a bit like Cary Grant. I suspect he was going bald, and grey, because he kept his hair very short and it was bleached. He's very toned. I would imagine he works out, and he definitely likes a sunbed. Does that help?'

'How old?' asked Norman.

'It's not easy to tell when they use a sunbed and work-out. I'd guess at about thirty-five, definitely not more than forty-five.'

'Anything else?' asked Slater.

'He rode a motorbike,' said Nico. 'In fact they might both have. I'm sure they came in once or twice wearing that leather motorcycle gear, you know?'

This made Slater and Norman take notice.

'What? Did I say something important?'

'Possibly,' said Slater. 'You've been really helpful. Thank you.'

'You'd better go now,' said Nico, looking around. 'They know you're the law, and you're making some of these people nervous.'

Norman grinned. 'Yeah, that's a pity,' he said. 'I quite like it in here.'

Nico smiled. 'You're not unwelcome, but, if you're going to come back, try to dress a bit more like a civilian, then people won't get nervous. And if you want to ask me any more questions, lunchtime is probably better.'

'Gotcha,' said Norman. He turned to Slater. 'Come on, Dave, time to go.'

* * *

'Now, wasn't that worth a little discomfort?' asked Norman when they were outside.

'What? I wasn't uncomfortable,' said Slater.

Norman smiled. 'No, of course you weren't. But it was worth it, right?'

'Yeah,' admitted Slater. 'No one's ever mentioned a boy-friend before. We need to find out more about him.'

'We can get onto it first thing tomorrow,' said Norman. 'Right now, I need my bed.'

CHAPTER THIRTY-FIVE

With time working against them, they had split up so they could work separate angles: Norman on the laptop and Slater out and about. Slater was on his way down to Winchester to see the former school bullies' erstwhile victim, who was now a dentist with his own practice. It was probably going to be a waste of time, but they had agreed they couldn't afford to miss anything.

Norman was secretly pleased Slater had gone out. He was supposed to be checking out the James Radford/Jimmy Huston name change cock-up, but he had started early because there was something else he wanted to have a look at first. Something had been bothering him ever since Slater had first told him about the case and what they knew, but he hadn't been able to put his finger on what it was. Then, this morning, as soon as he woke up, he knew exactly what it was.

He was going back over the CCTV recording from the rear car park at the police station. He was looking for the images of the mystery courier's motorcycle. He thought it strange that no one seemed to have done the obvious and followed up on the registration number, or at least if anyone had, he could find no evidence to say what they had found.

He stopped the footage running at the appropriate place and studied the images. The explanation was there right before his eyes. It was crystal clear the bike was a Suzuki, but there was no registration number. It had been covered with black tape. Norman stared at the image in frustration, but then something caught his attention. He enlarged the image a couple of times, then studied it again.

It had just been an indistinct smudge at the bottom of the number plate at normal size, but now it was blown up it was quite easy to see it was a name, and it was one he recognised. 'Bikerzwurld' was a grubby little motorcycle repair shop tucked away down a back street in Tinton which did servicing, and supplied spare parts. The shop wasn't licensed to make number plates, and had been in trouble with the police before for doing it. It was a start, although whether it would be any good without the full registration number was debatable.

He looked again at the blacked-out number now it had been blown up to several times the original size. Was it his imagination, or could he just make out the base of the last two letters? He looked away for a minute, and then looked back at the image. There was definitely something there, along the bottom of the black tape on the right-hand side. He studied it for several minutes, writing some letters on a pad as he studied. Finally, he sat back and looked at his pad. He had narrowed it down to a few possibilities. He thought the last letter could be T, I, P, F or V. The letter preceding that could be R, K, H, X or N. He leaned forward and crossed out the P and the F. Whatever the last letter was, it had to have its lowest point in the centre.

Gathering up his writing pad, he headed for the front door. It was all going to be a bit vague, but he figured a seedy backstreet shop like that probably didn't make too many number plates, so it had to be worth a try.

* * *

Norman drove slowly past Bikerzwurld and pulled in to the kerb. He climbed from his car and strolled back towards the shop, stopping to peer through the grimy front window. It looked as though there were no customers in the shop, which was just what Norman had been hoping for. He pushed the door open and walked in, flipping over the 'closed' sign as he pushed the door shut. Just to be sure, he slid one of the bolts across to make sure no one could get in and spoil his fun.

The shop was as grubby inside as the windows were on the outside. Assorted spare parts were stacked in boxes all over the place, with no apparent order to any of it. A long counter ran across the back of the shop, and from somewhere beyond it, a noise that could optimistically have been described as music blared from a radio that wasn't properly tuned in to the station. A sign on the counter asked him to 'ring for attention', so he did.

'Yer'll have to wait a coupla minutes,' called a surly voice above the noise from the radio. 'I've got me 'ands full of chains.'

Norman thought this was excellent news. Silently, he raised the flap in the counter, eased himself through, and made his way out through the open door into the workshop. A man was working at the side of a motorcycle, which was raised up on stands to enable him to work from a low stool on which he was perched, with his legs out in front of him under the bike.

He was dressed in a pair of overalls that had so much grease, oil and general dirt ground into them that Norman thought they had to be totally waterproof. An equally greasy and dirty ponytail hung down the man's back. He was hunched over, quietly muttering to himself as he struggled to replace the bike's drive chain. He had no idea he had company sneaking up behind him.

Norman watched patiently as the man fiddled with the chain. Just at the vital moment when it seemed the task was about to be successfully completed, he spoke.

'There's a much easier way of doing that, you know?'

Startled by the sudden voice right behind him, the mechanic nearly jumped out of his skin, letting go of the chain it had just taken him almost fifteen minutes to get into position. He sighed a big, heavy, impatient sigh.

'I told you I'd be there in a couple minutes, didn't I?' he roared.

He made to get up off his stool, but Norman was right up behind him and shoved a knee in his back, making it impossible for him to move.

'Hi, Georgie,' he said. 'Remember me?'

'I 'aven't got eyes in the back of me 'ead, 'ave I? An' wiv me face stuck in this bike frame, 'ow am I supposed to see oo you are?'

'Now I have to confess, that's a fair point,' agreed Norman. 'Lemme see if I can help you with that.'

With one deft move, he kicked the stool from under the man, dropping him onto his backside and then onto his back. He made a loud 'Ooooooff' noise as he hit the floor. Norman smiled down at him.

'Now you can see me, right?' he asked.

The man looked up at him. It was clear from his expression, and the way he swore, that he remembered exactly who Norman was.

'You're the law, aintcha?' he asked.

'So you do remember me, Georgie, that's very good,' said Norman. 'It's a pity you don't remember how we came to meet.'

'I learned me lesson. I don't do number plates no more.'

'I seem to recall there was actually a lot more to it than just number plates,' said Norman. 'But since you chose to mention it, I have to tell you I'm finding it hard to believe you.'

'Look, I'd need to be pig-shit stupid to keep on doin' that after I been done, wouldn't I?'

'That's an insult to pig shit,' said Norman. 'Not only are you stupid enough to keep on doing it, you're even stupid enough to keep on doing it and make it easy for us to know it's you.'

'I dunno what you're talking about.'

'You put your shop name on the bottom of the plate,' said Norman. 'Now that's a really special kind of stupid, and I doubt even the worst kind of pig shit could be that stupid.'

'That's a load of old bollocks,' said Georgie. 'You can't bluff me.'

Norman took out the photo of the blacked-out number plate and dropped it on Georgie's chest. 'Take a look,' he said.

Georgie picked up the photo and squinted at it. 'You can't prove I done that. The number's blacked-out.'

'Very good,' said Norman. 'But what's that across the bottom of the plate?'

'Can't see, it's too small.'

'Try this one,' said Norman, dropping one of the blown-up images.

Georgie looked at the second photo, and his face creased in frustrated defeat.

'I think that's called a fair cop, don't you?' asked Norman.

'Oh, come on,' pleaded Georgie. 'Gimme a break. I struggle to make a livin' as it is!'

'Well, maybe it's your lucky day. I'm prepared to overlook the fact you made this plate, as long as you tell me who you made it for.'

Georgie looked up at Norman as if he was mad. 'I'm not that stupid I keep bloody records.'

Norman had been smiling all the time, but now his face fell. 'Oh, now that's a pity,' he said. 'I thought we were getting on so well, but now I'm gonna have to call the boys in to turn your shop over and see what else we can find.'

'Nah, please, don't do that,' said Georgie, helplessly. 'I'll try and remember. But can I get up off this floor, it's bloody freezing!'

'I'll let you get up,' said Norman. 'But you need to understand if you try anything, there's a van with four bored uniforms right outside just waiting to come in and break someone's head, alright?'

'Aw, come on,' said Georgie. 'You know I don't do that sort of violent stuff. I'm all talk, me, I wouldn't 'urt a fly.'

Norman stepped back to give him some space. 'Okay, get up,' he said.

Georgie climbed stiffly to his feet.

'Right,' said Norman. 'I told those boys outside to give me fifteen minutes before they came busting in and breaking things. We must have wasted half of that already, so you need to start talking fast.'

'But I told you, I don't keep no records about stuff like that,' said Georgie. 'An' it's a blacked-out number. 'Ow the 'ell am I supposed to know who I did it for?'

Norman turned and started walking back towards the shop.

'Wait! Where yer goin'?' asked Georgie, following him.

'If all you're going to do is waste my time, I'm going to tell my boys they might just as well start turning your shop over now.'

'No, don't do that,' squealed Georgie. 'I'm tryin', honest.'

Norman stopped and turned around. 'Let's stop pissing around, shall we, Georgie? I know you don't keep records, and I know whoever it was would have paid cash. But I also know a crappy little backstreet shop like this, dealing mostly in stolen goods, has very few customers, and those you do have will probably be regulars and you'll know them all. And I bet you can count the number of plates you make on the fingers of one hand.'

Norman could see Georgie was thinking about it, but perhaps there was one thing that might really make his mind up for him. 'D'you really want to be dragged away as an accessory to murder?'

Suddenly, Georgie looked as if he'd been smacked. 'Murder?' he yelped. 'I ain't been involved in no murder!'

'But we think the guy who used this number plate has,' said Norman. 'And if you know who he is and don't tell me, you're withholding evidence. We can easily ramp that up to aiding and abetting.'

'I dunno his name,' said Georgie, suddenly only too willing to help as much as he could. 'He comes in 'ere now an' then, but he never says much, just finds what he wants, pays cash, and goes.'

'So who is he? I need a name.'

'I dunno, I swear.'

'When was this?' asked Norman.

'About six weeks ago, I reckon.'

'What about the full registration number?'

'You don't want much, do ya?'

'Don't let me down now,' said Norman. 'You see, I remember when we caught you doing this before. You used to keep a list of all the number plates you made up. At the time, you said it was to keep track of which numbers and letters you had used, but then later we found that wasn't the only use for that list, right? You were keeping it just in case you ever got the opportunity to blackmail one of those people. That's the sort of habit people like you never drop. So, either you find the list and give me the number, or I'll ask four clumsy PCs to come in here and do it for you.'

'You're an evil bastard,' said Georgie. 'You'll ruin me.'

'I think I've been very fair. I've given you a choice.' Norman looked at his watch. 'And just to help you with your search, I can tell you you've got about two minutes before the storm troopers arrive.'

Muttering and cursing, Georgie slipped his hand under the counter and produced a tatty notebook. 'Here,' he said. 'I'll read it out for yer.'

'No need for that,' said Norman, snatching the notebook from his hands. 'I'll look for myself.'

He looked at the number: RG15 AKV. He had been right about the last two letters.

'What's this guy look like?'

'He's usually got leathers on,' said Georgie. 'Late thirties. A bit on the short side, with funny eyes.'

'What do you mean "funny eyes"?' asked Norman.

'You know, one's looking at yer, the other one's doin' its own thing. They're different colours too.'

'What else?'

'He's a bit of a pansy, you know? Clean hands, bleached hair, that sort of thing. I think people that age with bleached hair must have something wrong with 'em.'

Norman took a long look at Georgie. 'Yeah,' he said. 'I can imagine you'd think anyone clean had something wrong with them. Actually it's quite normal. It's the result of washing. You should try it some time.'

He closed the notebook and put it in his pocket.

'You can't take that,' said Georgie. 'You ain't got a search warrant.'

'You really want me to get one?' asked Norman.

'But you can't bring yer 'eavies in 'ere wivout one.'

'You're right about that,' said Norman. 'But that's okay, there aren't any heavies outside.'

'But you said—'

Norman tried his best to look guilty. 'Yeah, I know I did,' he said. 'Telling lies is terrible, isn't it? Not that you would know, of course, seeing as you never tell any. I promise you, I do feel guilty about misleading an arsehole like you, but I just can't seem to stop myself.'

'You bastard,' snapped Georgie. 'I'm gonna complain to the nick about you.'

'Oh, did I forget to tell you? I'm not with them anymore. I retired.'

Georgie took a step towards him, but then seemed to realise Norman was both taller and heavier.

'Uh uh,' said Norman. 'Remember, you said you don't do violence. Best not to start now, huh?'

He walked back through the shop, slipped the bolt, turned the 'closed' sign to 'open', pulled the door open, and left the shop. As he headed for his car, he felt a spring in his step that had been missing for quite a while. There was no doubt about it: this is what he enjoyed doing, and this was probably what he did best.

CHAPTER THIRTY-SIX

'How was your trip to the dentist?' asked Norman when Slater got back.

'Well, Malcolm Jennings certainly remembers them all,' said Slater. 'He claims Ian Becks made the first two years of his life at senior school a complete misery, until Adam Radford got killed by a flying brick. The police were called in but no one ever got charged with anything. The only good thing to come out of it was that after the poor kid died, all the bullying stopped.'

'I suppose you'd have to be pretty hardcore to keep it going after something like that,' said Norman.

'According to Jennings, it was Ian Becks who threw that brick off the bridge.'

'How the hell does he know that?' asked Norman.

'He says he was hiding from the three bullies at the time but he saw it all happen.'

'So why didn't he say something at the time?'

'He says he never came forward because he knew it would be his word against three. He didn't think anyone would believe him, and he knew he'd get another good kicking afterwards. They'd just killed one boy who had done nothing to them, what would they do to someone who grassed them up? He says he regrets it now, and he wished he'd been brave enough at the time.'

'Was he any help to our inquiry?' asked Norman.

'He says he hasn't seen any of them in years, and made it quite clear he really wouldn't have wanted to.'

'We can't really blame him for that, I suppose. I expect we can all think of plenty of people from our past we wouldn't want to waste our time on.'

'Yeah, I suppose,' said Slater. 'So, all in all, he wasn't really much help.'

'At least we know,' said Norman, 'and we can tick him off the list.'

'So what have you done this morning?' asked Slater. 'You seem to be looking rather pleased with yourself.'

Norman looked suitable abashed. 'Well, I went a little off track this morning. There was something that had bothered me right from when you first told me about this case, and this morning, when I woke up, I knew what it was so I had to check it out. I didn't tell you because it might have been a waste of time. Anyway, the thing is, I know the registration number of the bike the mystery courier used.'

Slater looked impressed. 'How did you do that?' he asked. 'They told me it was covered in black tape and there was no way of reading it.'

'I'm glad you didn't tell me that,' said Norman, 'or I might never have looked at it. But I have to admit I got a bit lucky. When I blew up the images of the number plate, I realised there was a shop name across the bottom of the plate. It just so happens I busted the owner about twelve months ago for an assortment of charges, one of which was illegally selling number plates. I went over there and leaned all over him this morning and he coughed up the full registration number.'

'That's what's missing at Tinton right now,' said Slater. 'There's no one left with enough experience to listen to their hunches and then act upon them like that. That's why we made a pretty good team: if one of us left a gap, the other one would usually fill it.'

Norman smiled. 'Yeah, it did seem to work that way. Unfortunately, though, just like you, I'm human and I cock things up almost as often as I succeed.'

'Yeah, well, none of us is perfect, Norm. I've had my own fair share of cock-ups you've had to dig me out of, so I'm not going to make a big deal out of it. Anyway, where are you with the registration number?'

'Well, here's where it gets confusing,' said Norman. 'The DVLA database has that number allocated to a Suzuki motorcycle, registered in the name of Jimmy Huston.'

'But Goodnews reckons he's got a cast-iron alibi,' said Slater, 'and his bike is a Yamaha. So he must have two bikes.'

'If only it were that simple.'

'What does that mean?'

'Just bear with me for a few minutes before you rush off and arrest him,' said Norman. 'I've been going back over my earlier search into Huston. When I first checked him out, I just did a cursory search to see if there was anything obvious we should know about. I wasn't looking back far, just to see if he had any convictions, stuff like that. It was only later I found out about the name change. That's where I became very unprofessional and jumped the gun, subsequently dropping you in the shit with your girlfriend.'

'Yeah, well, don't worry about that. She still needs to apologise about that,' said Slater. 'And she's not my girlfriend.'

'Well, whatever she is,' said Norman, 'I think you might have a long wait for an apology. In fact, I think she had good reason to explode, and you probably need to apologise to her.'

'Why?' asked Slater, indignantly.

'I told you James Radford had disappeared, right? The thing is, he didn't disappear, he went to Australia and he's still there. If I had done my job properly and found all this out at the time, I could have saved you both a lot of hassle.'

Slater was getting confused.

'Hang on, Norm, I'm getting lost here. If he's in Australia, what was he doing changing his name here? And where's this all going?'

'James Radford hasn't changed his name,' explained Norman. 'He's still James Radford, and he's still in Australia. Jimmy Huston has always been Jimmy Huston. What we have is two Jimmy Hustons, but one of them ain't a real person.'

Slater sighed and rubbed his eyes. Now he really was confused. 'Am I stupid, or what?' he asked, 'because you've lost me.'

'Let me make it simple,' said Norman, 'although it's anything but. It looks to me like someone has cloned James Radford's identity and used it to change his name to Jimmy Huston. That person has then cloned the real Jimmy Huston's identity and added it to his fake Jimmy Huston to create a second version. He, or she, has used it to make us think the real Jimmy Huston killed Ian Becks. But I don't think Jimmy Huston is our killer, and I'm quite sure he's being framed. The real killer is the person who created the fake ID.'

'Are you sure?' asked Slater.

'I can show you the trail if you wanna check, and I wouldn't blame you if you did, after last time,' said Norman.

'I don't need to check up on you, Norm,' said Slater. 'If you've gone that far into it and you say it's right, then that's good enough for me.'

He paced up and down as he thought about what Norman had just told him. 'Nothing's ever bloody simple, is it?' he said. 'Whatever happened to good old-fashioned murder? Now we've got a villain who doesn't even exist in the real world. How the hell are we going to catch that?'

'The same way we ever did,' said Norman. 'Except now we're not looking for who killed Becksy, but who created the fake Jimmy Huston.'

'I suppose you're right,' said Slater. 'The question is, who are our suspects? I'm still not convinced Jimmy Huston's not involved in some way. Maybe he's created a fake Jimmy just to confuse us. And then there's this supposed boyfriend. Where is he? Why hasn't he come forward?'

208

'Yeah,' said Norman. 'He's the one that interests me. You'd think if he cared, he would have shown his face somewhere along the line.'

'What about the guy who bought the motorcycle number plates?' asked Slater. 'Did you get a description?'

'Of sorts,' said Norman. 'Georgie's not the most reliable, or helpful, witness. According to him, the guy was some sort of pansy, very clean, neat and tidy. Mind you, a tramp would look clean and tidy if you put him up against Georgie. He also said the guy has funny eyes that don't look in the same direction, but I'd take that with a pinch of salt.'

'Can we actually believe anything he said?' asked Slater.

'I think it would be fair to say he can be flexible with the truth,' said Norman. 'He would have told me it was a six-foot bunny rabbit if he thought he could have got away with it.'

'Right then,' said Slater. 'In that case I think we should go back to Dickie's Bar and see if we can find this boyfriend.'

'Come on then. There's no time like the present, and that young barman did say lunchtime was a good time to go if we wanted to ask questions. I have to say, the lunchtime menu looked pretty good too.'

Slater gave him a disapproving look.

'What?' said Norman, innocently. 'Let's be honest, it would be a shame to miss an opportunity to sample it.'

As Norman had hoped, they did learn the food at Dickie's Bar was excellent, but apart from that, they were left with pretty mean pickings. The only thing Nico could remember that he hadn't already told them was that whoever Ian Becks' boyfriend was, he always wore dark glasses.

'That wasn't much help really, was it?' asked Slater when they were back in the car. 'We're not really any further forward than we were.'

'Yeah, but on the bright side, at least we're not hungry,' said Norman.

'Oh, well, that's alright then,' said Slater, his voice laden with irony.

'Hey, you have to eat,' said Norman. 'I don't know about you, but I think better when I'm not hungry.'

'Well, I hope you do,' said Slater, 'because we need something right now, and it doesn't seem to be coming from my brain.'

'Okay,' said Norman. 'So let's just focus on this supposed boyfriend for a minute. We've got no reason to think this Nico, the barman guy, is giving us a load of crap, right?'

Slater nodded. 'Not so far at any rate.'

'Okay, in that case, we know the guy's about your size, looks a bit like Cary Grant, and is vain enough to bleach his hair and look after himself. And now we know he wears dark glasses.'

'Right,' agreed Slater, patiently.

'Do we know why he wears dark glasses?'

Slater sighed. 'How could we?' he asked.

'Bear with me,' said Norman, picking up on Slater's impatience. 'I'm not just rambling here; I *am* going somewhere with this. So why would someone wear dark glasses? Some people do it for effect, right? Or it could be because they have some sort of vanity issue, like maybe they have some sort of eye problem they want to hide.'

'You're sure this is going somewhere, are you?' asked Slater.

Norman gave him an indulgent smile. 'Have faith,' he said. 'Remember my biker friend, Georgie? He told me the guy who wanted the number plates made up had funny eyes, right? Wouldn't that be a possible reason to wear dark glasses?'

'So why wasn't he wearing them when he bought the number plates?' asked Slater.

'How many reasons d'you want?' asked Norman. 'Maybe he broke 'em. Maybe he can't wear them with a tinted visor on his crash helmet because it makes it too dark. Maybe he just wants to make sure different people give different descriptions. Shall I go on?'

'So you think the boyfriend is the same guy who paid for the number plates?'

210

'It's gotta be a possibility, hasn't it?' said Norman. 'You have to ask why hasn't this guy come forward? It could be that he's not come out yet, or maybe he's just a coward—'

'Or maybe he never was a boyfriend, but was someone just trying to gain Ian's confidence,' finished Slater.

'Exactly. It makes sense when you think about it.'

'But if we're going along with the revenge theory, and this guy isn't James Radford, what's his motive?'

'Heck, I don't have all the answers,' said Norman, laughing. 'Maybe we can ask him when we catch him.'

Slater started the car and began to head for home. Something was nagging away at the back of his brain, but he couldn't quite figure out what it was. Norman had known Slater long enough to recognise when he was deep in thought, so he kept quiet on the short journey back to Slater's house. It was only as Slater pulled on the handbrake outside his house and switched off the engine that the penny dropped and he realised what had been troubling him. He turned to Norman.

'You have that glint in your eye,' said Norman, 'and I'm sure it's not because you fancy me. You've just joined some dots, right?'

'We're agreed this guy wears dark glasses, right?' asked Slater.

'It looks that way,' said Norman.

'But we think it's unlikely it's James Radford trying to avenge Adam Radford's death.'

'From Australia? He'd need an accomplice,' said Norman.

'Agreed,' said Slater. 'You were bullied as a kid, weren't you?'

'All the fat kids were,' said Norman. 'I was just lucky I could make enough jokes to keep the bullies amused most of the time. But one or two of the others had their lives made a misery.'

'If you were one of those other kids, how long do you think you'd feel resentment towards your bullies?'

'That would depend on how bad they had affected me,' said Norman. 'I'm sure some would spend the rest of their lives wanting to get their own back. What's that got to do with this anyway?'

'Malcolm Jennings, the dentist,' said Slater. 'He wears dark glasses. He says he has a condition that makes his eyes sensitive to bright lights, but I've only got his word for it.'

'And he was bullied at school by Ian Becks and his pals,' added Norman. 'Why not? He's as good a suspect as we have.'

'Fancy a trip to Winchester?' asked Slater.

'Sure,' said Norman. 'It's a nice afternoon for a drive.'

CHAPTER THIRTY-SEVEN

On the way down to Winchester, Norman called Malcolm Jennings' dentist surgery on the pretext of needing some dental work done urgently.

'I've been told Mr Jennings is brilliant,' he told the receptionist. 'Is there any chance he could fit me in? I don't mind waiting until the end of the day.'

He listened to the receptionist's reply, and then ended the call.

'Crap,' he said. 'This is a wasted journey. She says he's taken the afternoon off.'

'We'll just have to pay him a visit at home then,' said Slater.

'You have his address?'

'Oh, yeah. When I spoke to him before, I asked if it was okay to come back if I thought of anything else. He said he'd rather I came to his home, and he gave me the address.'

'Is it right?'

Slater nodded. 'I didn't think he would give me a false address when I knew where he worked, but I checked just in case.'

'Well, in that case, he must be pretty confident we're not going to think it's him,' said Norman.

'Or he's got nothing to hide.'

'I suppose there is that possibility, but my gut's telling me different.'

'Are you sure your gut's not just telling you you've eaten too much again?'

'Trust me,' said Norman, not rising to the bait. 'I'm not wrong about this.'

* * *

Iverton was a small village about five miles south of Winchester. As they drove slowly along the one narrow road through the village, it was easy to see there was no shortage of money out here. Slater reckoned the smaller houses would cost in the region of half a million, and he had no doubt many were well about the one-million mark. When they finally found Malcolm Jennings' house, Applegate, it was obviously one of those.

Slater turned off the road and the car crunched its way up the short gravel driveway to the house. He parked the car and they climbed out.

'It's very quiet,' said Norman. 'You'd have thought anyone inside would have heard us crunching our way up that drive and be looking to see who it was. It'll be just our luck if he's out.'

'Let's find out,' said Slater. He marched up to the front door, rang the bell, and waited. 'Looks like there's no one in,' he said, and rang the bell again.

They waited another minute, but still there was no sign of life. Slater bent down, lifted the letterbox, and peered inside. Faint music seemed to be coming from somewhere deep inside the house, but there were no other sounds. He let go of the letterbox and straightened up.

'I can hear music,' he said. 'Maybe they're out the back.'

Norman wandered off to the right-hand side, looking for a way around to the back of the house. A double garage had been built alongside the house, but there was a passageway between the two.

'Round here,' he called to Slater. 'There's a back gate.'

Slater followed Norman round the side of the house and through the gate. An enormous paved area stretched all the way across the back of the house, past a stable door at the near end and two sets of French doors further along.

'Nice,' observed Norman, 'but I don't think my pension would stretch quite this far. Jeez, how much does a dentist make?'

'Yeah, it's pretty tasty,' agreed Slater.

He walked across to the stable door and knocked. Again, there was no answer. There was a small window to one side, and then on the other side, a much larger window. He looked through the larger window into a spacious kitchen. Everything was neat and tidy. It certainly looked as if no one was home. He thought perhaps they'd gone out and left the radio on.

While Slater was peering in the window, Norman was trying to imagine how much money this guy must have and was wondering what sort of car he might drive. A side door opened into the garage from the patio and there was a small window alongside it. He put his face to the window, and using his hand to create some shade, he looked inside.

'Come take a look at this,' he called to Slater.

Slater walked over and took Norman's place at the window.

'What's your gut telling you now?' asked Slater.

'It's a bit of a coincidence, right?' said Norman. 'I mean, we're looking for a Suzuki with black tape on the number plate, right? And we're also looking for Becksy's bike. And what do we see right here in this garage?'

'I can't believe he'd be so stupid as to leave it all here for us to find,' said Slater.

'Overconfidence,' said Norman. 'That's what this is. He's probably so convinced we'd believe it was Jimmy Huston, he hasn't cleaned up behind him properly.'

'I suppose I ought to call my boss. Perhaps she'll listen to me and follow this up now we've got some concrete evidence.'

'We're not gonna go off and leave this, are we?' asked Norman. 'For all we know the guy's figured out we're on to him and he's about to do a runner. Why don't we just wait for him and bust him ourselves?'

'We can wait down the road,' said Slater. 'If he comes back, we can maybe stop him leaving again.'

'This isn't really you talking, is it?' asked Norman. 'Only it doesn't sound like you. What's going on?'

'I just think I'd rather hand it over. Goodnews needs this more than we do.'

'Really?' said an amazed Norman. 'After that bust-up yesterday? You really have gone soft on her.'

'It's complicated,' said Slater. 'She has her back against the wall getting a load of shit she doesn't deserve. She needs all the help she can get right now.'

'Okay. I won't say I understand, because I don't really, but you're the boss, and it's your call.'

They got back in their car.

'I'd better make that call,' said Slater awkwardly.

'Go ahead,' said Norman. 'Don't mind me.'

Slater glowered at him but Norman just looked away and whistled a jaunty little tune. Eventually, he heaved a sigh.

'Fine, I'll leave you to it,' he said and climbed from the car.

The sun had decided to put in an appearance, so Norman ambled round to the front of the car and leaned against the bonnet to enjoy its warmth while he waited.

After about ten minutes, Slater wound down his window. 'It's okay, you can get back in now.'

Norman climbed back into the car. 'Did you convince her?'

'I think she got the gist,' said Slater.

'Are they on their way?'

'She reckons she'll be here in twenty minutes.'

'Jeez, you must have been pretty persuasive.'

'I think finding both bikes makes quite a convincing case.'

216

'Do I have to hide when she gets here?' Norman made a big pretence of looking around for a hiding spot.

'Don't be an arse,' said Slater. 'Why would you need to hide?'

'Because I'm not supposed to be here, am I? I don't want to get you into any more trouble.'

'Norm, I don't give a toss about that. What are they going to do to me, anyway? I'm leaving.'

'Don't start talking like that again,' said Norman. 'You know you don't mean it.'

'I do mean it,' said Slater.

'Yeah, well, I'll believe it when I see it.'

'That'll be next week, then.'

Slater had just started the car and put it into gear when an expensive-looking 4x4 turned off the road and up the drive, finally pulling up alongside them. Malcolm Jennings gave Norman an enquiring look, but then he recognised Slater and there was just the briefest flash of panic on his face before he regained his composure.

Norman clapped his hands together. 'Oh, my. It looks like we get to bust him after all,' he said. 'How cool is that?'

Slater shook his head in annoyance, but part of him was looking forward to confronting the man who had killed his friend. He eased the handbrake off and let the car roll down the drive, then slipped it into first and pulled up right behind the 4x4. He put the handbrake on and switched the ignition off.

'Just in case he was thinking about it,' he said to Norman.

'Good move.'

Slater reached into his pocket and fiddled with something for a moment, and then looked pensively out of the window.

'Well, come on,' said Norman. 'You're the only fuzz here, so you're going to have to do this whether you want to or not. I'm just here to make up the numbers, remember?'

Slater climbed slowly from the car.

'It's DS Slater, isn't it?' asked Jennings, who had climbed from his own car and was waiting by the front door.

'You did say you'd prefer it if I came here with any further questions,' said Slater as he walked up the drive towards Jennings.

'I thought you might have called first,' said Jennings, a small tic going in his cheek.

'Were you worried we might see something we shouldn't?' asked Norman, pitching up beside Slater.

'And who are you?'

'DS Norman,' said Norman, without pausing for breath, or thought.

Slater cringed as Norman came out with the reply, and then was relieved Jennings didn't ask to see any proof of ID. Mind you, he didn't really care too much about proper procedure any more, and it was probably going to be easier to go along with the lie than complicate things any further.

'So why are you here?' asked Jennings, making a big show of looking at his watch. 'What exactly is it you want? I haven't got all day, I'm a busy man.'

Slater gave him a sardonic smile. 'As you're such a busy man, I'll try not to waste your time. But I think you already know why we're here.'

'I'm sorry, but you'll have to do better than that,' said Jennings.

'How about you explain why Ian Becks' motorbike is in your garage,' said Slater. 'Is that better?'

'I haven't got time for this,' insisted Jennings. 'Like I said, I'm a busy man.'

'Oh, yeah,' said Norman. 'We know just how busy you've been. It must have taken a lot of planning to kill those three guys. I bet you thought you'd got away with it, too, but that was your problem. You got overconfident.'

'I don't know what you're talking about.'

'Wow, he's good, don't you think?' Norman said to Slater. 'You could almost believe him.' He looked hard at Jennings. 'Now the sun's gone in, why don't you take off those shades?'

'They're not sunglasses,' said Jennings. 'I'm sensitive to all light.'

'Or maybe you've got a lazy eye,' said Norman, 'you know, one that tends to do its own thing?'

'I haven't got time for this nonsense. I've got places to be.' Jennings made to move towards his car, but with surprising speed, Norman was across the drive blocking his path.

'How dare you! Get out of my way.'

Norman shook his head. 'You can't go anywhere anyway,' he said. 'Or maybe you're planning on murdering us too? The thing is, I don't see any syringe, and somehow I doubt you'd want a fair fight.'

'I've told you I don't know what you're talking about,' said Jennings, blustering. 'I'll be making the strongest complaint about this outrageous behaviour.'

'You can do that while you're at the station,' said Slater.

'What station? What are you talking about?'

'When you get arrested and dragged off to be interviewed. You can make your complaint then.'

'Interviewed? Why would I be interviewed?'

'Well, for a start I think you'd need to explain why you have not one, but two motorcycles we're looking for, parked in your garage.'

Jennings paled slightly. 'Someone must have put them there,' he said, lamely.

'Yeah, right, sure they did,' said Norman. 'D'you think that would've been the same someone who put the red leathers there? And that crash helmet that looks suspiciously like the missing one that belonged to Ian Becks?'

Jennings' jaw dropped and a sheen of sweat appeared on his brow. In the brief silence, Slater thought he could just about make out the distant sound of an approaching siren.

'You remember Ian Becks, don't you?' he asked Jennings. 'He was a colleague of ours, and a good friend.'

As soon as Slater mentioned Ian Becks, Jennings jerked his head.

'He worked with you, and you befriended him?' he asked. His expression was curious — not just the anger Slater had expected, but almost a twinge of regret.

'I suggest the police need to be a bit more selective about who they employ, and you should be a bit more selective about your friends. Ian Becks was a killer. He killed a young boy with a brick to the head. Why didn't you go after him back then? You tell me that. Why didn't anyone go after him?'

'If you're talking about the Radford boy, there was never any evidence to prove Becks was involved,' said Slater.

Jennings was looking slightly crazed, as if a whole life-time of torment had become focused on this very moment.

'I know what happened to that boy. I saw it with my own eyes,' he said. 'I've spent my entire life feeling guilty about it. It was me they were really after that afternoon. If I hadn't managed to hide they would never have seen him cycling by underneath. He would still be alive now.'

'Survivor's guilt,' said Norman. 'So why didn't you come forward if you were a witness?'

'What, my word against the three of them? Who would have believed me? And they would have made me pay even more afterwards, wouldn't they?'

The sound of the siren was getting nearer, but Jennings didn't seem to have noticed.

'So you admit you killed them?' asked Slater.

For a moment, Jennings seemed to be about to admit it, but then his expression changed. At first Slater thought he'd heard the siren, but the look of realisation that was dawning on his face was combined with sly cunning.

'I'm admitting nothing,' he said.

'We worked out how you did it on the way over here,' said Norman. 'You've got easy access to morphine as a den-tist, haven't you? You injected Terry Jones and John Willand with morphine and made it look like they died of natural causes and a drug overdose. Easy when one of them was a heroin addict, wasn't it? Bet you were clapping your hands with glee at that turn of events.'

Jennings gawped at him, but didn't say a word.

'And then,' Norman carried on, 'you had to be a bit cleverer with Ian Becks, didn't you? He was a forensic scien-tist, after all. You knew his death would come under scrutiny.

You befriended him at Dickie's Bar. You must have been stalking him and realised he was gay. What an opportunity, huh? You got to know him. Did he recognise you from years ago? Probably not, he probably didn't have a clue who you were. And that made you even more mad, didn't it?'

Jennings' face was turning puce but he still didn't say a word.

'You were very clever,' Norman said, shaking his head in mock admiration. 'You'd put the groundwork in a while ago, stealing Jimmy Huston's identity and James Radford's name. You were playing the long game. You must have been watching Ian for some time, learning all about his life. How did you arrange for the manuscript to be delivered? Had you paid off someone in the dispatch department at P&P to tip you off? That's my bet. They probably had no idea what they were getting involved in. Then all you had to do was phone the courier company and arrange for the parcel to be picked up and delivered to Ian Becks. You even told the courier that he might be waiting outside.

'Of course, it was *you* who was waiting outside, wasn't it? You pretended to be Ian Becks. You had even scoped the place out so you knew you wouldn't be caught on CCTV. You signed for the parcel then took it in to Ian. Had you called him to tell him you were coming to see his lab and asked him to meet you in reception? You must have known how proud he was of it. And from that point, it was easy. How did it go down? You waited until he was sitting at his desk and opening his parcel — did you tell him it was a present? What was it, just a load of blank paper that went up in smoke? — and then stabbed the syringe into his neck.'

The sound of sirens was much closer now, but Jennings seemed to be totally unaware.

'The rest of it was easy for you,' Slater cut in. 'You were already wearing the red leathers, so all you had to do was put on Ian's crash helmet, quickly open the fire escape, chuck your own helmet out so you could grab it when you got to the car park, and then leave via the front door. Nice touch, waving to Tom on the desk.

'Of course, the explosion must have made you confused when you read the paper the next day. That wasn't what you planned, but it worked well for you, didn't it? We went totally off on the wrong track. And you got complacent.'

Norman pointed in the direction of the garage. 'The motorbikes,' he said. 'You really should have got rid of them, Malcolm. But your arrogance has been your downfall.'

Jennings laughed, but his hands were shaking furiously. 'You're not a real policeman, are you?' he said. 'And you don't have a search warrant, do you? Nothing you've seen is admissible without a warrant.'

'I have to admit you've got us there, we don't have a search warrant,' Slater admitted. He nodded his head towards the police car, which was now crunching up the drive towards them, its wheels spitting gravel in all directions. 'But *they* do.'

The car skidded to a halt alongside them, Steve Biddeford spilling from the passenger seat even before they had stopped. Quick as a flash, Jennings was off, but Biddeford was fast, and big, and fearless. Jennings barely got ten yards before he found himself being rugby-tackled to the ground.

More cars could be heard screeching to a halt out in the road, and the sounds of car doors slamming and running feet began to fill the air.

Goodnews approached them, looking suitably unimpressed to find Norman with Slater. She made a point of ignoring the former detective and focused her attention on Slater.

'Did he confess?'

Slater took a small Dictaphone from his pocket, and handed it over to her. 'Not exactly,' he said. 'Everything's on there, but you probably won't need it.' He pointed in the general direction of the garage. 'There's enough evidence in the garage round the back.'

'I'll need a statement,' she said, heading off towards the garage.

'Yeah, right. I'll get onto it,' he said half-heartedly, but she had already gone. He turned to Norman. 'Come on, mate, let's get out of here, while we can. They don't need us anymore.'

CHAPTER THIRTY-EIGHT

Goodnews had told Slater she wanted to see him on Monday morning. She hadn't specified a time, suggesting he should come in when he felt ready. It was just after ten when he parked in the car park and made his way through reception. To his relief, the desk sergeant, Tom Sanders, was occupied with a weeping woman, and he managed to sneak past without signing in. He figured this way he could avoid as many of his colleagues as possible, and thus avoid the need to answer any awkward questions.

Unfortunately, what he hadn't allowed for was the unexpected in the form of a non-colleague, and he had barely got inside the building before he was confronted by DI Grimm. As usual, DS Fury was in attendance, following just a short distance behind him.

'Ah, Detective Sergeant Slater,' said Grimm, an ugly grin on his face. 'Just the person I've been looking for. We still have an interview to conclude.'

'I'm afraid I'm a bit busy now,' said Slater. 'I've got a meeting to attend.'

'If you mean the one with DCI Goodnews,' said Grimm, 'you don't need to worry. She's aware of my need to interview you, and she says she's happy to wait.'

Slater didn't believe that for one minute, but he knew he was going to have to go through with this interview whether he liked it or not. Avoiding it was only postponing the inevitable, so he might as well get it over with. On the positive side, maybe he could find a way to speak up in defence of Naomi Darling.

'Alright,' he said. 'Let's get this over with.'

'That's better,' said Grimm. 'I was beginning to think you might be trying to avoid me.'

'Good heavens, no,' said Slater, sarcastically. 'It's always such a pleasure being interviewed by you people. You have such a worthwhile purpose, I can't think of anything I'd rather do.'

Grimm gave Slater one of his grimaced smiles. 'Yeeeessss.' He hissed the word, rather like a snake might hiss. 'Come along then, follow me, let's try not to waste too much of your precious time.'

He walked past Slater in the direction of the interview rooms. As she passed him, Fury rolled her eyes, gave him a long-suffering look, and then a small smile.

'Right,' said Grimm, when they were settled on opposite sides of the table. 'Let's get this show on the road. Are you ready with your notebook, Fury?'

'Yes, sir,' said Fury from her position alongside him.

'I told you before,' said Slater. 'I wasn't on duty at the time of the incident between DC Darling and the so-called victim.'

'I'm not interested in what you know about DC Darling,' said Grimm, dismissively. 'She's going to be charged with GBH. She's finished. We've moved on to bigger fish now. What I want to know about is DCI Goodnews.'

For a moment Slater's stomach lurched, first at the news of Darling's impending doom, but then even more so at the mention of Goodnews's name. Surely Grimm couldn't know anything about that. No one else seemed to know, so how could he possibly know?

'I'm not sure I follow,' he said. 'What do you want to know about DCI Goodnews?'

'Well,' said Grimm. 'How can I put this? Let's just say we have reason to believe she may not be totally suited to her position, and we're trying to find evidence to prove it.'

'We?' asked Slater. 'Who's we?'

'People way above me.'

'You mean the chief constable.'

'It doesn't matter who I mean,' said Grimm. 'I'm just given a job to do, and I get on and do it.'

'And you think I'm going to help you by stabbing her in the back, is that it?' asked Slater.

Grimm beamed at him. 'Well, I understand you're the one who works closest to her, so it seems logical you'd be the one who would see all the flaws when they appear.'

'Have you ever heard of a thing called loyalty?' asked Slater.

'Come, come,' said Grimm. 'That's all very well in theory, but where does it get you in the real world?'

Slater looked down his nose at Grimm. 'How do you sleep at night?'

'Just give me what I need,' said Grimm. 'You never know, I might even be able to put in a good word. Wouldn't you like to be a DI?'

'I'm not interested. As far as I'm concerned, she's not a bad boss, and I have nothing to say against her.'

'From what I've heard, you and her have been known to argue,' said Grimm.

'We've had a couple of barneys, yeah,' said Slater. 'There's nothing strange about that. I used to argue with DCI Murray.'

'Doesn't it annoy you that a woman is above you in the pecking order?'

'Not really. She's got ambitions for her career, and I haven't. As long as she's not using other people to advance her career I don't have a problem. Why would I?'

'But she's younger than you, and bossing you around. Doesn't that bother you?'

'No, that doesn't bother me, but I can tell you something that does.'

Grimm sat back and beamed a self-satisfied smile in Slater's direction. It was plain from the look on his face that he thought he'd finally cracked it.

'Please, DS Slater,' he said. 'Do go on.'

'What really bothers me,' said Slater, looking Grimm right in the eye, 'is having a total twat of a DI wasting my time asking me stupid questions in an attempt to undermine a DCI who's ten times the copper he'll ever be. I always thought the idea of the police service was to solve crimes, not undermine people who are working their arses off to try and make things better for everyone.'

Out of the corner of his eye, Slater could see a broad grin break out on DS Fury's face. Hastily, she angled her head away so Grimm wouldn't see. Meanwhile, her boss was spluttering and coughing, so angry he was unable to form any words. But it didn't matter, Slater wasn't going to give him time to speak anyway.

'If you're trying to bury Goodnews, you must have realised by now that you're not going to get any help from anyone here,' said Slater, getting to his feet. 'That should tell you everything you need to know about how highly regarded she is around here. We all know she's not perfect, but then, who is? And compared with what they had to put up with before, she's a saint. The fact you're still hanging around here waiting for me suggests I'm your last hope, but I can assure you you're hoping in vain because you certainly aren't going to get any bloody help from me.'

He set off for the door, but he hadn't yet finished speaking.

'You can shove your interview up your arse,' he said, 'and if you try to ask me just one more question I'm going to take that notepad and ram it up there myself.'

'Come back here,' shouted Grimm. 'You can't speak to me like that. I'm going to make a complaint. You'll be up in front of a disciplinary hearing—'

'Yeah, you go ahead and do that,' said Slater, and then he stalked from the room.

* * *

When Slater got up to Goodnews's office the door was open, but he knocked anyway and poked his head around the corner. She looked up from her desk and smiled.

'Come on in,' she said.

He walked in carrying a tray with two coffees. 'I got you a skinny latte, is that right?' he asked.

'Perfect,' she said. 'Let's go and sit in the comfy seats.' She led him across to the two comfy chairs. 'That was great work tracking down Malcolm Jennings,' she said.

'He made it easy for us,' said Slater. 'He did all the hard work and then got complacent. All he had to do was ditch the motorbikes and the red leathers and all we would have been left with was purely circumstantial evidence. I wasn't expecting to find Becksy's bike there, and I never actually asked him how it got there. What did he say when you interviewed him?'

'He admitted the whole lot,' she said. 'I think he's actually full of remorse now. He wanted to murder Ian Becks the school bully, just like he had killed the other two bullies, but he hadn't got to know them. When he started dating Ian, he found he actually liked him, and now he's regretting what he's done.'

'So, did we get it all right?' asked Slater.

'More or less,' she said. 'Just a few details were wrong, but then you didn't know Becks had actually stayed at Jennings' house the night before he died. The reason his bike was at Jennings' house was because Jennings had taken him to work. He was supposed to meet Becks in reception so Becks could show him round the lab, then he was going to take Becks back to his house again.'

'Or, at least, that's what Becksy was supposed to think, right?' said Slater.

'Exactly,' said Goodnews. 'The poor guy was taken in completely. It was even Becks who told Jennings about the manuscript being ready. The reason it was late was because Jennings phoned them and insisted it had to be delivered that afternoon. Originally it wasn't going to be until the next day. Becks was actually waiting for Jennings in reception and wasn't expecting the manuscript.'

'Did they really bully Jennings that badly?' asked Slater.

'It wasn't just that. He's been carrying a lot of guilt inside himself for the past twenty odd years.'

'Yes, he said something about having seen it happen with his own eyes when he was ranting to me and Norm, but it was never his fault the other kid got killed,' said Slater.

'Aye, but he thinks it is, and after twenty years of feeling guilty he felt driven to do something about it.'

'By murdering three other people?' said Slater. 'And has it cured his guilt?'

'What do you think? Now he's got that guilt on top of what he had before.'

'Christ. What a bloody mess,' said Slater.

'Aye, but it's a nice finish,' she said. 'At least now we can prove Becks didn't commit suicide.'

'I bet your boss is none too pleased about that.'

'There's nothing he can do about it,' she said. 'He can still give me hell over the security, and he's got Sneaky Pete downstairs doing his best to find reasons to get rid of me.'

'I wouldn't worry about him,' said Slater. 'He's just realised he's been wasting his time. You might not be perfect, but no one wants to see you go.'

She smiled.

'That's a back-handed compliment if ever I heard one,' she said, 'but I'll take it. Does this mean we can get back to normal and I can expect you back at work?'

Slater pulled a face and took a deep breath.

'No, I don't think so,' he said. 'I reckon you owe me at least four weeks' leave.'

'And you want to take it now?' asked Goodnews. 'I suppose that would be alright. You certainly deserve a break.'

'That's not quite what I meant.' Slater reached in his pocket and withdrew an envelope. He pushed it towards her.

Goodnews looked aghast.

'Christ, you're not,' she said, alarmed. 'I thought that was all said in the heat of the moment.'

'It wasn't just that,' said Slater. 'I've been thinking about it for a while now. Everything seems to be designed to make it harder and harder to do our jobs. And now we have people pointing bloody guns at us, and we can't even fight back. I've had enough. I just don't want to do it anymore.'

'This isn't because of what happened the other night, is it?' she asked. 'Because it doesn't have to be a problem.'

'I think it might always be a problem for you,' he said. 'Like you said, it wouldn't do much for your career if anyone found out, would it? And I wouldn't want to be the one who stopped you. For what it's worth, I think you've been like a breath of fresh air for this place, and I told that idiot Grimm exactly that.'

'You didn't have to do that.'

'I didn't do it because I had to. I did it because it's right.'

Her eyes were reddening now, and he could see she was very close to tears.

'You don't really mean this,' she said, desperately. 'I don't want you to resign.'

'I'm sorry,' he said. 'I'm flattered you want me to stay, but I'm afraid it's not your call.'

'What about your notice?'

'I think I've enough leave to cover that, don't you?' he said.

'So that's it?' she said. 'You're just going to walk out of that door, and that's it?'

He fished his warrant card from his pocket and laid it on the table. 'I'm afraid so,' he said.

'You'll have to come in and do some paperwork before you're officially finished,' she said.

'Yeah, I know.'

'Make sure you come in and see me when you do, right?'

He stood, not quite sure how to handle this situation. 'Well, I'd better get going,' he said, awkwardly. 'I've got a new life to plan.'

She looked up at him sadly. 'Would you close the door on the way out, please? I think I need some time to myself.'

He closed the door quietly behind him and took a long, deep breath. The whole thing had taken less than fifteen minutes, but he felt as though it had been hours. He walked slowly down the stairs and out through the back doors. He stopped to look back at the doors, and to say goodbye to the last twenty years of his life. To his surprise he didn't feel sad, but surprisingly good, as though a massive weight had just been lifted from his shoulders.

He walked across the car park and climbed into his car where Norman sat in the driver's seat waiting for him.

'Have you done it?' asked Norman.

'I have.'

'Are you sure you're doing the right thing?'

'Absolutely,' said Slater as he buckled up his seat belt.

Norman looked enquiringly at him. 'Are you okay?'

Slater looked back at Norman and smiled. 'Never felt better, mate. Honestly, it's like I just escaped from prison.'

Norman smiled, started the car, and drove slowly up to the barrier.

'So, what are you going to do now?' he asked, putting the car into gear as the barrier lifted.

'I haven't got a clue,' said Slater as Norman drove under the barrier and turned right. 'But I'm sure something will come up.'

Norman turned to Slater, grinned and winked. 'I'm sure it will,' he said, knowingly.

THE END

THE JOFFE BOOKS STORY

We began in 2014 when Jasper agreed to publish his mum's much-rejected romance novel and it became a bestseller.

Since then we've grown into the largest independent publisher in the UK. We're extremely proud to publish some of the very best writers in the world, including Joy Ellis, Faith Martin, Caro Ramsay, Helen Forrester, Simon Brett and Robert Goddard. Everyone at Joffe Books loves reading and we never forget that it all begins with the magic of an author telling a story.

We are proud to publish talented first-time authors, as well as established writers whose books we love introducing to a new generation of readers.

We won Trade Publisher of the Year at the Independent Publishing Awards in 2023. We have been shortlisted for Independent Publisher of the Year at the British Book Awards for the last four years, and were shortlisted for the Diversity and Inclusivity Award at the 2022 Independent Publishing Awards. In 2023 we were shortlisted for Publisher of the Year at the RNA Industry Awards.

We built this company with your help, and we love to hear from you, so please email us about absolutely anything bookish at feedback@joffebooks.com

If you want to receive free books every Friday and hear about all our new releases, join our mailing list: www.joffebooks.com/contact

And when you tell your friends about us, just remember: it's pronounced Joffe as in coffee or toffee!

Made in United States
Troutdale, OR
05/27/2024